T.M. CROMER

HUMAN
AUTHORED
AG THE Authors Guild
9689304

Wilder Thorne woke in a cold sweat, his body both burning and freezing.

She was there again. Calling him from somewhere out of reach, even for a man with magic.

Abbie.

Goddess, he missed her. The feel of her silky skin against his, the smell of her minty shampoo, her constant teasing and laughter. She'd brought light and life wherever she went. Without her, he was a dried-up husk. Dead inside. Two years gone, and he was very well aware he needed to call a meeting with his inner demons to establish boundaries. But getting his shit together wasn't easy. He dreamed of her nightly. Sometimes with crystal clarity, where she begged him to find her. At other times, she was a presence, faceless and silent, but still condemning him, a nightmare he couldn't wake from.

"That fucking mountain," he muttered.

He wished he'd never agreed to climb it. Wished they hadn't been anywhere near the thing when the Thornes' enemies cast their spell, stripping him of his power. Despite his objections, she'd insisted, trusting him to keep her safe. But Wilder had failed her, and there was no sugarcoating it.

He lay still, eyes sightlessly on the ceiling, with the fan's hum the only sound. A haunted man with little hope left. His mind circled back to his relentless dreams and the feeling that Abbie was waiting for him, suspended between worlds. *Alone.*

And the hell of it was, he couldn't be sure those dreams were real or not. They felt like memories or, if he was being fanciful, premonitions. Maybe he'd cracked and finally crossed the line between grief and delusion. It continually gnawed at him that his brother Laszlo had never encountered her spirit on the earthly plane. Did it mean she'd crossed over to the Otherworld? And if so, should Wilder appeal to his cousin Alastair in hopes the Goddess could confirm his fear?

These constant visions of her lingering in the distant past, beyond the present, were killing him. Yet what other explanation was there? Time travel? Yes, that type of magic existed for a rare few. Yes, Abbie's mother was a witch, but she, herself, had no abilities to speak of.

The glowing digits on his phone told him it was early morning. Weird. He'd assumed it was just past midnight, given how little he'd slept. Lately, time blended, one giant melting pot of fucking blah.

"Enough!" he shouted to the empty room.

He needed the truth.

Today.

Wilder showered and dressed, giving his clothes a quick cleanliness sniff. Then he looked around the bedroom in disgust. Laundry was piled high. A handful of plates, along with an endless number of cups, littered the tops of dressers, side tables, and nightstands. The layer of dust on all available surfaces was thick enough to engrave his name. Yeah, he'd been a neat freak...before. But now, well, he couldn't exactly blame anyone for staging an intervention, could he?

Closing his eyes, he visualized the room as it had once been: spotless, organized, and spring-fresh. A snap of his fingers brought it all back. When he opened his eyes, it was as if stepping into a memory, and it almost made him smile. It felt good to move in the right direction.

Next would be Ebba. If anyone could sniff out a magical anomaly, it was Ebba James. He needed her help.

Five minutes later, Wilder paced outside the building, stopping now and again to glance upward at her apartment. She was his sister's best friend and his brother's now-steady girlfriend. They'd known her since the girls were kids, and she possessed the kindest of souls. If Wilder were anything but obsessed with his own problems, he'd take the time to appreciate that she and Laszlo finally got themselves sorted after years spent dancing around each other.

But he promised himself there'd be cause for celebration if he could find Abbie.

He shuddered, recalling the day she'd slipped from the rock face.

"On belay?" Abbie called, clipping to the anchor. Her voice was stable despite the biting wind trying to whisk the sound away.

"Belay on," Wilder answered, double-checking his Grigri and footing on the ledge. "You're good."

She flashed him a grin, fearless and radiant, before pushing upward. Once she started, her natural rhythm kicked in, and she flowed up the granite as if part of it. Her movements were clean and confident, those of a pro. The crampons bit into the ice-dusted rock while her chalked fingers sought the next hold, finding it with remarkable precision. She was poetry in motion, even on a class-five nightmare.

They were two pitches from the summit when it all went to hell.

The sky darkened, and clouds rolled in fast.

"Abbie?" he hollered, giving the slightest of chin gestures.

Although she noted the threat, she shook her head, not wanting to turn back.

He let her convince him, and deep inside, where his arrogance resided, he didn't believe anything could go wrong, so he gave in. Still, a warlock with his power could become complacent, assuming they could handle any situation as it arose. It wouldn't do to not take precautions.

A low rumble split the air.

Without missing a beat, Abbie reached for the narrow crack and slid a cam into place, tugging to test the hold. She gave a slight nod as if assuring herself it was secure.

Then, everything changed.

A pulse rippled through the air, and it felt like the mountain exhaled. Wilder knew the instant his magic abandoned him, and the sensation was similar to ice water gushing straight into his chest. His heart sank into his stomach, and a chill embraced him, refusing to let go. The cold was nothing he'd ever experienced on the mountain. In the past, he'd kept Abbie and himself warm in hostile conditions by heating their cells.

The weather shouldn't be so fucking frigid!

Something was wrong, and the urge to teleport the hell out of there was intense.

"Abbie, wait!" he shouted.

But her next placement missed. The rock she'd weighted broke loose, clattering down as warning shots. Her terrified scream ripped through him as her body pitched backward, and the cam she'd set yanked free.

Wilder locked the rope and braced to catch her weight, only to feel nothing. The rope went slack. He lunged, fumbling for her line, heart in his throat.

But she was gone. Simply vanished. No resistance. No impact. Hell, not even a secondary cry.

Just silence.

The kind that echoes for years.

"Abbie!" he screamed. Scrambling forward, he scanned the wall below, along with the ledge and slope.

He stared, hollowed out and disbelieving.

Two years later, and he still couldn't wrap his mind around it. The perpetually lost sensation created a haze wherein he dwelled.

Wilder glanced up at the window where light glowed behind half-drawn curtains. His stomach was twisted in knots, and his hands were shaking. Asking Ebba to shift into her wolf and search was a desperate move. The last one he had.

***

The apartment door swung open, and the stranger greeting him caught him off guard. Wilder stared, mute. It didn't stop the man from introducing himself or ushering Wilder into the foyer.

Alexander Castor, the Traveler, in the flesh. The man was a living legend and, coincidentally, best friends with another formidable warlock, Alastair Thorne, Wilder's cousin. Odd how they'd never met before. But if they had, he'd have immediately known who the man was.

Laszlo entered with a smiling Ebba in his arms.

"Wilder?"

His brother's confusion wasn't surprising. Wilder hadn't sought anyone out since Abbie fell. He'd kept to himself, avoiding conversation and comfort, feeling disinclined for the first and undeserving of the second. But here he stood, in the doorway, with his proverbial hat in hand, prepared to apologize if need be. Anxiety was eating him up, but not because of his brother's expected reception. Hell, he had no fear where family was concerned; they were all tight. It was the Thorne way.

No, mainly his apprehension stemmed from the worry that time was running out to find Abbie, if she could indeed be found.

"What is it?" Ebba asked, her concern written all over her face.

There was no need for her to ask if he was okay; she'd probably already guessed he wasn't.

"I have a favor to ask you, Ebba," he said, trying not to choke on the words. "You can say no, but I hope you'll consider it."

"Of course."

She gave Laszlo a pat, silently demanding to be let down. When her feet were on the ground, she crossed to Wilder and hugged him. The gesture was unexpected, and he didn't realize how much he'd needed it. If he held on a little too tightly, for a little too long, she was kind enough not to complain.

"You may want to wait until I explain before saying yes," he said in a quiet warning.

She waved him to the kitchen like it wasn't a big deal. "You can tell me over breakfast. Do you still take your coffee black?"

Castor set a mug and a platter of bacon in front of him. "If you want anything else, you'll have to conjure it yourself."

"I'm good. Thanks." He wasn't, but it had nothing to do with food.

"If this is family business, I can leave you to it," Castor said.

"Actually, I'd like you to stay, Mr. Castor," Wilder replied. "I'm beginning to suspect something else was off about the day our magic went on the blink, and could use another perspective."

Once they were settled, he detailed the climb, the emptiness where his abilities should've resided, and his abject failure to catch Abbie when she'd needed him the most. He did his damnedest to hold it together, but when he reached the moment she'd slipped, he dropped his face into his hands.

They didn't rush him or insist on filling the quiet.

"With no magic, I couldn't save her," he finally said. "And as Lo knows, we never found her body." He looked at Ebba, voice raw. "It's been a long time, and it could be a fool's errand, but will you search in your wolf form?"

"She's not a fucking rescue dog," Laszlo snapped.

His anger was justified. Hell, Wilder would feel the same if the situation were reversed, but his last bit of hope was hourglass sand slipping through his fingers.

"I'll do it," Ebba said, placing a calming hand on his brother's wrist.

Wilder's heart quickened, causing a deafening pounding in his ears. Uncertain what he would've said, probably a weepy thank you, he was nevertheless cut off by his brother's indignation.

"No way," Laszlo argued. "You have zero climbing experience. How will your wolf manage those mountain passes alone? It's stupid to try."

"I'll be with her," Wilder blurted, somewhat desperately. "I'll rig up slings and extra safety measures. We'll go when the weather conditions are perfect."

"You're risking her life! Wasn't Abbie's death enough to tell you that fucking mountain is too dangerous?"

Wilder flinched. The words stripped him bare. It wasn't as if he needed the fucking reminder. He lived it every damn day. He dropped his gaze to the table, seeking stability in a world gone mad, and the weight in his chest was heavier than granite.

Laszlo was right, leaving Wilder unable to argue the point. And he sure as shit couldn't defend himself.

Ebba was on her feet in a second. "Get out!"

Wilder was halfway out of his chair when it registered she wasn't yelling at him. All her focus was on Laszlo, and his disbelief was priceless. Had the situation been less dire, Wilder might've laughed.

"*What?*" Laszlo's brows were at his hairline.

"How fucking insensitive can you be?" She shoved him. "I said, go! You can come back when you apologize to Wilder for being a dick."

"Jaysus, I think I love you, Ebba James," Castor said, grinning appreciatively. "Fierce and beautiful, what an intoxicating combinat—" He caught sight of her death glare. "I'm shutting up now."

When the man mimed locking his lips and tossing the key, Wilder fought a second laugh. It was such an Abbie move. But he curbed the impulse and prepared to step in to defuse the fight no one wanted.

Yet Laszlo, once riled, was hard to calm. "You're being ridic —" he began.

Wilder kicked him under the table.

"Don't say it," he warned. "Trust me, man. You don't want to go there."

"No. By all means, Laszlo, say what's on your mind," Ebba cut in, crossing her arms.

Both Castor and Wilder frantically shook their heads, trying to signal him to abort with a slicing motion across their throats, but Laszlo forged on, stubborn fucker he was.

"You want me to tell you I think you're being ridiculous?" he demanded. "Fine. I do."

"Because I refuse to allow disrespect in my home? Or because I intend to help your brother?" she challenged.

"The second one." Laszlo's voice grew softer. "I love you, Ebba. I don't want to see you risk your life on an unstable mountain. We've searched." He turned to Wilder. Waiting.

But Wilder stayed quiet, unprepared to give up on Abbie.

Laszlo's eyes reflected his disappointment. "Come on, man. Don't make me out to be the bad guy here. Tell her. We searched and searched. We scryed. When our magic was restored, Liz and I went up there with you and did everything we could to clear the peaks and hold back the inclement weather to get a better view." Laszlo placed a hand on Wilder's shoulder. "Tell her there was no trace. We found a few deceased climbers, but none were Abbie."

Shutting his burning eyes, Wilder nodded, acknowledging the truth.

"Ebba, Sweet, I'd never forbid you to do what you think is best," Laszlo said. "Hell, you'd castrate me if I tried. But the risk is great for zero chance at a reward."

Wilder should've let his brother have the win, but he couldn't. Lifting his gaze from his coffee mug, he cleared his throat and said the one thing he knew they couldn't ignore.

"I dreamed she spoke to me through Ebba."

Silence followed Wilder's announcement, and his heart hammered with dread as he awaited a response.

Finally, Castor leaned in, pale-blue eyes narrowed consideringly.

"What are you thinking?" Laszlo asked.

"I'm intrigued by the mystery, and I'm bored enough to help." Castor grinned and slapped the table. "Count me in, Thornes!"

Wilder blinked. The unexpected offer cracked open his chest, warming what had been frozen before. With the thawing came hope. He couldn't say with one hundred percent certainty how a Traveler's magic worked, but if the man could somehow alter time…

He inhaled a ragged breath, forcefully pushing down the desire to sob his gratitude.

Laszlo shot him an assessing glance, then turned his focus on Ebba to judge her reaction as he spoke. "I'm sorry for being a dick, Wilder."

She didn't move, and her expectation hung on a raised brow.

"And I'm sorry for saying you're being ridiculous, Sweet Ebba," he added. "I'm scared for you."

A soft smile curled her lips. "Was that so bad?"

Laszlo held his fingers an inch apart and shrugged.

"I have questions," Castor said, suddenly all business. "The first one is for you, Wilder. Was your girlfriend a witch? If so, why didn't she teleport?"

"No, but her mother was. She never knew her father, but I suspect he was incredibly powerful in his own right."

"Why?"

"It wouldn't have mattered," Laszlo cut in before Wilder could answer. "Anyone near us that day had their magic subdued. Had she been a witch, and she was within touching distance, she couldn't have teleported."

"But she fell down a mountain," Castor said. "At some point, she'd have been far enough away to save herself."

Wilder didn't answer. He'd wondered the same thing a thousand times.

"Can we talk to her mother? I'd like to get a sense of who Abigail was." Castor sipped his coffee before adding, "At the very least, if I've ever encountered the mother or your girl-friend, I may be able to travel back to that time. Possibly warn one or both."

And finally, he was given the first inkling of how the Traveler's gifts worked.

"Do you remember every face you've seen?" Ebba asked the question on Wilder's mind.

"Yes. Every interaction, too. It's a curse," the Traveler replied.

"What if we speak to Death?" Laszlo suggested. "She's your son's mother, right? She might help locate Abbie on the other side."

Wilder's heart slammed in his chest, and he recoiled from the idea she wasn't alive.

"Abbie's not dead!" The denial was torn from him. "I'd feel it. *Here.*" He pressed a hand to his chest. "She's not dead."

The looks he received were a mixture of shock and pity.

"May I see her picture?" Castor asked gently.

"Oh, wait! I have one!" Ebba ran to the mantle and returned with a framed photo. "Here."

He stilled. "Her mother," he rasped, expression pale and tight. "What's her name?"

"Beth Monroe," Wilder replied. His pulse quickened in anticipation of the answer to his next question. "Why?"

Castor turned the frame. "The blonde is Abigail, I presume."

His brother's jaw dropped, but Wilder had seen the connection the second Castor greeted him. The resemblance was uncanny, the white-blond hair unmistakable.

"You guessed?" Laszlo asked him.

"I came here to ask Ebba's wolf to see what she could find. When he opened the door, I knew." Wilder didn't look away from Castor. "You and Beth had an affair, didn't you?"

"I'd have thought the picture was enough evidence for you. You're asking for a DNA match?" Castor asked dryly, appearing to have recovered from his shock.

"What does that mean for her?" Laszlo turned thoughtful. "Wouldn't she have similar abilities to yours?"

"I don't know. One would think she'd be powerful, but that's not how magic works. Sometimes it's diluted. There are those with witch DNA whose powers never develop." Castor rubbed the back of his neck as he studied the image. "I can't believe Beth never told me."

"How could she? Weren't you in hiding for years?" Ebba asked. She clasped Castor's free hand, squeezing it.

"Yes. I suppose you're right." He exhaled a heavy sigh. "How old is she? Abbie."

Wilder sipped his coffee and swallowed hard. The man should know when he'd been with Beth, but his curiosity made Wilder consider whether traveling altered one's perception of time.

"She would be forty-one next week."

"Older than Quentin." Castor's expression cracked, giving a hint of deeper emotions. "Christ! I need to tell my son he had a sister."

"Has," Wilder stressed, unable to keep the edge from his tone. "Has a sister."

The Traveler's regretful eyes locked with his, and resolution settled on his face. "If she's alive, I'll find her, Thorne. Get some rest. We leave tomorrow morning for the mountain." He stood and hugged Ebba. "You won't be needed on this trip, love. I've got it covered."

Wilder hung around a while longer after Castor teleported away. "Is this guy on the level? And yes, I know he's a friend of Alastair's, but I need him to take this seriously."

"You can count on him, Wilder," Ebba assured him. "He saved my life, a virtual stranger, not once, but twice. I imagine he'll go to the ends of the earth for his own flesh and blood."

"Yeah, man," Laszlo added. "You can trust him to do the right thing."

The pressure on Wilder's chest lightened, making it easier to breathe.

"Okay. That's good," he said, almost to himself.

"I'm sorry I failed you the first time," his brother said equally as soft, as if the words were difficult to voice. "We shouldn't have left that fucking mountain until we had solid evidence one way or another."

"You did all you could, Lo." Wilder couldn't downplay it. His family had stepped up, not stopping until they'd run out of options. "You were right about the rescue effort. No amount of scrying was going to find her if what I believe is true."

"And what's that?" Ebba asked with a tilt of her head.

"Some witches have latent magic. It only comes out under high-stress situations." Their bewildered expressions said they had no idea what he was talking about. "If Abbie is Castor's daughter, it stands to reason she'd have magic, despite all the sometimes-they-don't shit he was spouting. He wouldn't have agreed to go there if he thought she didn't."

Ebba shot a sharp look at Laszlo before speaking. "You believe Abbie had latent power, and once she was far enough from you, the trauma of the fall sparked it to life? And maybe she sent herself to a different time without knowing how her magic works?"

"Something like that." Wilder studied them both closely. "It's possible, right?"

"Dude, I'm a wolf shifter. I've only read about it in para-normal romance novels. Anything is possible."

Laszlo laughed. "Wait! *You* read paranormal romance books? That's the best ironic twist of fate ever. You've become part of a trope you love."

"Stuff it," she growled, but her grin gave her away. "Truth-fully, I wasn't mad to learn you had magical abilities."

"You totally were."

"No, I was angry you lied to me throughout our entire friendship," Ebba corrected.

Wilder wisely remained silent as his brother apologized yet again.

"So, back to Abbie," Laszlo said. "It would be a miracle, but they've been known to happen. I, for one, am hoping it did."

"But where would she have gone that she couldn't return from?" Ebba asked. "Why not try to get a message to someone if she were in the recent past or return to Wilder if she went to the future?"

"That's just the thing. I don't know," Wilder confessed.

"I think I do. And your dream, the one where you believe

Abbie spoke to you through Ebba, it actually happened," Laszlo said.

Wilder fumbled his coffee cup. "What? What the fuck are you talking about? How?"

"Castor and I changed the timeline when we went back the night of Ebba's accident. In the first one, you stopped by here when she was in her ghostly state. She channeled Abbie."

"And you didn't think to tell me this?" Wilder's desire to punch him in the fucking face was an acid burning through him, destroying his brotherly affection. "Why wouldn't you tell me, Lo? For God's sake! Why?"

"With everything that happened, I didn't have time." Laszlo embraced him. "I swear it was next on my list. Today, as a matter of fact."

"You could've mentioned it earlier, while Castor was here," Ebba said with an edge in her voice.

"Yes, and I should've, but I wanted to hear what he had in mind. To see if he'd volunteer to help."

"You were testing him?" Wilder could believe it. His brother didn't have much faith in others.

"Something like that." Laszlo refilled their coffee cups. "Look, I didn't recall the thing about Ebba channeling Abbie until this week when the timelines merged. It all sort of clicked into place, and I've been trying to make sense of it in my head. It's a total mind fuck."

Wilder could see where warring memories might be. "Do you think my dreams are shadows of that time, too?"

After giving it thought, Laszlo nodded. "Possibly. Spirits leave an echo, so it would make sense, somewhere in the ether, their residual energy is floating about."

"It helps to know I'm not going crazy."

"You're not, Wilder. I swear."

"If anything happens when Castor and I go to the mountain, and I don't get back—"

"Don't say that," Laszlo snapped. Softening his tone, he said, "Please, brother. Remain positive. It's so important you do."

"I can't continue to exist without Abbie, Lo. I don't want to."

"I had much the same thought about Ebba," his brother confessed.

She gasped and pressed her hand to her mouth. Cupping her cheek, Laszlo smiled so lovingly it caused Wilder's heart to ache.

"When I thought I would lose you forever, I finally understood what my brother was going through with Abbie," Laszlo confessed to Ebba. "You and I hadn't even begun, not really, and I was nearly destroyed by learning Death stalked you." He turned and met Wilder's gaze. "So I get it, man. Whatever it takes, we'll find her."

Closing his eyes against the sting of fresh tears, he nodded his gratitude. The thickness in his throat refused to allow anything else.

"We love you, Wilder," Ebba said with a fierce hug. "Come back to us."

"I'll do my best," he lied.

If Abbie weren't with him, he wouldn't be coming back.

Afternoon sunlight filtered through the branches of the massive pecan trees lining the Monroe property. It cast dappled shadows across the fluted columns and the lightly swaying porch swing. The place hadn't changed much since Alex saw it last. It sported a fresh coat of paint and new flower baskets with a fern or two, making the overall look homey and inviting.

Like Beth.

Alex stared at her house from the edge of the gravel drive. Although his feet felt rooted in the red Carolina clay, like an anchor to the earth, he swayed. He'd been off-kilter since learning of his daughter. How the hell had he never known about Abbie? Beth had his number and should've called. And how was he supposed to casually stroll onto that wraparound porch and knock as if he had the right after forty-plus years?

He stepped forward, hesitated to gather his courage, then closed the distance to the porch. When he reached the base of the wide steps, the door swung open, and there she stood—dark hair and heartbreakingly haunted eyes.

"I was hoping you'd eventually come," she said in that soft Southern drawl of hers.

Jaw tight and throat thick, Alex dragged a hand down his face. "I only found out I had a daughter three hours ago, or I'd have been here sooner."

Beth's pale face crumpled, and tears welled in her large blue eyes. "Oh, Alex."

He bounded up the steps, catching her in his arms as she sank to her knees.

"I'm going to save her, Beth. Count on it."

She drew back to meet his eyes, and he hoped like hell they reflected the promise in his heart.

"I'm not doubting you, but how do you plan to do it? She's been dead for two years."

"I'm formulating a plan. Will you tell me about her?" he asked as he guided her to the swing.

"She was so much like you. Quick with a quip, adventurous, never encountered a challenge she wasn't going to meet head-on." Beth smiled, and the bittersweet sight tightened his stomach. "I looked for you when I discovered I was pregnant, but every source said the same thing. Alex Collins didn't exist."

"I was on the run, but if I had known…"

Her hollow expression said she didn't believe him.

"Do you know what I am?" he asked.

"I suspect I do." She trailed her fingers over his cheekbone. "You haven't aged a day in forty-two years, and even for a warlock, that's odd."

"I'm a Traveler, Beth. My birth name was Anton O'Connor—"

Her face froze, and wariness entered her eyes. Rightfully so. The surname carried a lot of baggage. "O'Connor? From the Irish O'Connors?"

"Yes. Loman was my brother and was put down like the feral beast he was. He's who I was running from, along with the Désorceler Society, which he worked for." There wasn't anyone in the witch community unfamiliar with the name of the organization intent on murdering them.

Alex touched her hand, and when she flinched, he said, "I'm nothing like him. No more than Abbie was like him. When I was a teenager, I ran away from home. It was good fortune Alastair Thorne and Damian Dethridge found me first."

"But there's only one Traveler—Oh! *Ohmygod!* Alexander Castor!" She covered her mouth as she shook her head. "I'm so stupid!"

"No. You're not. You saw what I wanted you to."

"You're a legend." Beth fingered a strand of his hair. "The white-blond hair and the icy-blue eyes are a dead giveaway. We've all heard talk of you, but I still didn't piece it together. It's a wonder no one did after Abbie was born."

"From the picture, it seems her eyes are darker than mine, and being female, no one would make the leap."

"I suppose not," she said in a soft voice. "I can hardly manage it, and I knew you. But how did you avoid everyone you know?"

"Glamouring, teleporting, and time jumping throughout the world. It was a helluva lot easier after staging my death."

"That's why you spent so long here, wasn't it? You were using my home to hide," Beth concluded.

"Primarily, yes, but I also enjoyed your company, or I wouldn't have stayed. It happens to be close to where my best friend lives, and it allowed me to keep tabs on him from afar."

"Yet you never thought to check up on me afterward?" she asked without a hint of the bitterness one would expect.

"I did, actually, but I didn't want to lead anyone to your door. You were safer without me around."

She watched him for a long beat, as if to test his sincerity. Finally, she nodded and held out her hand. "Come. I want to tell you about her life and her boyfriend, Wilder."

"I've recently met him. Turns out, he's a cousin to that best friend I mentioned."

She smiled a moment before her heartbreak seeped through. "He's in a worse state than I am, if you can believe it."

"Yes, I saw for myself," Alex said as he entered the foyer and cataloged the changes four decades had wrought. His gaze swept the family room, and the pictures nestled on the mantle beckoned. He drank in all the images of Abbie at various stages of life. "Why didn't her magic evolve, Beth? You and I are both witches. Did you bind her powers?"

"No. And I never understood it either. We tried everything we could to bring them out, even enlisting the aid of a local coven."

A picture of young Abbie gracing the camera with a gap-toothed grin was his favorite of the bunch, and he traced her face with a finger. "She's beautiful."

"Have you looked in the mirror?" Beth replied dryly.

He chuckled and spontaneously hugged her. "Thank you. It's easy to tell she was loved and well cared for."

"She was my everything, Alex." Raw honesty shone on her face. "I've been so broken for the last two years."

"I have a special talent and very powerful friends, love. If Abbie can be returned to you and Wilder, I'll make it happen."

Wilder spent the afternoon tying up legal loose ends. He wanted to ensure his will was in order in case things went sideways. After visiting his mother and younger brothers, Heath and Coleman, he paid a call on his sister, Liz.

She opened the door with a broad smile, but it faded in slow increments.

"Wilder? What's going on? Are you okay?"

He snorted as he crossed the threshold. "I haven't been okay for two years, Liz. But I have news."

"What is it?" she asked as she led the way to the kitchen.

Wilder wasn't surprised to see her husband, Rafe, at the counter with a glass of wine and a laptop. Ever the diligent businessman, he barely looked up as he toasted them.

"Wine or coffee?" she asked Wilder.

"Coffee, please. I still have a few things requiring my attention."

After starting a fresh pot, Liz faced him. "You don't ever seek anyone out. Start talking."

He couldn't prevent the grin. His little sister was born bossy.

"Maybe I've turned over a new leaf and have become social again."

"Right, and pigs fly." She withdrew a couple of hand-thrown pottery mugs from the cabinet before adding, "But if you've suddenly rejoined the world, I'm happy for it."

Wilder waited until she filled the cups and handed him one.

"I'm going back to the mountain to search for Abbie."

"What?" She shared a horrified glance with Rafe, then refocused on him. "Wilder, what the hell are you doing? You know I love you and want to see you happy, but this has reached so far past the obsession stage that it isn't healthy."

"I spoke to Alexander Castor today. He's Cousin Alastair's friend—"

"I know who he is," she said with an impatient wave. "Did he convince you to do this? The man's a wildcard. Do you know he—"

Wilder captured her hand mid-flutter. "Liz. Please."

"Okay. Fine. Tell me."

And so he explained about Abbie and Castor's relationship, the dream that wasn't a dream, and how Abbie's newfound father intended to help uncover her whereabouts.

"Wow." She looked as stunned as he'd felt when the Traveler first opened Ebba's door. "That's a lot to take in, but if anyone can alter time and save her, it would be him."

"I thought the same, and I have to try."

Shaking her head, Liz said, "I can't believe this. But let me get this straight. Ebba channeled Abbie in some alternate time-line? Which you believe is, what, the Wild West?"

Her brow was furrowed as she tried to fit the pieces together.

"Something like that," he replied. "It's possible, under the high-stress fall, her powers manifested. If they did and she doesn't know how to control them, she could be stuck in the past."

"But why wouldn't she have found a way to contact you? Left a note for you to find or something?"

He smiled wryly. "Ebba asked much the same thing."

"Because she's smart. And what did you answer?"

"I don't know."

"You don't remember how you answered her, or you don't know how to answer me?" she asked tartly, raising a brow.

"My kid sister, always the wiseass." He sipped his coffee as he considered her question with a clearer mind. "If Abbie's timeline is similar to ours and two years have passed, it's possible she made the best of a bad situation and moved on. Maybe she met someone and created a life there if she couldn't get back."

"Oh, Wilder."

"Yeah. I may have to accept she doesn't love me anymore, but I can't rest until she tells me herself."

Liz covered his hand with hers and squeezed. "You forget, I've seen you two together. Abbie isn't a woman who would move on easily. You're made for each other."

"I've always thought so. But maybe not. We don't know what she's gone through. Despair does strange things to a person." His voice held a catch, but he wasn't embarrassed by his intense emotions. His sister would understand. She had fallen in love with Rafe while on vacation, only to have him disappear one morning. It had taken four years for the two of them to reconnect, and their romance hadn't gone smoothly. She knew what loss and separation felt like.

Hell, their mutual enemy was the one responsible for taking down the Thornes' magic the day Abbie fell, making it impossible for Wilder to save her.

"I'm not sure," she replied. "But for a good ninety-five percent of us, it works out."

He met her sorrowful gaze and could tell she believed he fell into the pitiful five-percent category.

"Do you have anything stronger to drink?" he asked.

"I do, but I'm not giving you a crutch to lean on. It's taken until now for you to visit my home, and you'll remain sober, brother mine."

"Nag." He turned his hand over, weaving his fingers with hers. "Thank you for caring, sister mine."

"You've always looked out for me, growing up. Of course, I care."

"Would you like us to join in your search?" Rafe asked. He'd been quiet and thoughtful the entire conversation, as was his way, but he was always willing to assist whenever he could.

"While I appreciate the offer, I'm going to let Castor take the lead on this one. She's his daughter, and if all else fails, he can cast a blood-to-blood location spell."

"Those are always useful," Rafe replied dryly.

Wilder chuckled. Once again, he was surprised by how much lighter he felt. Perhaps it was finally taking action after so long, or maybe his once-inherent optimism was returning. Either way, the burgeoning hope felt good.

"That's the first time I've seen you crack a smile in over two years," Liz said tearfully.

He hugged her, holding on for dear life. If he didn't, he'd likely break down, too. When Liz patted his back, he kissed her temple, cleared his throat, and released her.

"As soon as I find Abbie, I won't be able to stop smiling," he promised.

"Then I hope you return with her immediately." Liz shot him a watery grin.

"Me, too." He hesitated, then forged on with what he'd originally come to say. "If I don't make it back—"

"Wilder—"

"Liz."

She sighed in resignation but didn't interrupt again.

"If I don't make it back, I want you to be the executor of my will. The bulk of my estate can go to charity, but I have a few collectibles I'd like to pass on to the proper people. Can you do that for me?"

She nodded, lips compressed as if she wanted to argue the outcome of his journey. He appreciated her restraint. There was a time, before Rafe's influence, when she'd have read him the riot act.

"You are the best sister a person could hope for. I've been blessed to have you in my life."

"Don't talk like you aren't returning," she ordered, unable to hide her unease.

"I don't know what we'll be facing. And from what Laszlo has told me, I may have to leave my body to cross through time with Castor. The process is risky as fuck."

A sickly expression settled on Liz's normally serene visage. "Goddess, I hope not. I forgot he had to do that to save Ebba."

"Yeah. I didn't, but I'm willing to try whatever it takes."

"What if you don't find her, Wilder? What then?"

"I don't want to think about a life without her, Liz. It's too dismal to consider."

"When is all this happening?" she asked.

"Tomorrow morning. We're going to the mountain."

"Wilder! That place is dangerous!"

"Not for those with magic in their back pocket," he said, giving her a careless grin.

"Need I remind you our abilities failed once?" she snapped. "I—"

"*Qalbi*, stop." Rafe wrapped her in a hug. "Your brother knows what he's doing and doesn't need you adding your worry to the mix."

She rewarded him with a vicious arm pinch. "Don't manage me."

"That's not what you said last night—oomph!" He doubled over slightly as her elbow found its mark, a grin still tugging at his lips.

"On that note, I'm outta here," Wilder said with a laugh. "You two try not to kill each other, okay?"

"Be safe! And call us as soon as you're home!" she hollered after his retreating back.

4

ilder's heart took up residence in his throat as he stared at the pulsing blue wall centered on the rock.

"What the fuck is that?"

"A portal." Castor's tone was as grim as his expression. "Fuck, I hate portals."

"They're bad?"

"You watch movies, Thorne. Ever see where one led to anything good?"

The urge to laugh was weirdly strong, but Wilder suppressed it. In the short time he'd come to know Abbie's father, he understood where her sarcastic humor and unstoppable drive originated.

"She's alive, sir," he told Castor. "I feel it."

"I'm counting on your feeling." Castor's determined, ice-blue eyes settled on him. Lifting a vial wrapped in a piece of paper, he tucked it into Wilder's shirt pocket, then sealed the material with a finger across the open seam. "I've concocted a foolproof spell to get you back here. And no matter what

26

happens on the other side of that door, you find her and get her out of there. Got it?"

"You're not sounding too optimistic about your chances." Wilder touched his bulky pocket.

"I'm a survivor, so don't worry about me. But my goal is for you and my daughter to return here in one piece."

"Sweet, because it's my goal, too," he assured the Traveler.

A wry smile curled Castor's lips as he drew back his long, white-blond hair and tied it in a ponytail. "Be prepared for anything and utilize your magic if you have to."

Wilder nodded, facing the pulsing portal with determination. "I'll do whatever it takes. Abbie's coming home."

"Thanks to this gateway, you won't need to be in spirit form. But keep hold of my hand until I tell you, Thorne. Traveling is an art form, and if you misstep in time, no one is going to save you."

"Noted."

Castor paused long enough to capture his attention.

"What is it?" Wilder asked.

"It's been two years. We may not find what you're hoping for. You need to be prepared for that possibility."

His throat tightened, and his voice was gruff when he asked, "Do you believe she's dead? Is that why you're warning me?"

"No." Castor looked pained. "I'm not sure why I am, truthfully. Maybe I'm preparing myself, too."

"You have the blood-to-blood location spell handy?"

He tapped his temple and grinned. "I memorized it years ago to find Quentin when needed. It'll work for Abbie when the time comes."

"Good. Let's go." Wilder braced himself.

The Traveler's grip was ironclad. If they got separated, it wouldn't be because of him. Just as they were about to step through, the blue light flickered and dimmed, causing Castor to tug him back.

"Shit!"

"What? What's going on?" he asked.

"It's not stable. I need something to shore it up."

"Like what?"

"Give me a damn minute to think," Castor snapped.

Patience used to be a plentiful commodity in Wilder's world. Yet in this moment, he had a harder time staying calm as Abbie's father paced, stopped to study the portal, and then resumed his nervous activity. Finally, with fingers laced behind his head, he stared at the wavering opening.

The longer Castor contemplated the gateway to Abbie's world, the more Wilder's control gave way to his building anxiety.

"It's fading. What do we do?" he asked.

Instead of answering, Castor whipped out his phone and thumbed through the screens, punching in text or numbers. For a heartbeat, it seemed like a Dr. Who scene, like maybe he was working out a scientific calculation. He spoiled the visual by putting his cell to his ear and speaking.

"I need Frankie and The Heart of Artemis. I'm sending the coordinates." He paused to listen, and his expression was pure frustration. "Please. I wouldn't ask if it wasn't important. You know that." With a heavy exhale, he added, "Yes, I'm aware she's only four years old, Quentin." He pinched his nose. "Nothing is required of her other than to activate the bloody orb." He nodded as if his son could see him. "Yes. Thank you."

Two minutes later, Quentin Buchanan and his young daughter, Francesca, appeared nearby. Perched high in her dad's arms, she cradled what looked to be a large pink-tinted marble to her chest. As they drew near, a colorful mist formed inside the glass, matching the portal's and swirling wildly as if seeking an escape.

Castor was a man transformed, and he held his arms out to the girl like the proud grandparent he was. "Frankie, my darlin'!"

With a giggle, she rushed forward to be swept up into his loving embrace. "Peepaw Alex! I got the art-e-must for you!"

"Thank ya, love. You've done me a good turn, ya have," he replied, falling into his native accent and laying it on thick. Wilder guessed it was for the child's benefit because she laughed with delight.

He cast a glance at Quentin, who appeared to be caught between disbelief and amusement. "Peepaw? Tell me she's got an equally creative name for my cousin Alastair."

The other guy's evil grin brought a matching one to Wilder's lips.

"Papa said I have a new aunt," Frankie said.

Father and son shared a look filled with silent communication. And it struck Wilder how much Abbie would love knowing she had a brother and niece. She'd always longed for family to spoil, and it hurt his heart they'd never gotten around to creating their own. If they got a second chance and she was willing, he would give her as many children as she wanted.

"Aye, that you do, love. And she's who we're hoping to find with that nifty globe of yours," Castor said.

"Is she pretty like me?"

"No one is as lovely as you are, to be sure," he assured her.

An adoring smile transformed Castor's visage, taking it from handsome to stunning, and Wilder's heart ached at the sight. Abbie used to smile at him the same exact way, and her loving gesture always stole his breath away.

"Will you tell me what I need to do to help her?" Frankie asked, full of hope and utterly positive she was required to save the day as only a child can be.

"We need you to hold the portal open long enough for us to

enter. Afterward, you can go home and tell your mam about your adventure with your old grandda, yeah?"

"You're not old, PeePaw Alex," she assured him with a pat on the cheek. And to many, he appeared no older than thirty-five or forty tops.

"I'll take your word for it, me darlin'. Though *Pee*Paw makes me sound like I soil me britches, it does."

She giggled.

Castor shifted her to his hip and pointed to the flickering opening. "Ready, love?"

"Yep."

"That's my girl," he said approvingly as he set her down. "Okay, approach the portal, but don't touch it with your hand, only the globe."

She did as instructed, with her father and Castor on either side to pull her back if needed.

"Clear your mind and, when you've focused only on the gateway, take hold of my hand," he said.

Her childlike enthusiasm shone brightly on her face as she stared at the magical tool, wide-eyed and solemn. With a resolute nod, she gripped his fingers as Castor and Quentin chanted the spell.

"Heart of Artemis, bright and true,
Lend me your strength to let us through.
Secure the thread through time and space,
Then hold the gate for this Traveler's grace."

Lightning shot from the center of the orb, arching up and around the opening. The blue light grew blinding, then remained steady, as it had been when they'd first discovered it.

"Ah, you're a natural, me darlin' girl," Castor exclaimed with a wide grin and a dramatically loud smacking kiss to her forehead. "A chip off the ol' block, ya are!"

She laughed in pure joy and hugged her pink globe to her.

Wilder shook Quentin's hand before kneeling in front of her and bowing his head like a knight promising fealty to a queen.

"You have my eternal thanks, Miss Frankie. I'll be your champion in life, should you ever need me."

Her eyes glowed with happiness. "Will you save her?"

"You can be sure of it," he promised.

"Okay. Hurry," she urged. "I'll wait for you."

"It could be a long time, Frankie, my love," Quentin said, picking her up to sit on his shoulders. "We'll scry from home, and the second they return, we'll come back so you can meet Abbie."

"But, Papa!"

"Do *you* want to be the one to tell your mother you're camping here for the duration?"

With a grimace, she shook her dark head. "Mama only lets *you* get away with mudder," she complained.

They all laughed, understanding the reference regardless of her mispronunciation.

"We should go," Wilder eventually said.

"Yes." Quentin locked gazes with his father. "Be careful. And if you need help, etch a C into the rock face next to the portal."

"If I need you to retrieve me, we're well past trouble, son."

"You aren't as young as you once were. Your feeble-mindedness can be a hindrance," Quentin retorted.

With a laugh, Castor gripped Wilder's hand. "You're just jealous I'm going on an adventure with my future son-in-law and not you."

"Keep telling yourself that, old man."

Giving a short tug, the Traveler urged Wilder toward the portal. Leaning in, he said, "Wait for me to get the last word before you step through. I can't have that young—dammit! He anticipated my comeback."

And sure enough, when Wilder glanced over his shoulder, Quentin and Frankie were nowhere to be seen.

"You're crazy, aren't you?" he asked. "I'm about to step into a wormhole with a madman."

"Perhaps a little batty, but all the best people are. Tighten your belt and gird your loins, Thorne. It's going to be a helluva roller-coaster ride."

5

TWO YEARS EARLIER…

$\mathcal{A}$bbie paused her ascent as dark gray clouds gathered around her and Wilder. The weather had turned with such unnatural speed that it was hard to process the abrupt temperature shift. Always before, he'd regulated their bodies, making the climb bearable no matter the conditions.

"Abbie!" he hollered.

With a shake of her head, she signaled she intended to push on. They were close to the summit, and it was safer to camp there for the night.

Fifteen minutes later, she cursed herself for a fool. Never had it been more apparent than when a low, distant rumble filled the air, causing the mountain to react. It breathed as if coming to life and grumbled its displeasure. Around them, the atmosphere became staticky, like pulling apart two socks after forgetting a dryer sheet.

"Abbie, wait!"

But she was already in motion, trusting the cam she'd placed. Her confidence in her skill was strong. Second-guessing only led to undermining it, and eventually, to mistakes.

The rock she'd weighted gave way, and the ricocheting tumble of stone sounded like rapid gunfire. A scream tore from her throat as she pitched backward off the cliff face, her terror multiplying when the cam slipped loose.

It seemed as if she fell through space for an eternity, and each second carried the expectation of brutal impact. She braced for jagged rocks, sheared skin, and crushed bones.

But it wasn't what she experienced at all.

In the distance, she heard Wilder's frantic shout and somehow *felt* his horror ripple through her. Her heart thundered in her ears, drowning out the sound along with the rushing wind. If she'd have thought about it, she'd have expected to freeze as the distance between them widened. Yet her cells warmed all on their own, growing hotter until her insides were an inferno.

A kaleidoscope of colorful images flashed through her mind, impossibly bright. They appeared and vanished again as if a bored teenager were flipping a TV remote in a manic haze. Abbie tried to grab one and hold on before she lost what was left of her sanity.

Suddenly, it all stopped.

The impact stole her breath.

Her ribs ached like a bitch, and every inhale was a struggle. When she dared open her eyes, she was sure she'd died and landed in an alternate version of hell. Nothing was familiar. The mountain she and Wilder had climbed was gone. If she didn't know better, she'd say she was in a different area of the United States altogether. One with a shit-ton of dirt.

The only other explanation was a magical vortex. When she next saw Wilder, she intended to ask if those were possible.

Closing her eyes, she took mental stock of her body.

Nothing hurt to excess, and Abbie prayed it meant no broken bones.

"What the Sam Hill was that?" The grizzled voice came from a distance, yet echoed off the surrounding canyon walls.

"Never seen nothin' like it in all my thirty-nine years," another male voice said, slow and filled with suspicion.

Leather creaked, and a horse snorted.

"Should we check it out?" asked a tentative third.

"Well, what else we gonna do, ya lunkhead? God's honest, boy, you got sawdust rattlin' 'round that skull. I should've left your ma's letter unopened."

A sixth sense told Abbie she didn't want to be found by these three. She jackknifed into a sitting position, muffling a groan by biting down on her knuckle. A frantic glance around revealed few decent hiding spots. Pulse pounding, she scrambled for the nearest gap in the rocks.

The unmistakable ch-ch-ch of a rattle stopped her cold.

Shit.

Every cell in her body screamed, "Move!" but even the twitch of a finger might earn her a venom-laced bite. Her breath hitched, the desert air scraping down her throat like sandpaper. The situation had officially gone from bad to biblically worse.

The air shifted beside her.

Thwack. Thunk.

And the rattling stopped.

Abbie stared, wide-eyed and disbelieving, as the snake writhed then fell still. An arrow pinned its triangular head to the ground with surgical precision, and dust curled up in lazy spirals around the shaft.

With a scream locked in her throat, she searched for the source.

Tucked into the rocky outcrop above her, a man stood half-shadowed, his expression unreadable. In his hand, a bow with another arrow at the ready. He was lean, but solid in a way that said he didn't run from a fight, and his skin was sun-bronzed. Long black hair blew over his shoulders, making him appear like a warrior from another time. He didn't move or speak, just stared at her, waiting.

Abbie glanced back toward the approaching noise.

Gruff and arguing, the cowboys made no effort to deaden the sound of their advance.

"You shouldn't be here." Her savior repositioned and slung the weapon across his back. "They're hunting for trouble. Best not to let it be you."

"I—" She gestured toward the rock. "There was an accident. A metaphysical anomaly."

"You're born of a Traveler."

She gaped and shook her head, not knowing what the hell a Traveler was or how this man might know anything about her heritage.

The stranger gave her a quarter smile. "I've seen you in dreams. But we must go."

He extended his hand and waited, steady and patient, as if they had all the time in the world, when they both knew they didn't. She hesitated only a second before scrambling forward and accepting his offer of help. Together, they climbed a shallow ridge, ducking into an opening just as the cowboys rounded the corner and spotted the pinned rattler.

"I'll be, Pa! You ever seen anythin' like that?"

"Shut up, ya fool boy." The burly man in charge had no softness for his son. He was harder than the stone Abbie rested against. "This is a fresh kill. Eustace, find that blasted savage. He can't have gone far."

Abbie wanted to scream at the injustice of it, but settled for squeezing her savior's hand. The real "savage" was the bigoted white man in the saddle, prepared to harm whomever he encountered, with extra hatred reserved for a proud Native American man.

"Blink us higher up the canyon," the low-voiced stranger urged.

"I'm not a witch," she whispered back. "I don't know how."

His intense gaze bore into hers, and a frown tugged at his brow as if he were trying to figure out why she was lying. He gave one decisive nod, then eased to her right, preparing to climb higher.

No equipment or fail-safes.

Abbie froze.

She began trembling, and her feet refused to budge when he gestured for her to follow.

"I don't think I can," she said. Her words were barely audible, yet he heard and understood.

An emotion similar to compassion shone on his chiseled visage. That sensitivity was at odds with what history books had claimed, and Abbie was grateful they'd gotten his people's "barbaric" behavior wrong.

Instinct said she'd be in dire straits had he not happened along. If the rattlesnake hadn't gotten her, the predatory cowboys would've.

The stranger scanned the ledge above them before looking for an alternate route. Below, loose pebbles fell under the pressure of Eustace's booted feet as he advanced toward their hiding spot.

"We must go, Traveler's child," her companion stated quietly. "He'll be upon us soon."

She nodded, taking his proffered hand.

You can do this, Abbie. You've free climbed plenty of times.

But nerves ate at her, and the fingers she stretched toward handholds shook as she moved along the cliff's edge. She tried to block out the snake scare, praying she wouldn't encounter another in the shaded hollows.

"Do you—"

The stranger held a finger to his lips and halted her ascent, gesturing for her to back into the shadows of the rock wall. His gaze locked with hers, sharp as the arrow that saved her life.

"Quiet," he whispered, as if fearing she hadn't understood.

Closing her lids, she concentrated on breathing evenly, hoping to control her anxiety. What fresh hell had she landed in this time? How had she gotten here, and where the fuck was Wilder?

Twelve miles away, leaning against the bar of The Broken Halo Saloon, Jonas Thorne waited impatiently for his friend to finish his poker hand, but Draven Masters was in no particular hurry.

"Masters," he barked. "Anomaly."

Other than a sharp nod, the gambler remained silent and appeared relaxed as he tossed down two of his five cards. The dealer shot a worried glance toward the only individual willing to bet against Draven.

"Clive?"

Whether the man was asking for permission or if Clive Cabbot, notorious hot-head, intended to gun him down for dishing out cards, Jonas didn't know.

Clive slammed his fist on the table. "Fucking deal already!"

The dealer's gulp was audible.

"This is a friendly game, Cabbot. If you cannot keep a civil tongue, I'd advise you to walk away," Draven said in his heavy French-accented drawl.

Jonas wanted to bang his head on the bar. No way would Clive not view the rebuke as anything but an insult. And they didn't have time for an altercation. Somewhere out on the plains, a magical disturbance had just taken place. Already, a handful of townspeople were speculating about the colorful burst seen from this distance away.

Draven's job, as a potential Guardian assigned by the Goddess Isis and the Fates, was to monitor supernatural events and ensure the mortal world never got wind of them. Powers like theirs were too advanced for the average individual's comprehension. But the man was rebellious at best, refusing to do as he was told.

Fifteen minutes had passed since the event. Sure, Jonas could go it alone, but magical mishaps weren't supposed to be his responsibility.

They were Draven's.

Town sheriff was his.

Jonas considered conjuring a winning hand for Clive, but he despised the bastard. The entire town feared the man's temper whenever he was in his cups, and as far as Jonas was concerned, everyone would sleep better if the guy took up residence in the local cemetery.

But then again, someone else would take his place. Perdition Ridge was a hotbed of thieves and prostitutes. No one was who they appeared to be. A preacher who drank too much and failed to quote the good book as it was written, a sexy-as-hell eye-patch-wearing madam with secrets, and a jail that hasn't locked properly in years. Locals say if you stay in this godforsaken place long enough, you'd either die, go insane, or vanish when the moon turns red.

Jonas tended to agree. He was halfway to mad himself.

"You're a filthy cheater!" Clive slurred, his hand heading south for his revolver.

"For the love of the Goddess," Jonas muttered.

There was little point in catching Draven's eye. His young friend's attention was all reserved for the surly outlaw. His smirk dared the man to act, assuring Clive that if he did, he'd be a dead man before he cleared his holster. Of course, the

Guardian had time manipulation on his side if he chose to use it, so he wasn't required to be faster with a gun.

Jonas rested his fingers loosely on his belt. Forty-plus years of kicking around the world had taught him to stay calm but be lethal when needed.

Movement on the second-floor landing caught his eye.

Then *she* appeared.

Roxanne Vale, affectionately known to him as Red.

The woman in emerald silk moved through the shadows like she owned them. Her body was a sensual ripple in a world full of grit. An off-the-shoulder dress skimmed the floor, the slit useful for either freedom or seduction. Her corset wasn't boned, and Jonas couldn't fathom how it stayed up—clearly, it had to be magic—but it displayed creamy breasts to spellbinding perfection. Light caught the green threads, setting them aglow as she glided down the stairs of her establishment.

She ran both sides of this business, the saloon and the attached house of secrets and sin, The Velvet Ember. With deceptive ease, she could wrap the patrons around her little finger. And right now, she had all eyes in the place focused on her, with the exception of Clive, the dealer, and Draven.

Strolling among the tables as if the world bent to her will, Red touched the shoulders of a working girl here or there, positioned to show their wares to full advantage. Whether to offer silent support or remind them to keep their clients leashed, Jonas didn't know, but she was a master of manipulation.

Red paused beside Draven, resting her hip against his broad shoulder as she peered at his cards. Her exquisite face was emotionless as she categorized his hand and lifted her gaze to meet Jonas's. Though a black leather patch covered her left eye, the glittering amber of her right one pierced his soul. Such was the impact of a single look from her.

Without breaking her hold over him, she addressed Clive.

"Mr. Cabbot, I've known Mr. Masters for a few years now. He's aboveboard and skilled enough not to swindle other players." Finally, she fixed her attention on the troublemaker. "I realize you've indulged more than you usually do, but it's no reason to lose your temper. Is it?"

Clive was no match for her warm smile, however fake, and melted into a surly schoolboy from the outraged outlaw he'd been mere moments ago. "No, ma'am."

"Excellent. Mr. Masters will be kind enough to buy your next bottle, and for being a fine upstanding patron of my establishment, Ginger will see to your needs for the next two hours."

"Thank ya, ma'am. That's more than kind."

"My pleasure." She'd taken only two steps before turning back and gracing him with a schoolmarm glare. "And other than worn out from a rowdy round of pleasure seeking, Ginger is to remain unharmed as per house rules. Do I make myself clear?"

"Yes'm."

"Excellent," Red purred. "I knew I could count on you, Clive. Ginger will be upstairs with fresh water for your bath."

"Bath?" he hollered. "I don't—" He gulped as her expression turned downright frigid. "It's just that bathin' leads to sickness, Miss Vale. Everybody knows that."

Without looking his way, Red called out to Jonas. "Sheriff Thorne, would you say you're a healthy specimen?"

"Yes, ma'am," he replied with wry humor.

She knew damned well how healthy a specimen he was.

"And how often do you bathe, Sheriff?" she asked.

"Daily."

"Thank you." She shot him a sultry smile over her shoulder, then faced Clive again. "And look how handsome he is. I bet a little soap and water will make *you* just as charming and pleasing to our girls, Mr. Cabbot."

Clive spat in his palm and smoothed his hair down. "Do ya really think so, Miss Vale?"

"I know so, you darling scoundrel." Dimples flashed along with her straight, gleaming-white smile.

"Even you?" Clive ventured with a crafty glint.

"If I spent quality time with my patrons, absolutely," she assured him, lying expertly through those perfect teeth. "Now, Barnaby will give you a bottle, but be sure to pace yourself, my dear. No one likes a limp whiskey cock." Her wink earned two jaw-drops and one smirk from the table's occupants.

By all appearances, she was calm as she sashayed toward Jonas, but he detected the underlying irritation, as only one close to her could.

"Take Masters out of here until cooler heads prevail," she ordered.

"Sure thing, Red."

"And make sure he pays for Clive's bottle." Out of the blue, she swayed but was quick to grip the bar, catching herself. With a clouded expression, she met his gaze in the mirror's reflection. Her brows clashed as her mouth tightened.

"What's wrong?" he asked, straightening.

"There's a disturbance west of town, Jonas. A woman needs your help, right now. No time to ride," she said in a low, urgent tone.

"A premonition?" He threw back the last of his brandy and slammed the glass on the polished wooden top.

"Yes. Hurry, before she's injured beyond repair."

"Shit." He snatched up his Stetson, stalked to the poker table, and scooped Draven's winnings into the hat. "Let's go."

His commanding tone brought Draven's head up from the deck he'd been shuffling.

"Premonition?" he murmured.

"Yep. Red said for us to get there, like yesterday."

6

In her fatigue, Abbie missed the next foothold, sending loose gravel skittering down onto Eustace's unsuspecting head. His startled shout echoed off the surrounding canyon walls and confirmed what she feared. They'd been spotted.

Panic-fueled, she climbed faster, only pausing to swipe her sweaty palm on her pant leg.

A gunshot cracked, and the bullet pinged right above her head.

Her scream was involuntary.

"Move," her companion snapped, all pretense of stealth gone.

She wasn't optimistic enough to believe she'd survive, but she was certainly stubborn enough to try like hell. Renewing her efforts, she scrambled up and to the left, intending to make herself less of a target. An approving nod from her savior told her the action was wise.

Another shot. Another ping.

Fire lanced through her right bicep with such suddenness, and she swore. She risked a glance. The sight of torn flesh and rapidly spreading blood turned her stomach. Burying her horror along with her gag reflex, she soldiered on. Movement meant survival, though she wasn't sure how much more she had left in the tank.

A second bullet struck her savior's back. He grunted, staggered, and barely managed to keep his footing.

If they continued, she risked his life, and that, she wouldn't do.

"Wait!" she shouted at Eustace, voice cracking. "Just wait. Please! I'm coming down!"

She looked up into the warrior's sorrowful eyes. He'd view it as a failure, but she needed to assure him none of this was his fault.

"Thank you for trying, but you need to save yourself."

"Don't—"

The next shot caught her shoulder and threw her off balance. Her world tilted, and she lost her grip.

The raw scream pulled from her throat was chillingly familiar, an echo of her first tumble off the mountain. The Native man's cry carried the same anguish Wilder's had as she plummeted toward certain death.

"Wilder," she gasped, for no other reason than she wanted her last thoughts to be of him.

The jarring impact onto a jutting boulder halted Abbie's free fall. Her bones snapped on contact, the sound sickening and final. Agony stole her breath as she sprawled facedown on the boiling-hot rock, paralyzed. Her cheek burned like a motherfucker, as if someone flayed it open with a fillet knife. She didn't possess the strength to move her arm, and she was too dazed to tally her numerous injuries.

A line of red caught her attention. Blood flowed from her head across the craggy, sun-washed surface and spilled over the edge in the faintest of waterfalls.

Cold. She was so unbearably cold. And wasn't it odd on such a scorching day?

She shivered once, then again as she blinked to lessen the glare of the overbright sunlight.

As her life force grew weaker, she closed her eyes against the salty burn of tears. Never once could she have imagined dying this way. Alone in a brutal, untamed land, with no one to mourn her passing in whatever timeline she'd been transported to. Goddess, let her wake from this, and it have all been a nightmare!

A man's fetid breath against her cheek made her want to recoil, but she couldn't move. Her nose twitched, curling at the offensive stench.

"Breath mint," she croaked.

"Ya brought this on yerself, woman. Me and—"

The wind carried away the rest of his words. Or perhaps it was her soul drifting. Didn't matter. He was of little concern anymore.

⁂

Jonas and Draven materialized at the exact moment the woman fell. That son of a bitch Eustace Larkham was already bending over her, intent on more harm.

"Can you freeze time?" Draven asked, not bothering to lower his voice. They were cloaked from sight and sound thanks to an age-old spell.

He could, but then, so could Draven if he weren't a stubborn jackass who refused to use his upgraded powers if he didn't have to. The thick-headed fool had a death wish, and one day soon, Jonas intended to discover why.

"Yes, but how the hell do we explain popping from here to there when time snaps back?" he asked.

Draven shrugged. "We kill them, *non*? Make it look like an accident."

Jonas shot him an irritated glance. "I'm the blasted sheriff, Masters."

"And still, you ride with the likes of me, *cher*," Draven said with a sly grin. "You cannot tell me those renegades aren't on the wanted posters papering your walls."

They were. But Jonas despised using magic on mortals unless absolutely necessary. It always raised questions if anyone looked too closely. He'd prefer to use human methods to capture and punish the unsavory elements. But damned if he hadn't run out of time. Eustace was gearing up to hurt the woman further.

Thoroughly frustrated by his friend and left with no choice, Jonas lifted his hands, curling them into fists.

"Praemorare!"

Though only he and Draven were able to hear, the word still cracked through the air, older than the canyon crags and heavier than gravity's pull. The current stilled, and previously billowing dust hung in place like frozen motes of copper.

Eustace was caught mid-kick, his face twisted into a hateful mask, arms suspended beside his head like a puppet on strings suddenly stilled. The rifle in his grip added depth to the scene, making the threat of death very real.

"I should kill that blasted trio," Jonas muttered. The only reason he hadn't was because, until that moment, he'd been unable to associate them with anything but cattle rustling. And he wouldn't fault people trying to fill their bellies. What was a missing cow or two compared to starvation? Unfortunately, it was becoming clear they were more than mere rustlers and had a deadlier mischief in mind.

With another wave of his hands, Jonas created enough airflow to lift himself, and he stepped onto the rock ledge.

"Stay cloaked, Masters," he called. "I'll bring her down after I deal with Larkham."

Time rebounded with a snap, but he was prepared. Drawing on his elemental magic of air, he pushed outward. The force threw Eustace off balance and tumbling to the ground thirty-five feet below. Based on the awkward angle of his neck, the blackhearted villain wouldn't be harming anyone else.

"What do we do now, Pa?" Gus Green cried.

"What the hell do ya think, ya demmed fool?" Harlan gave the reins a vicious tug, whirling his mount and digging his spurs into the poor creature's sides. The horse gave a screeching whinny before galloping east toward town.

"One more thing to hold the bastard accountable for when we get back," Jonas muttered as he knelt to check for the woman's pulse.

Gus was slower to react, splitting his concern between Eustace and the pale blonde. Opposite his sire, it seemed the boy had a conscience. Swinging out of the saddle, he began the arduous climb.

"Fuck." Jonas ran through the catalog of spells he knew, hoping to recall one to dissuade the youth.

Other than as a witty companion with a fast fist and faster gun, Draven was little use to him. Having shunned his latest gifts, he was on borrowed time with the Witches' Council for refusing to bend to the Goddess's and Fates' will and accept his new job as Guardian. Jonas had been picking up the slack to keep the stubborn bastard from a showdown he couldn't win.

Movement behind him caused Jonas to round on the potential threat, gun palmed in his left hand and his right prepared to blast whoever or whatever to perdition.

"Shadow," he murmured before becoming disconcerted that the man could see him despite the cloaking magic.

Stands-in-Shadow gingerly picked his way toward Jonas,

keeping his attention on Gus's progress. The fact he'd ventured out of the darkened cliff crevice suggested he didn't believe the young man was a viable threat.

"You can see me, yes?" Jonas asked.

The Apache man nodded. "Traveler's child," he said in a low voice, indicating the injured woman. "Came through the rocks."

Damnation.

They could only hope no one would follow her. The last thing Jonas needed was a group of witches turning Perdition Ridge upside down. Despite their town being a hellhole, the residents weren't mentally equipped to handle any level of supernatural chaos. Only the Witches' Council had a snowball's chance in Hades of keeping the magical community in line. Well, them and the Aether, Damian Dethridge.

Jonas considered summoning him and dumping his latest headache in Damian's lap.

Though Stands-in-Shadow didn't display any outward signs of suffering, he moved with a caution unnatural for him, and the skin around his eyes was pinched.

"How badly are you injured, Shadow?" he asked his old friend. "Be honest."

"Bullet to the back from Crooked Neck." Stands-in-Shadow didn't bother to glance at Eustace's broken body.

"Lodged?"

"Yes."

Double damn!

"Okay." Jonas rose and whistled to Draven. "Larkham shot Shadow. Get your ass up here and get the bullet out while I heal the woman."

"What about the runt?" Draven asked as he materialized beside him. "He's gaining ground, *cher*."

"Yeah, I know. I can't seem to recall any spells to deter him." Squinting one eye, he studied his friend. "But you can."

"*Mon dieu!* Kindly fuck yourself in the face if you believe I'll play with Guardian *magie.*"

Leading Stands-in-Shadow back toward the wider part of the shelf, Draven removed his duster and rolled up his sleeves. "This will hurt like the very devil, Shadow. You are ready?"

The Apache withdrew a strip of leather from a pouch attached to the cord slung across his chest and slipped it between his teeth. Without hesitation, he sat, presenting his back, and rested his palms on his knees. With a grim nod, he indicated Draven should proceed. His trust alone was courageous.

Jonas ignored the surgery to concentrate on the woman's predicament. First, he needed to detour Gus. After stepping outside the cloak and silently adjusting the spell to encompass Draven and Stands-in-Shadow, Jonas kicked gravel over the rock ledge.

"Lady? Lady, are ya alright up there?" Gus called.

"No, she's not, Green," Jonas replied, bracing himself to see below. "That good-for-nothing Eustace Larkham caused her to fall, and she's badly injured."

"Sheriff?" Gus's voice squeaked in fear.

"Yes. It's Sheriff Thorne. I was chasing rustlers through the canyon when I heard the shots." He paused for a beat to let his plausible lie sink in. "You wouldn't know anything about those rustlers or the gunfire, would you, son?"

"Uh… well… no, sir." The unmistakable panic returned the boy's voice to prepubescent.

"I see." And he did. Having dealt with the underbelly of society, Jonas saw a heck of a lot. No words needed. "Gus, climb back down and ride away. For your own safety, mind. I don't want those murderous rustlers to stumble upon you, son."

"But the lady… how will you get her down?"

Lord love the kid for the tender spot Harlan hadn't yet beaten out of him.

"Don't worry your head none. I've already rigged a sling from my rope," Jonas lied. "Go on, now. Get. I don't want to worry about your neck in a gunfight."

"Yes, sir."

Sounds associated with Gus's scrambling down reached Jonas. The following silence indicated the young man was rethinking leaving.

"Sheriff?"

Jonas sighed and shot a Goddess-help-me glance skyward. "What is it, Gus?"

"Should I have Doc come out here?"

"No. It'll take too long, and I don't want Doc to run afoul of those bandits. I've some medical training. It comes with the job."

"Alright."

A rare protective feeling washed over him, and he leaned over to meet Gus's worried brown eyes. "Stay clear of Harlan. He'll be your death, son."

"He's my Pa."

"Don't mean you have to follow him to the noose."

The young man paled.

"If you need a job, come see me tomorrow afternoon. I'll find work for you. Maybe we can get you out from under his boot."

The offer extended, Jonas returned to examine the Traveler's child, wondering who and what the hell she actually was.

As one of the Six—the original families blessed with magic —he'd learned early on that only a select few could manipulate time to their will, as he had. But he'd never met anyone able to travel through time and space. Yes, he'd heard tales of one legendary man's ability, but no one knew the guy's name or from whence he came.

Perhaps the Traveler would come looking for his daughter one day soon.

7

Fevered dreams took the Traveler's child from pale and knocking on death's door to scarlet and raging about something called a carabiner. And no amount of medical knowledge, human or otherwise, could cure her. Jonas had appealed to the Witches' Council on the woman's behalf, pleading for a Healer from The Authority's ranks, but he was continually denied.

"Red sent me to check on you," Draven spoke from the foot of the bed, startling him.

"Christ alive! You walk as soft as a cat."

Other than a twist of his lips, his friend said nothing.

"If I'm being honest, I'm exhausted. It's been five days, and I'm worried the fever is cooking her brain. She's been rambling something fierce." Jonas met Draven's gaze. "I think the Witches' Council is holding back to force your hand, but I have to do something."

"Why do you care so much, *cher*? It's one woman, and no one's come lookin'."

"Perhaps that's why. No one should be helpless or alone in the world. It doesn't seem right."

"I've lent my *magie* to yours, Thorne, but I'll not accept the anchor of Guardian, not even for you or your need to save the world."

"I'm not asking you to," Jonas snapped.

"Aren't you?"

Maybe he was, but he wouldn't admit it aloud. Draven could do so much good if he'd get over his rage at being manipulated by his mother, one of the three sisters of Fate. But perhaps betrayals like theirs didn't allow for forgiveness or acceptance.

"I'm going for the Aether," Jonas decided aloud. "Damian will help her. He must. And if not him, Uncle Nate won't let her suffer."

"We will pray to the Goddess you are right. I wouldn't bet my last coin on her chances after tomorrow."

Leaving Draven in charge of her welfare, Jonas teleported to the Thorne estate in Leiper's Fork, Tennessee, to confer with his uncle. He swore as he stepped into the dining room, having failed to note the hour.

"I'm sorry, Aunt Evie," he apologized, Stetson in hand. "You know I'd never interrupt your supper if it wasn't important."

"Think nothing of it, dear boy. Are you hungry? Darling, dish Jonas up a plate," she directed, smiling at Uncle Nate down the length of the table. "No, not the cornbread, dear. He loathes the stuff."

If Jonas weren't so damned tired, he'd have laughed. Though tiny, Evelyn Flemming-Thorne was a force to be reckoned with, and her husband did her bidding with zero complaints.

"I don't really have time, Aunt Evie. I need to find Damian."

"He's not here, dear. The last I heard, he was watching the

Enchantress's tomb from Ravenswood until the next Guardian took his place."

"Does he never leave his estate these days?" Jonas asked, desperation creeping in.

"What's all this about, my boy?" Uncle Nate asked, handing him a full plate, having ignored Jonas's refusal. "Sit and tell me what's happening."

So he did. Between mouthfuls of Evie's delicious stew and freshly conjured biscuits, he explained his current circumstances.

"Oh, the poor woman!" Evie rose in one fluid motion and snapped her fingers. In a blink, she was wearing a traveling costume and had a small satchel in hand. "I'll go back with you while Nathanial finds Damian."

"Evie—"

"No, darling. I'll not hear another word about it. Bring Damian to… where is it you live now, Jonas?"

He bit back a grin. "Perdition Ridge. Arizona."

"Right, well, that sounds like a dreary place, doesn't it?" she mused. "Nothing for it. That sweet woman needs our help."

"Evie—"

"I won't be gainsaid, Nathanial."

Uncle Nate blew out a breath, rose to his feet, and swept her into a one-armed embrace, using his other hand to remove the bag from her grasp. He dropped the satchel at her feet and proceeded to kiss her senseless. Though brief, the kiss was pure seduction, and when he straightened, there were stars in her eyes.

"I have no intention of gainsaying you, my love," he said huskily. "But we need a plan of action before going off half-cocked."

"I'd say you're more than half cocked, darling," she purred, letting her fingers wander with blatant appreciation.

Jonas choked on a carrot. There were certain things he

didn't need to witness. Foreplay between his older married relatives was at the top of the list, only second to his parents going at it.

Uncle Nate's deep laughter rang out.

"But I do have a plan," Aunt Evie countered, returning to the main topic. "I'll nurse Jonas's young woman—"

"Not mine. I only found her."

"—while you bring Damian to Predilection Ridge," she said, as if he'd never spoken.

"Perdition," he said, waving his fork. It earned him a tap to the back of his head.

"Manners, Jonas Thorne!" Uncle Nate scolded.

"Sorry," he mumbled, ducking his head to hide a grin.

His uncle was a proper British viscount by birth, despite making America his home. His stately Tennessee residence had once been a scaled-down version of the massive family estate, Thornewyck Castle, nestled in the misty hills of Wiltshire, before burning down and being rebuilt in the modern, High Victorian style it currently was.

Although Uncle Nate was lax about most things, manners weren't one of them.

Having been born and raised in the United States, Jonas tended to be less formal in his dealings with others. His persona as an amiable sheriff—unless crossed—saved a lot of lives and headaches.

He finished his stew, drained the last of the beer Uncle Nate had so kindly poured for him, and pushed back his chair to stand. "I'll see Aunt Evie is well taken care of. You have my word, no harm will come to her."

"That's good enough for me." His uncle tucked one of Evie's stray blonde locks behind her ear. "I know you're prone to trouble, my love, but please, stay safe. Life would be dismal without you."

She patted his chest. "Charmer."

Bending, he whispered into her ear, causing her cheeks to pinken prettily.

His chuckle lingered after he'd teleported away.

"Don't tell me what he said. I don't want to know," Jonas said with an exaggerated shudder.

"Good, because it was private," she replied pertly. "Now, take me to your young woman."

"Not mine, Aunt Evie. I told you, she's merely a lost lamb I found. Or who found us."

"If she's out of her time, I'm surprised The Authority isn't trying to rectify the situation." She tucked her arm through his. "Transport us to your home, dear."

***

Fire raged through her veins, licking beneath her skin with every breath. Only the cool press of a washcloth against her brow brought the tiniest sliver of relief. Her caretaker placed wrapped ice compresses beneath her arms and along the sides of her neck. The moment was pure heaven.

"Her fever is breaking. But it's vexing that she won't allow anyone to heal her wounds. It's almost as if she possesses a built-in defense mechanism," a woman said. "I've never seen anything like it."

"We encountered the same issue when we tried to repair the damage to her face and treat the skull fracture," replied a deep-voiced male. "She only accepts mortal medicine and rejects all supernatural intervention, but at least we were able to set her broken bones."

"Damian should be here soon, dear. He'll know what to do."

"It looks like she may be coming around, Aunt Evie." The man perched on the edge of the bed and gently clasped her hand. "Hey. Are you with us, ma'am?"

Her lids felt weighted, but she managed to open them long

enough to search his face. Although his sharply chiseled features teased her brain, she couldn't say she knew him. Next, she studied the female. The same sense of familiarity, but no true recognition.

"Wilder?" she rasped, hoping one of them knew the person whose name was prevalent in her mind.

They looked as confused as she felt.

She closed her eyes, unable to contain her disappointment.

God, her body ached. And fatigue pulled at her like a riptide, dragging her back under. She frowned, but her burning cheek stopped the motion cold. Reaching up, she touched the side of her face, fingers skimming the eight-inch gash from temple to jaw.

She recoiled in horror.

"Mirror?"

"Not yet, honey. Not until we get you stitched up good and proper. All right?"

The woman's tone was firm, conveying authority and making her seem older than she appeared, given her clothing and hairstyle. Yet she couldn't have been much past forty.

In trying to recall her own age, she hit a brick wall. Again, she frowned, but like before, the pain stopped the motion.

"It's okay, ma'am. No need to fret. If you give us your name, we'll contact your people," the man offered with a smile.

Her brain stalled, and her throat tightened as panic struck in earnest.

What the hell was her name?

A jagged bolt of dread pierced her chest. She shrank from his touch, clutching her head and willing the answer to surface.

Nothing but a yawning, black void.

"No..." Her voice trembled. "I don't know. Oh God! I don't know my name."

Her caregivers exchanged an apprehensive glance, but then the woman squared her shoulders and smiled.

"These things happen, and you're not to worry, honey," she soothed. "I'm Evie, and this is my nephew Jonas. He's the sheriff here in Perdition Ridge."

Breathing labored, she shook her head before admitting, "I don't know this place."

"I don't expect you do."

More questions arose, but every word uttered was sandpaper scratching the inside of her throat. She pressed a hand to her neck, swallowing hard. "Water, please."

"Sure thing." Jonas poured some, then went a step further, supporting her upper back and head as she greedily gulped the cool liquid.

"Easy now, ma'am." He touched her wrist. "We've barely been able to get anything inside you. Too much and you might get sick."

Although she wanted to keep the tin cup, she recognized the wisdom of his words. Mid-handoff, her fingers tightened on the cool metal.

Tin? What an odd choice for drinkware! Why not plastic or glass?

Her gaze drifted around the small space. It was rudimentary: a bed, a dresser with a washbowl, and wooden walls of a log cabin.

Perdition Ridge, Evie had said.

Not a place she recalled.

"Ma'am, we—"

The door burst open.

Two men entered, both familiar to her, but not. Their clothing was all wrong.

One was light-haired with sapphire eyes, damned near angelic in appearance; the other was dark, creating a perfect foil. With his black hair, obsidian eyes, and carved angles, the intense stranger was beyond compelling.

He was fucking beautiful!

Exactly as she imagined Lucifer would look.

"Oh, Damian! I'm so happy you've come." Evie greeted him with a welcoming smile and a hug. "This poor dear needs your help."

His assessing gaze missed nothing as it swept over her, leaving her feeling exposed despite the covers.

"Why was I called for a simple healing, Evie?" he asked. His voice was cultured, laced with the hint of a British accent, as if America wasn't his homeland.

"It's not so simple," Jonas replied grimly. "She has a protective shield. Magic won't touch her, so we can't."

Interest sparked in Damian's eyes, and his mouth curled slightly, taking his handsome visage to a dangerous new level.

Not that she cared. She hurt too damned bad to think about anything but her discomfort. Yet even her pain-numbed mind couldn't completely ignore his appeal.

She shifted her attention to his companion, and a name surfaced. "Alastair?"

Everyone froze, and tension rippled through the group.

Damian recovered first. "His name is Nathanial. Nathanial *Alastair* Thorne."

"Not right," she whispered to herself.

"What's not?" Nathanial asked softly, stepping closer.

"Your name. You're Alastair." Emotion caused her throat to ache worse than it already did. "Must be."

"You're not the first person to mistake me for another, my dear." He crouched beside the bed and tenderly brushed the hair away from her throbbing temple. "But I'm not the person you believe me to be." He smiled. "I'm Nate to friends."

She winced as she swallowed hard, and Jonas was quick to offer the tin cup. After sipping a bit of water, she returned it and met Damian's thoughtful gaze.

"What's your name?" he asked.

Mutely, she shook her head.

"I see." His gaze sharpened. For a moment, it felt as if he peered straight into her mind.

The sensation was similar to a thousand bugs crawling across her skin, and she desperately tried to shove it away. A raw, unseen force surged up in defiance. Her body reacted with a furious jolt, primal energy lashing outward in defense. A blue glow filled the small space, crackling as loud as a lightning strike as it gathered into a sphere around her.

"Get down!" Jonas shouted, pulling Evie to the floor as the bolts exploded in every direction.

Drained, she slipped into sleep.

"Good Goddess!" Nate said. "Is that normal?"

"It's been happening since we found her," Jonas replied, helping Evie to stand. "Everyone okay?"

The Aether ignored them, stepping closer to examine the unconscious woman. "Incredible. Other than a Goddess or Guardian, I've never seen such power."

"What is she? Fallen angel?" Uncle Nate wrapped an arm around Evie, leaning in to assure himself she was unharmed. With a satisfied sigh, he kissed her forehead and tucked her close.

"Do angels even exist?" Jonas asked, having never considered the possibility before. Since gods and goddesses were real, it stood to reason they might create winged creatures in their image.

Damian shook his head with a chuckle. "One never knows, but so far, I've not encountered any."

"That you know of," Uncle Nate replied dryly. "Could be they are hiding in plain sight. This lovely young woman, for instance."

"Then why not heal herself?" Aunt Evie countered with a jab to his stomach to free herself. Approaching the lady in question, she fearlessly began the fever-cooling process again. "No. She's merely lost her way."

"Nate explained she appeared from thin air in the canyon west of here," Damian said. "What did the Guide say, precisely?"

Jonas tried to recall the exact conversation. Failing, he said, "He called her a Traveler's child."

A secretive smile curled the Aether's mouth. "Did you summon Isis?"

"I tried. She was reticent. Her message was along the lines of suggesting Draven Masters should make the first overture."

With a dark chuckle, Damian nodded. "That sounds like the deity we all know and love. I'll reach out to her, the Council, and the Authority. Perhaps I might gain answers where you could not."

"Can you heal her?" Jonas asked, reluctant to let him leave without trying.

"Not without a nasty shock. She's holding her own for now. If she takes a turn for the worse, send Draven to me." He turned to go, but paused. "Is Shadow still hanging about?"

"Yes. He's keeping watch over Gus Green."

"I'm not familiar with the name."

"No, you wouldn't be." Jonas gave a single-shoulder shrug. "He's a mortal with the devil for a father. Poor kid."

"Well, we weren't all as blessed as the Thornes."

"Thorne," their patient mumbled in her delirium. "Wilder."

Damian stilled, and a dangerous expression settled on his face. "She recognized the name. She's definitely more than she seems."

"Should we be concerned? Is it possible she's a Death Dealer seeking one of our extended family?" Uncle Nate asked.

"I don't believe so," he said slowly. "In my experience, they regenerate faster than a standard witch." Damian turned to Jonas. "Nate said she was like this for five days?"

"Yes."

"Then, no, she's not a Dealer."

Aunt Evie waved them off. "You're distressing her with your morbid talk. Go on with you boys."

"Evie, my love—"

"You, too, Nathanial. The woman needs rest and care at the moment." She gave him a pointed look. "Go investigate the name Wilder. Ask Isis about future generations. I have a sneaking suspicion it's attached to our family."

"You think she somehow tumbled through time to find other Thornes, Aunt Evie?" Hopping about time was difficult for Jonas to wrap his head around, but based on the female's manly clothing and tools, she certainly didn't belong in their century.

"Perhaps." His aunt gave her a considering look. "I doubt it was by design. More likely, it was accidental. If Stands-in-Shadow is correct and she is a Traveler's child, she may not be in control."

Damian shifted closer.

"You make a great point, Evie. If she was injured first, she might be falling through time, instinctively searching for her people."

Uncle Nate grunted. "Bloody fantastic."

"The only thing we can do is nurse her to the best of a mortal's ability. If, at a future juncture, she allows the use of my gifts, I can restore her mind and heal her more serious injuries," Damian said. "Continue to ply her with willow bark tea. It should control the fever. Slippery elm and honey might soothe her throat as well."

"You're able to remove her power," Jonas said, hating himself for suggesting it. "Why not do it?"

"It's a painful process, and some don't survive. Separating a witch from their magic requires a directive from the Authority or Isis. I'll not take it upon myself to destroy her life."

"You may not have a choice, son," Uncle Nate added.

"Certainly, it may come to that, Nate, but I'd rather exhaust all other possibilities first."

"I agree. In her weakened condition, it's doubtful she'd make it." Jonas pressed the back of his wrist to her forehead and cheeks. With a grimace, he retrieved the empty bucket by the dresser. "She's flushed. I'll retrieve another block of ice."

Aunt Evie protested. "It's a simple matter to conjure more."

"I need to stretch my legs and find Draven. I'm still required to fulfill my duties as sheriff of this godforsaken town, and he's likely the one stirring up trouble."

"He's a young man with the weighted expectations of the Fates. Let him enjoy his freedom for a while longer," Uncle Nate suggested.

"Wise," Damian replied with a warm smile. "I'm glad I had you and Evie to raise me, sir."

"Your mother was to thank, son. Her last act was to save you."

His expression hardened, and the room grew chilly. "I must go."

"That boy," Uncle Nate muttered after he was gone.

Jonas barked a laugh. "Boy? He's what, fifty-six, fifty-seven? He's no more a boy than I am."

"You'll both always be boys to us," Aunt Evie cut in with an affectionate smile. "We love you like our own."

He kissed her smooth cheek. "I love you, too."

"Leave the bucket. Nathanial can conjure ice while you patrol the town and check on your friend."

"Yes, ma'am."

"Oh, and I want to meet your young lady. Soon," she said with a stern look.

"Young—"

"The one you call Red," Uncle Nate supplied helpfully.

Jonas groaned and hightailed it from the room. How the hell did they find out about her so quickly? There was no way in hell he'd introduce Red to Evie. Not that he didn't feel she was good enough, more like she didn't need to be corrupted any more than she was by his aunt's and uncle's inappropriate humor.

***

6 MONTHS LATER...

Nightmares continued to plague her. Relentless and haunting, with the shadow of knowledge lingering on the edges of her consciousness. And one man was at the center.

Wilder.

Whoever he might be, the phantom without a face.

There were dreams so vivid, creating such a desperate longing for him, she would wake crying. But on other nights, even the merest glimpse of him triggered a level of anxiety, causing her to scream herself awake. Snowstorms, mountains, magical doorways... none of it made sense. Nothing and no one was familiar. Over the months, she'd had to relearn the basics, like dressing herself.

Jonas and Evie had dubbed her "Mary," but the name didn't fit. They tended to speak in hushed conversations, sending her sidelong glances and falling silent if she drew near. Whenever she chose to eavesdrop, the primary topic was the Aether and the removal of her powers. What abilities she could possibly have were beyond her scope of imagination, but she couldn't shake what she'd heard from Nate: she was a woman out of time.

Lately, she'd begun to believe she was on her way to insanity.

Especially those nights she woke, reaching for a lover who wasn't there. How could she explain the phantom feel of a man curled around her? Or the echo of him calling her name during intimate acts? A more fitting one she could never recall come daylight.

Although the Thornes were kind, the overall feeling of oppression wouldn't fade. Tonight, after dinner, she'd made her excuses, claiming she was turning in early. Once alone, she crawled out the window and crept toward town. Maybe, by spending more time there, she might recognize something or someone.

One block from the saloon, Mary paused and tugged at the bodice of her borrowed gown, wishing for anything less constrictive than her ridiculously tight clothing. Happily for her, Evie and Jonas had given up trying to force her into a corset and bustle, agreeing that neither was suited for the sweltering Arizona heat anyway.

"Well, what do we have here?" sneered the voice of a man she'd come to despise.

Harlan Green.

A real-life nightmare.

He actively stalked her whenever she left the safety of Jonas's home, and anytime she glanced up, it was to find him smirking as if he knew a secret she didn't. He probably did, since she couldn't recall a damn thing before six months ago. But it annoyed her, instilling unease she couldn't seem to shake.

"Cat got your tongue?" he taunted, shifting closer. "Or maybe you really are too dumb to talk. That it, Crazy Mary? Ain't got a thought in that broken head of yours?"

Jaw tight, she averted her chin. Speaking was difficult for her, as most of the townspeople had eventually guessed. Her brain had not only locked away her memories, but it had also half-paralyzed her vocal chords, effectively limiting her speech.

"Folks say you're touched," Harlan drawled, circling as he sized her up. "But me? I think you're fakin' it. Playin' the mute so you don't have to answer no questions about where you came from." He flipped the lace at her collar. "Is that right? Maybe you're smarter than what they say."

Anger simmered within her, gathering strength like an unchecked storm.

His foul breath teased her gag reflex. Did no one believe in mouthwash in this godforsaken town?

Mouthwash.

A memory tried to surface. There had been no mention of it before, she was sure of it. Yet she was certainly familiar with the word and the minty liquid used as a rinse. How else would she know he needed it?

"Pa?" Gus Green stepped onto the boardwalk and met her gaze. His expression held discomfort with his father's behavior.

"Go away, you fool boy," Harlan grumbled. "Can't ya see I've captured the filly loose from her pen?"

His menacing leer tightened her stomach.

"And I'm just the man to break her," he concluded.

Mary gave a slight shake of her head, hoping Gus would understand she wanted him to stay.

His answering nod was infinitesimal.

"Pa, if ya don't come now, Cookie said he's givin' up our table. Said those ribs don't stay good for long."

"That's because they're already older than dirt with no meat on 'em," Harlan snapped. "Go on with ya. Get. And don't be eatin' my meal, or you'll face my belt."

The suggested abuse caused Gus to pale, but he remained stubborn in the face of the threat. "Cookie said he ain't holding no food, neither."

Harlan rounded on him, prepared to settle the matter with his balled fists.

Unable to let the young man be punished for his father's obsession, she stepped in his path.

"No," she rasped, through her faulty vocal cords.

Rage clouded Harlan's pockmarked features, but then he grinned, the expression so evil, her stomach shriveled.

"Would ya look at that, boy? She fancies ya."

No, she damn well didn't, but she wasn't capable of voicing it.

"But that's only 'cause she hasn't had a real man, like your pa."

Dear God! As if he were anyone's poster boy for a real man. She shuddered.

"Don't worry if you're cold, gal, I'll be warmin' ya soon enough," Harlan promised.

"That's going to be mighty difficult, considering *la dame est* with me, Green."

A match flared in the darkness, then died, leaving smoke to signal Draven Master's approach, and as he stepped into the light at the alleyway opening, he shifted a cheroot from one side of his mouth to the other without lifting his hand from the pearl-handled gun butt he caressed.

"Isn't that right, *ma chère?*" Although he didn't look at her, he was aware of the exact second she nodded. "There you have it, Green. *C'est confirmé.*"

There was a pecking order in Perdition Ridge, and Draven was at the top. Many had challenged him since her arrival, but none had won, as the graveyard upon the hill attested. Unfortunately, Harlan knew better than to challenge the top dog, and he tended to slink away to save his hide.

His glare promised retribution as he disappeared into the shadows.

"I'm sorry, Miss Mary," Gus said, eyes downcast.

Despite wishing to touch his arm in understanding, she didn't. Harlan didn't know it, but Draven Masters had saved him from a nasty shock. If he'd come in contact with any part of her skin, her body's selective process would've likely registered the threat and acted accordingly. The force field protecting her was temperamental, allowing some contact but denying it for others. With any luck—and of late, she'd had little—it would remain on high alert for those of Harlan's ilk.

"She understands," Draven said in her stead. "He's your *père* and difficult to challenge, *oui*? One day, you'll get there, Gus." His unspoken "you'll be forced to" hung in the air between them.

Or perhaps only Mary heard what he hadn't voiced aloud. As an outsider, she observed more than most, relying on body language and a person's energy.

"It seems Jonas's plan to separate them isn't workin' all that well," Draven commented casually as he joined her to watch Gus scurry after his father.

Mary placed a hand to her throat. "Works."

"*Oui*, however, it will not be enough. Harlan Green will get that boy killed one day, *ma chère*. It's a sad *fait*."

She looked up at him, meeting his warm whiskey gaze.

"But perhaps his *père* will meet his end first?" he suggested with a wink. "For now, let's introduce you to the Ridge's finer *plaisirs*." With a smile promising sin, he held out an arm, waiting for her to tuck her hand into the crook. "Do you fancy a taste of Perdition's underbelly? Cards, whiskey, and *péchés* folk pray the good Lord don't see."

She hesitated.

"You can't shock me, Marie," he said, giving her new name a poetic flair, *Mah-ree*. "I mean you no harm. But if it makes you feel better, I can conjure for you a pair of gloves."

With breath held, she touched her fingers to his coat sleeve and sighed happily when nothing happened. His grin was pure triumph.

9

ONE YEAR LATER...

"Shots fired at the bank, Sheriff!" Gus hollered as he skidded to a halt in the open doorway of The Velvet Ember's parlor.

"Blasted thieves," Jonas swore, slamming his whiskey down. "Sorry, Red. Gotta run."

Gus's pale face prompted him to pause. "What is it, son?"

"I think it's my Pa. He's rounded up a few—"

Red's expression arrested. "Mary is in the bank."

"Goddammit! I swear, that woman attracts trouble like prairie flowers attract bees."

Jonas was on the move, not waiting for further explanation.

It was pure bad luck that Mary was in the Perdition Ridge Exchange & Trust when Harlan decided he needed to make a withdrawal. And worse, the bastard didn't have an account and had added others to his one-person gang.

Teleporting would be faster, but there was no way to do it with a town full of spectators. He dashed through the saloon, expecting and finding Draven, with Red and Gus on his heels.

"Bank robbery," he barked. "Mary's at the center of trouble again."

With the grace of the gunfighting gambler he was, Draven flung his cards facedown on the table and rose. "We'll pick this back up when I return. And should one of you peek at my hand, I'll remove yours. *Compris?*"

In unison, his three tablemates gulped and nodded.

Locking gazes with Red, he said, "Keep them honest, *chère.*"

She waved them off.

Outside the bank, they formulated a plan. "Gus, you keep watch from atop the mercantile," Jonas ordered, intending to keep the young man from harm's way. "Draven and I will enter as soon as you're clear. If they escape, don't leave your spot, but monitor their route. Got it?"

"Yessir."

The instant he scurried off, Jonas turned to Draven. "Bulletproof yourself, Masters. We can't stop time with witnesses."

"Understood."

They spared a moment to cast their spells, making it seem as if they were deep in conversation while reciting the words to protect themselves.

"Let's go." Jonas led the way, not hurrying, though everything inside was screaming he should.

When he tried the handle, the door was locked, but it didn't deter him. The shock on Harlan's cronies' faces was worth the price of admission.

Harlan, the sneaky bastard, was already on the move, grabbing Mary and putting a gun under her chin. "Just turn back 'round now, Sheriff. Ain't nothin' here for you to see."

White-hot rage burned Jonas from a cellular level, and containing his fury wasn't easy. This was on him for developing a soft spot for Gus and not wanting to hurt the boy. But he should've ended Harlan much sooner, right about the time the sonofabitch cornered Mary the night she snuck out.

With Draven and him as her champions, he'd expected the bounder to back off. But it seemed as if Harlan viewed hurting her as a challenge. Which meant she wouldn't get off scot-free today. Not unless he was put down for good.

"Can't do that, Harlan. Too many people rely on their pay to survive." He shrugged, casting the man a wry smile. "You'd know something about that if you ever worked an honest day in your life."

Draven leaned against a nearby column, struck a match, and lit his cheroot. After a deep inhale, he blew smoke Os, scaling them down to fit one inside the other. The trick caught the attention of Harlan's two partners in crime. As distractions went, Draven's was expert-level.

"I thought you'd understood. Touchin' *ma dame est* a sentence of death," he said, squinting through the haze he'd created. "Let her go, Green, and it will be painless."

Mary's eyes widened, and like a wild animal scenting a mountain lion, her nostrils flared with the panicked glance she cast around the room. Why her standard electrical force field wasn't working was in question, but magic, especially a wounded person's, wasn't always reliable. Other than randomly electrocuting a threat, she hadn't learned the standard arts of survival: conjuring food, shelter, or warming her cells against the cold.

Jonas maintained an air of calm, hoping to reassure her.

"You say that, but I'm holdin' all the cards this time, Masters," Harlan sneered, pressing the gun barrel harder against her jaw, forcing her head at an awkward angle. "Unless you're wantin' to see your scarred woman's face made uglier, you'll back off."

With a resigned sigh, Draven threw down his cheroot and crushed it under his boot. Casting Mary a half smile, he asked, "Why is it always to be hard with stupid people, *ma chère?*"

She registered his intent a second before Harlan and

sagged, straining her captor's hold. His gun shifted as he scrambled to lift her. But what none of them expected was for the weapon to fire.

The bullet tore up the side of her face, exiting her frontal lobe and lodging into the wall above Jonas's head.

"Fuck!" Harlan paled as her dead weight became a useless shield.

Four rounds were fired.

Two from Draven, taking out Harlan and the closest outlaw to him.

One from Jonas, taking out the last standing bandit.

The fourth was a mystery until one registered the shattered glass and saw the smoking rifle held by the man above the mercantile store.

Harlan's body rested beside Mary's, one bullet in his chest, and the other in the center of his forehead. Until Jonas questioned Draven, he wouldn't know which was his and which belonged to Gus.

Diving to his knees, Draven felt for Mary's pulse. From the flash of relief, he found one. Without a backward glance, he swept her away, stalking for the rear exit.

Jonas had to trust him to save her because he couldn't leave the crime scene with all the traumatized onlookers and staff.

"Why the hell can't we seem to heal her?" Jonas ran his hands through his hair and exhaled heavily. "Three months in stasis, and no signs of life."

Seraphina Valentine observed her lover from the vanity mirror, feeling a sense of sadness for his plight. Had she been anything other than a whorehouse madame and business owner, she might've felt a tinge of jealousy over Jonas's obsessive need to save Mary.

But she didn't.

Her not-so-illustrious career as Roxanne "Red" Vale and a murderous past refused to allow the finer emotions associated with being the sheriff's mate. Not that she considered herself anything more than his passing fancy piece. If she did, it was a sure bet the Fates would come knocking, prepared to destroy the only good thing in her life.

Speaking of the Fates...

"Perhaps you're not meant to, Jonas." She never allowed herself to call him by anything but his given name. Pet names were for lovers without secrets. Those who were at liberty to spend their lives together.

He glanced up from his pacing.

What a sight he made! Shirtless, with the top of his britches unbuttoned, displaying his flat, muscle-ridged abdomen and the fine hairs leading to an impressive member. With his blond hair mussed and a day's growth of facial hair, he looked rough, like she preferred her men.

"What the hell's that supposed to mean, Red?"

"Only that the Fates have a plan for all of us." She shrugged and leaned in to apply a rich burgundy lip rouge.

The shade was reserved for nights with him alone ever since he'd told her he loved the dark contrast of her mouth against his paler skin as she pleasured him. Spinning around, she rested her elbows against the table, displaying her breasts to advantage. It was doubtful she could completely pull his thoughts away from his concerns about Mary, but she wasn't above trying.

"Perhaps Crazy Mary—"

"Don't call her that," he snapped.

With a frustrated sigh, she straightened, drawing her wrap over her shoulders and cinching it. "Perhaps *Mary* has escaped their design long enough. It's possible she was never meant to survive Eustace, but we interfered with their plan for her."

Jonas scowled before turning away and drawing on his shirt. "I have to go check on her."

"Of course you do," she muttered. Upon receiving his sharp glance, she shrugged. "It's always Jonas with his God complex to the rescue."

"Want to tell me what this is all about, Red?"

"No, I don't." If he hadn't already guessed, a third person in their bed was one too many. Rising, she moved toward the door. "If you don't mind, I'd like to be alone."

Sure, he'd already started dressing, and the effect of her precious supply of lip rouge was now a waste, but sending him on his way afforded her control. Of which she'd had little until opening The Velvet Ember. It was fortunate The Broken Halo's owner had adored her and given her the first option to purchase the saloon after his consumption diagnosis three years ago.

The same day Jonas had walked into her life and accepted the job as sheriff.

Her position as his lover and her two businesses provided a deep sense of security, however false. Any affection he felt for her was fleeting and would easily die in the face of a "good girl." Innocent Seraphina Valentine might've been marriage material. The eye-patch-wearing Roxanne Vale was not.

Jonas halted mid-shirt tuck and stalked toward her. His piercing sapphire eyes swept her face, lingering on her mouth. When his gaze locked with hers, he wore a contemplative look.

"Are you jealous, Red?" he asked huskily.

Her heart hammered, but she lifted her chin in defiance.

"Please." She scoffed. "I'd have to be in love for that, Jonas, and while I hold you in high regard, I'll never be so foolish as to fall for you."

Goddess, she was the greatest liar in the west. However, pretending was everything in her line of work.

Disappointment twisted his lips, but in a breath-stealing

move, he wrapped an arm around her, hauled her against him, and kicked the door closed.

"We'll have to see what I can do to change that," he growled before crushing his mouth against hers.

Seraphina, the silly girl, melted against him as Roxanne, the practiced courtesan, fell into what she did best—seduction.

There was a quality to Jonas tonight so different from before. A desperation she attributed to his inability to save Mary. Oh, if only she'd had a man like him in her corner seven years ago. One who defended the innocent Seraphinas of the world as well as the jaded Roxannes, should the past ever meet the present.

His touch was bold yet reverent, his kisses pure fire. And when he sank into her welcoming warmth, she pretended love was still an option for her and that Jonas wanted to claim her as his forever.

10

Wilder had no fucking idea where they were, but the Native American man made up to resemble figures only seen in movies or history books gave him the first clue.

Expressionless, the guy observed them exit the portal. Either he'd witnessed the same in the past, or the guy killed at poker. They had yet to discover which.

Castor ignored his presence as he leisurely surveyed the surrounding cliffs and the plains beyond.

"A bit dusty and barren for my tastes," he deadpanned.

Wilder was torn between laughter and a roll of the eyes.

Without missing a beat, Castor asked their observer, "Do you speak English?"

Amusement flashed in the dark-haired man's eyes.

"*Parlez-vous—*" Castor began.

"I speak English," he said.

"Thank the Goddess. Other than French, my foreign-language skills are shit."

Wilder snorted. "It's uncanny how much you and Quentin are alike. Never serious."

"Well, he is a chip off the old block, Thorne." He gestured for the stranger to move closer. "Since you've not lost your tan or soiled yourself, I imagine you've already witnessed a Traveler pass through this portal. Can you tell me where she is?"

"Traveler's child."

With his heart pounding hard enough to crash through his chest wall, Wilder met the man halfway. "You've seen her? You've seen Abbie?"

"I do not know Abbie. But Mary lives near."

"Mary. Right." His disappointment was keen, causing the man's face to blur. His lungs shut down, refusing to function as they were designed.

"It doesn't mean she's not here, son," Castor reminded him as he joined them. "Only that he didn't see her."

"Traveler's child was here. Climbed rock and fell."

Had the man witnessed Abbie's fall from the mountain? Hope once again gave Wilder life. "Who is the Traveler's child? What does the rock climber look like?"

The man gestured to Castor.

"It's her! It's Abbie!" Excitement thrummed through him, and he had to hold himself back from kissing the stranger on the mouth. "Can you tell us where she is?"

"Perdition."

Did he mean she was dead?

Wilder traded a concerned glance with Castor. "What the fuck?"

Brows drawn together in consternation, the Traveler considered the stranger. "What is Perdition? Hell?"

"Some call it that, but it is a town. Perdition Ridge," the man replied. "Due east."

"So she's alive? This rock climber you call Mary?" Wilder asked.

Why go by Mary and not Abbie? It made no sense.

"Yes." Sympathy clouded the man's face. "But she is not whole. Not the same as before."

Bile swept up from Wilder's gut, burning his esophagus and throat as the urge to vomit rode him hard. If he spoke, he'd lose control and puke.

Luckily, Castor wasn't similarly afflicted.

"What happened to her?" he demanded, no longer the jovial time-jumper and every bit the enraged father.

"Find the Guardian and the Thorne."

"Guardian." His tone was razor sharp. "Would his name happen to be Draven Masters?"

"Yes, this is he."

Castor's grin flashed his delight. "This is excellent news! Come, Thorne, let's find Masters. He'll help set things to rights."

Things felt off, but Wilder couldn't pinpoint quite what.

"Has this portal always been here?" He gestured to the rock wall, then swore upon seeing the solid stone. "Uh, Castor, our way home… It's gone."

"Abbie can create another, and if not her, we'll petition Isis."

The careless response was as annoying as the missing portal was concerning, but since it wasn't his expertise, Wilder remained mute on the subject.

"She stepped through two years ago by the white man's calendar," the stranger said. "Like your door, hers closed behind her."

Two years had to seem like a lifetime in a strange place.

"What is the date? As in the year?" Castor asked.

"1877."

"Jesus," Wilder muttered. They'd gone back almost a hundred and fifty years. What would that mean for Abbie, with her modern clothing and ways? "Do you know if she's been back here or attempted to reopen it?"

"No. She has not returned. She is ill. Here." The man tapped his temple. "They say crazy."

What happens to people deemed insane in this century? Asylums?

The urge to scream was too overwhelming to deny, and Wilder stalked away to vent his pain, pacing off his agitation. After a while, the continuous murmur of voices caught his attention, and he rejoined the conversation.

"We would appreciate any help you can provide, Stands-in-Shadow," Castor was saying, having learned the stranger's name in the short span Wilder had taken to regroup.

"How far to Perdition Ridge?"

"Twelve miles. But with no horses, you will move like the Guardian and Thorne."

If they were magical—and with the term Guardian involved, there was a high chance they were—they probably teleported everywhere. Yet Wilder wanted to be clear.

"Move like them how?" he asked.

"Through space. Like all of your kind."

"So you know other magical people?"

Stands-in-Shadow's grin flashed. "Yes. I am the spirit Guide and Seer."

Wilder exchanged a glance with Castor. They only knew of one Seer in their time. Were they more common here?

"You keep saying thorn. The Guardian, we know. What is the thorn?" Castor asked.

"Like him. Thorne."

With another delighted grin, he slapped Wilder on the back. "Ah! More good news, Wilder, my boy. It seems you have a relative in this land that time forgot."

"Sheriff Jonas Thorne. He is a good man and will help you," Stands-in-Shadow replied.

"How do we teleport to a place we've never seen?" Wilder asked. Moving from one spot to another without a general idea of what lay ahead could be deadly. If they misjudged, they might end up half in and half out of a wall, their guts torn from their bodies. Or a beam through the brain. Neither option was appealing. It wasn't as if they could rely on cell service, WiFi, or Google Maps to investigate a location beforehand.

"We put out feelers and tap into this gentleman's mind."

"What? How?" As a Thorne, Wilder was well versed in witchcraft, but without tanzanite and his cousin Alastair's spell, sharing thoughts was virtually impossible.

"If Stands-in-Shadow isn't opposed, he will pilot us through touch. You and I conjure the magic to teleport, using his image of the town. We only need to get to the outskirts." Castor addressed the Native man. "Are you willing?"

"I cannot leave my *ħí*."

"Is someone else here?" Wilder asked.

"Horse," Stands-in-Shadow replied with a half smile.

"I can return you immediately. Your *ħí'* will not suffer," Castor assured him.

"I will not leave him. He is all I have anchoring me to this world."

Anchoring him? What the hell did he mean? Mentally? Physically?

"My spirit drifts," Stands-in-Shadow explained as if reading Wilder's inner thoughts.

"How does a horse stop you from drifting?"

"You would call it love." The man met his gaze. "It is how you found this place."

Let him believe what he would. Wilder wouldn't argue that he hadn't controlled their time hop.

"Okay, what if I stay with your horse and you show Castor the town? He can return you here once he has the coordinates, then I'll go with him to find Mary."

When he received an affirmative nod, he looked at Castor. "I'm assuming you can tap into his mind without me?"

"It may be easier without your thoughts crowding ours." Holding out a hand, Castor waited as the Native man considered it. "Trusting a stranger is difficult, but I mean you no harm. You have my word that I will bring you there and straight back, Stands-in-Shadow."

His forthright nature did the trick, inspiring trust. But within five minutes, they realized their plan was a bust. Their powers didn't work in this past world.

"How is it we don't have our gifts here?" Wilder battled the tidal wave of panic threatening to wash over him. In the only other instance he had been without his abilities, tragedy struck.

"I've never gone beyond the boundaries of my natural life," Castor replied. "Perhaps it has something to do with not existing yet?"

"Christ, we're screwed."

"What would your cousin Alastair say in the face of your pessimism, my dear Wilder?"

Although his pale eyes didn't contain their standard amused light, Castor didn't appear to be as deflated as him. Still, a hint of displeasure tugged his mouth down, so it wasn't only Wilder's bout of pessimism.

"He'd make some ridiculous quip about courage and the challenge being fun, I'm sure," Wilder replied dryly.

"Exactly. Twelve miles isn't a particularly long trek. I've suffered worse."

"In the desert, during the middle of the day, with no water?"

"Are you *trying* to annoy me, son?"

"You will use my horse," Stands-in-Shadow interrupted. "I will run beside you."

"To save your horse the burden, I can run for part of the journey," Castor stated. "I jog at least five miles every morning."

Wilder didn't volunteer for cross-country. He hadn't done

anything particularly athletic in two years and would likely die from his lack of fitness.

"Show-offs," Wilder muttered. The sooner he got to Abbie, the better. "Let's go."

"Not now," the Native man said. "We wait until the sun is lower in the sky. Even the Diné take care when the desert burns hottest."

It went against the grain for Wilder to wait, but this was not a time or place he was familiar with, and he had to trust the Guide-Seer had their best interests at heart.

"Will you tell us what you know of Abbie, er, Mary?"

11

Despite the late-afternoon sun, the scorching heat of the Arizona desert was brutal, and the journey to Perdition Ridge was pure hell. Wilder hoped the town wasn't aptly named.

"When we arrive, I will procure new clothes for you," Stands-in-Shadow said after they paused to rest his horse, and likely because he realized Castor was quite literally running on empty.

It was rare to see a warlock red-faced from exertion since they usually handled most tasks with their abilities. But healing, teleporting—hell, even stopping time—was now outside their range.

The Guide's instincts were good. Their clothes were too modern for anyone not to notice.

"Should we be proficient in gunfighting?" Wilder asked. He'd hate to delay, but if it was a matter of survival and getting Abbie out of a bad situation, he'd do whatever he had to.

Although he frowned, Castor didn't weigh in and instead looked to their new friend for answers.

"It would be helpful, yes. Perdition is a town of outlaws, of every nation. They test their skills on newcomers."

"Fucking fantastic." Wilder sipped his water, hoping to preserve as much as he could for the two doing the actual exercise. One canteen and a single bladder for three men and a horse would've been dire if they had left earlier in the day like he'd wanted to. Thank the Goddess for levelheaded strangers. "I know how to shoot, but I can't claim to be skilled."

"It's about appearances," Castor replied, ripping off a piece of buffalo jerky from Stands-in-Shadow and passing the rest on to him. "You only need appear ruthless, and most of those cowards will leave you be. Very few want to tangle with a killer."

"And the few who do?"

Castor's grin flashed. "Well, they're liable to shoot you down in the streets."

"How does my cousin tolerate you?"

His laughter rang out, tugging a reluctant grin from Wilder.

Even without his abilities, Alexander Castor possessed a magic all his own. It lived in his charm and easygoing façade. Underneath, the deadly opponent existed for anyone who cared to challenge him. But if one was smart enough not to rattle his cage, the likelihood existed that he'd live and let live. The actual problem was Castor's smartass tendencies. He rattled *others'* cages for the hell of it. Although his arrogance was well-earned, it stemmed from his descent from a god, with the looks and skill to back it up.

Wilder had a touch of it himself. It came with the name Thorne.

Those in his family had been taught from a young age what they were, the power they held, and the empathy and kindness they should offer. But it didn't mean he wasn't used to having it all and living comfortably in his skin because of it.

Only when he lost Abbie did he understand. Life had a way

of making the haughty humble. The day on the mountain, when he was left vulnerable, thereby leaving her unprotected, he'd learned a valuable lesson.

"You see much," Stands-in-Shadow said quietly.

Wilder glanced up and met the wisdom in his dark-eyed gaze. "Not as much as you."

"What will you do if Mary doesn't remember you?"

"Abbie. Or at least I hope it's her." He swallowed another sip of water and passed the canteen. "I don't know. I guess I'll play it by ear."

The very real worry existed that she might not know him, and if she didn't, she'd fear him. Making her whole again could be a problem without someone of their magical caliber.

"Earlier, you mentioned a Guardian and a Thorne. Why were they unable to heal her mind?" Wilder asked Stands-in-Shadow. "Does that level of magic not exist here? Is there some sort of interference?"

"They cannot get close. She allows few to touch her."

"Why?" Castor asked, leaning in and accepting the canteen.

"Her mind is broken, Traveler."

"Is she lucid?"

"This word is new to me," Stands-in-Shadow said.

"Awake and able to speak. Can she hold a conversation despite the claims she's crazy?" Wilder clarified.

"Ah. Yes, if she chooses. But Mary lives in her head and draws pictures in the dirt of faraway places."

Wilder looked at Castor. "Are you thinking what I am?"

"Those far-off places could be future events?"

"Maybe she's trying to reconnect in some small way." Yes, he was grasping at any bit of hope available, but he couldn't bear the thought of her mind being destroyed from either her trip through the portal or the following injuries.

"Don't get ahead of yourself, Thorne. We need to find her first. After, we can assess the damage and make a game plan."

"What is game… plan?" Stands-in-Shadow asked curiously.

"It is a strategy worked out by sports teams, politicians, and business people," Castor supplied helpfully. When the Guide remained curious, he elaborated. "In the future, teams of men or women, sometimes both, are built to display athleticism or skills. They compete against each other for money, awards, and such."

"This is an interesting concept. The Diné also display skills in these sports teams, but not for money."

"Many people play for fun, like I imagine the Diné do," Wilder said. "But I'm sure teammates come up with a plan to beat the other players, right?" He waited for the guy's nod before adding, "Hence, game plan."

"I like this game plan."

"It's always wise to have one," Castor agreed.

"We will make one for you."

They shared a grin.

Night had fallen by the time they arrived in Perdition Ridge. Lights poured from windows above closed shops, illuminating the way to The Broken Halo Saloon. On the far side of the bar sat The Velvet Ember, with two men lounging against the wall outside, shotgun barrels resting over their shoulders and holsters with very real revolvers on their hips.

The scene was from every Western movie or show Wilder had watched. The small boy inside him was thrilled, but the adult, who understood the lethal consequences related to this century, wasn't so happy. In fact, he was downright uneasy.

"This way," Shadow, as he suggested they call him, gestured to an alley behind the mercantile. "Bartholomew Mercer lives above the store. Most call him Bart. He will be sitting for his meal."

So saying, he pulled a cord, then stood back to wait.

"What is that?" Wilder asked.

"Bell pull. The rope runs to a bell inside an upstairs apartment," Castor said as if he'd witnessed it a thousand times.

At the top of the stairs, a door opened, backlighting a heavyset man. "If it ain't about trade, it'll wait 'til daylight. It's suppertime, and a man should be allowed to eat in peace."

"We're sorry to disturb, but my friend and I are looking to be outfitted with clothing, horses, and pistols. It can't wait until morning, Mr. Mercer," Castor replied.

"I ain't a horse trader. You'll go to the stables for livestock," Bart barked. He softened to add, "But I've got tack if ya need it."

He shifted, displaying the girth of a man who ate well off his steady profits rather than manual labor. Though not necessarily built for fighting, his barrel chest and thick arms indicated he'd lifted a heavy crate or two in his day.

"Understood. Are you willing to open your store tonight, friend, or should I offer my gold to one of the drifters loitering about the saloon? They might look more favorably upon selling goods after hours."

Bart sighed, knowing when he was beaten.

Wilder was awed by Castor's ability to blend seamlessly into the current timeline. Perhaps his confidence came with his Traveler abilities, but his boldness could only benefit them in a town like this.

"I'll be down as soon as I get my keys. Best have that gold ready. I ain't in the mood for games."

"It's a straightforward transaction, nothing more."

"All right, then."

Wilder wasn't surprised by the offer of gold. They'd both conjured the mineral and stored it on various parts of their bodies to account for payment should they need it. What he didn't know was the going rate in this century. He just hoped to hell they weren't about to get swindled.

As if reading his mind, Castor turned to Stands-in-Shadow. "Are you able to tell me if he's fair in his dealings? I wouldn't care to be taken advantage of. And should you require it, there's payment for your services."

He nodded. "Bart's fair, or he would not last here among these people. But be wary, and don't show more than you must. A few ounces at most, or it will bring the wolves to your door."

"Thank you."

Castor slid him two of the smaller pieces as a gesture of thanks.

"I do not need your gold," Stands-in-Shadow protested.

Wilder folded the fingers of the man's outstretched hand. "He can afford it, and you've given us a lot already, Shadow. We'd be grateful if you would take it for times you may need to board your *ħi'* or pay for his feed."

Bart returned, slamming and locking his door with a grumble. They chose to ignore his surliness.

The Guide slipped the gold into a pouch hanging from his waistband. The sleight of hand was performed in Wilder's peripheral vision, but was definitely magician-worthy. At some point in life, Stands-in-Shadow had learned to be cautious of strangers and merchants. Wilder hoped it wasn't from being screwed over in the past, but feared it was.

"From the looks and sound of ya, yer not from these parts. Back East?" Bart asked after unlocking the shop and striking a match to light a lantern.

"I am," Wilder said. "My father-in-law is from Europe, though he lives in New York now."

Though Castor shot him an amused look, he didn't deny the claim.

"What brings you fellas to The Devil's Backbone?"

"I thought this place was called Perdition Ridge," Castor said sharply.

"It is, but only those owin' their souls to Old Scratch reside in these parts," Bart said, eyeing them from head to toe. "Yer needin' it all, I'm guessin'."

"Yes," Wilder said.

"Them's mighty fine duds. Ya rich, then?" Greed gleamed in the merchant's eyes, urging caution.

"No. We're here on business."

"Business? What business?" Bart asked suspiciously.

Behind his back, Castor flared his eyes in warning.

"Actually, Mr. Mercer, we're looking for a woman. Perhaps you know her? She would've shown up about two years ago," Wilder said.

In a calculated move, Bart scratched the expanse of his belly and narrowed his eyes, as if in deep thought. "Well, let's see here..."

"It's understandable if you don't have recall, a man of your years," Castor said with an airy wave. "Don't bother yourself about it, my good man. Let's resume our shopping expedition, shall we?"

"I didn't rightly say I didn't know of her." When he got a stone-eyed stare for his comment, Bart tried another tactic. "It might be Crazy Mary you're referrin' to. But if it is, good luck to ya, friend. Me and some of them others made fair offers. But Masters thinks he's high and mighty, protectin' her like she's somethin' sacred."

"Masters? Where might I find this, Masters?" Wilder asked, using every ounce of his willpower not to beat the information out of the sleazeball. As beautiful as Abbie was, there was little doubt what his "fair offer" was for.

"This time of night? The Broken Halo or the whorehouse if he's not stickin' it to Crazy Mary."

Wilder saw red, and only a cautionary hand from Stands-in-Shadow curbed his impulse to pulverize the store owner.

"Are ya tradin'?" Bart asked, ignorant of his impending demise.

"No," Castor said succinctly. "Though dusty, our clothes are in good condition—for church—and we're willing to pay a fair price for your wares and add a small fee for your time."

Wilder choked.

The idea of two warlocks in church was one ridiculous claim too much.

"Ya said clothes, guns, and tack." Bart stacked two pistols and bullets on the bar before tallying the clothes and the handful of things Stands-in-Shadow brought to him, including a bowler hat and a floppy-brimmed cowboy hat. "That'll cost ya two hundred and twenty-six dollars for what your injun is pilin' up."

A glancing look at Stands-in-Shadow had Castor raising his brows in the face of Bart's claim.

"I said fair, Mercer," Castor returned coldly. The chill in his voice made them all stand straighter. "I already know what those things should cost, and I won't be fleeced."

"Ya wake me—"

"You claimed you were sitting down to dinner. In addition to the profit on your goods, I've added an extra fifteen dollars to compensate you for your time. Don't mistake us for fools. It will be the last thing you do."

Castor's challenge was awfully bold for a man without a weapon, but his confident superiority subdued the merchant. Men, no matter their level of importance, recognized an alpha and bowed in defeat.

"You plannin' to try these on?" Bart shoved denim pants and cotton shirts at Wilder.

"No need, but tell us where we can get a room and a bath."

Crazy Mary felt a chill. The icy sensation slithered along her spine, and she knew exactly what it meant. Trouble, most likely aimed at her. She frowned, and the uncomfortable pull of skin served as a grim reminder of the unsightly puckered scars that marred her face.

The light clink-clink-clink of spurs and the distinct tapping of boot heels on the wooden floorboards drew her attention to the approaching man. He strode forward with purpose. The pearl-handled revolver rode low in a holster, lovingly clinging to his upper left thigh and declaring he meant business.

Licking her dry lips, she let her eyes roam upward from lean hips, over a trim, flat stomach and muscled chest, to broad shoulders straining the threads of his cotton shirt. She lingered long enough to release an appreciative sigh before continuing her visual journey.

God, what a face!

His was seemingly strong, but a full beard hid the lower half. For all she knew, he could possess a weak chin, but somehow, she didn't think so. Intense amber eyes touched on her, locking on the jagged mark running from her left temple across the bridge of her nose, then shifting, likely to the one running from mid-eye to the right side of her mouth. Disfiguring blows had created a permanent, gruesome half-smirk that mocked the world and invited fists, kicks, or hair-pulling.

But revenge was always hers. Tormentors always received a nasty electrical shock, which usually deterred anyone else smart enough not to risk a strike.

The dark-haired man crouched in front of her, one knee braced on the sawdust-covered floor. A wide, beaming smile transformed his features from worried to radiant. Joy bloomed across his face. A pure, soul-deep happiness, as if his heart found what it had lost.

Her own heart thumped in her chest, skipping a beat when he addressed her.

"Hello, sweetheart. You don't know how long it's taken me to find you."

Mary jerked at the familiarity in his husky voice.

"Y-you know m-me?" she rasped, her words scratchy and broken. It was the first sentence she'd spoken in over six weeks. Until now, head gestures, grunts, and single-word responses were all she'd needed. No one cared to make conversation with a wounded bird.

He frowned. His eyes dropped to her scars again, and with a cautious hand, he traced their path.

She flinched, expecting the familiar zap her body utilized to defend her. Instead, his touch flooded her with warmth, wrapping around her mind and coaxing it to remember. Yet any knowledge of her previous life stayed stubbornly locked away, despite the stirring shadows and whispers of recognition. It was as if her brain had woken to possibility.

His frown deepened. "I do. I—"

"Step away from her, *mon ami.*"

Mary's blond Guardian didn't look up from his poker hand,

but the tension in his body gave him away. He didn't need to move to make his presence threatening; his energy was far-reaching.

"I'm not your friend," the newcomer snapped over his shoulder, not taking his gaze from her. "And she's with me, so feel free to fuck all the way off."

She sucked in a breath so hard she choked.

No one talked to Draven Masters that way. No one. Even the most foolish recognized his air of authority. But this man with his hardening features? Yeah, he couldn't care less. If anything, he was furious Draven had the nerve to address him.

"Go," she whispered. "Go... or he... kill... you."

The stranger's amber eyes were turbulent. "I'm not leaving you, Abbie."

"Ab-bee?"

The scrape of chair legs signaled Draven's rise. He loomed large and ominous as a funnel cloud. Yet the man with the beseeching expression ignored him, except to motion for him to wait.

"Look, it seems you've forgotten, but your name is Abigail Monroe. Your mother and I call you Abbie, and we've been so worried about you."

Mary tried the name on for size, but it didn't fit. Tears stung her good eye, and she blinked rapidly. "Not... familiar," she whispered.

"It's okay." The stranger's voice turned tender. It soothed, easing the panic threatening to overwhelm her. "It's going to be all right. I promise."

Before Draven could intervene, her hands acted of their own volition, sandwiching his face between her palms. "No shock... when touch?"

He grinned, and the love in his smile radiated to her toes. "Oh, I always feel a shock when you touch me, my dearest, but not in the way you mean."

Heat rushed through her. After all this time, all the insults and slurs cast her way, she wouldn't have believed she could be embarrassed. Yet here she was, blushing like a sixteen-year-old debutante at her first ball.

"Are we…? Did I…?" She was helpless to form the words and dropped her hands to her lap. "Never mind."

"Yes. You're mine, and I'm yours. And I've come a very long way to take you home."

"Mary? Do you know this man, *ma chère?*" Draven's question was gentle, but his eyes were granite-hard as they locked onto the stranger.

She wanted to say yes. Part of her encouraged the lie, but she shook her head in slow, heartbreaking denial.

The man's brows clashed together. "You do, Abbie, and you need to come with me. There's no time to lose."

"She's goin' nowhere," Draven declared. "Move out, now."

The newcomer stood, and his hand dropped to the gun at his side. "I'm not telling you again. Back the fuck off. I'm taking her home."

"Pausa!"

Everything around them froze at Draven's snapped command. The world went still, motion suspended in time. Only Mary, Draven, the dark-haired stranger, and Jonas Thorne remained in motion.

Movement by the door drew her eye.

A man with white-blond hair—*hair just like hers!*—sauntered toward them.

"Far enough, fella," Jonas said, sweeping his fan of cards closed and setting them neatly on the table.

The big blond grinned. "You must be Sheriff Thorne. Those sapphire eyes, the golden hair, and the blood-borne arrogance give you away." He jerked his thumb toward the man still kneeling by Mary. "Wilder is, too, but he gets his coloring from his mother's side."

Jonas blinked, then stared hard at the man by Mary. "Thorne. Is it true?"

"Yes."

"And a young Draven Masters," the blond giant crowed as if delighted. "It's certainly a mind fuck."

Her Guardian scowled. "Are you claiming to know me?"

The weird electric tension grew too much, and Mary curled in on herself, pressing her forehead to her knees.

Go away. Go away. Go away, she chanted silently.

Fire built beneath her skin, rising until she worried she might combust, and as with every instance before, her wishes failed to carry her away. No escape. Only pain. With a choked sob, she tore at the silver bracelet encircling her wrist.

"Go away!" she screamed.

The gambler whom Castor called Draven swore as his pinky ring flared to life.

"She's tryin' to teleport!"

Wilder dropped beside Abigail and wrapped his arms around her.

"Abbie," he whispered, his throat thick with emotion. "Abbie, you're safe, sweetheart. I promise, you're safe now."

Seeing her curled in the corner of this godforsaken saloon had been a fucking head punch. But he'd used the few precious seconds before she looked up to school his expression. He hoped like hell she hadn't seen his horror at finding her so broken.

The scars didn't bother him other than to remind him of the pain she'd suffered. Though why a Guardian and warlock with powers such as theirs hadn't already found a way to restore her to full health was in question. When Wilder got Abbie home, he intended to bring her to the Aether and bargain for his help.

But if those angry, disfiguring marks were now part of her, so be it. He'd love them, too. Abbie's true beauty had always resided in her soul, anyway. Outside trappings didn't matter in the entire scheme of things.

What absolutely shredded Wilder's heart was her nonexistent memory and fragile mental state.

But he had hope.

She hadn't shied away from him as Shadow mentioned she had with others. Hell, she'd touched him and searched his face, as if seeking the familiar. Her confusion wrecked him, bringing to light the terror she must've felt when she first landed in this time.

"I'm here, sweetheart. It's me. Your Wild Man," he crooned, using the name she'd always called him when he came back from a climb, scruffy, dirty, and in dire need of a shower. She'd never minded. Her smile, when she saw him, was always enough to melt stone.

"I'm sorry I took so long to find you," he said achingly, rocking her gently, uncaring how long the Guardian could freeze the world. In the back of his mind, he was vaguely aware Draven had to be nearly as powerful as Castor to manage it.

Lifting his gaze, he met Jonas's eyes. Wilder was counting on their familial relationship. If his Thorne code of "family first" was as strong here as in the present day, he might be able to aid in their return to the future. Without magical abilities, they were dead in the water.

Resting his cheek on her tangled mess of hair, he said, "Thank you for looking after her, Mr. Masters, but I'm taking her with me."

"*Non.* Not gonna happen," the gambler said, stepping forward. "*La dame est* mine."

"She's not chattel," Wilder snapped, feeling feral and protective of his mate. "She doesn't even know who she is, and she's certainly not staying where she's banished to a corner like a mongrel."

A calculating light entered Master's whiskey-colored eyes as he studied them.

"I swear to the Goddess, if you've taken advantage of her, you're a fucking dead man," Wilder promised him.

"Stand up," Draven ordered.

"Go to hell."

"Time's about to reset," Jonas warned, scanning the room. "If you're not back where you were, there'll be questions. Do it now, friend."

Reluctantly, Wilder eased his arms from around Abbie, hesitating when she clutched at his sleeve. "I'm not leaving without you, sweetheart. I promise."

She let go, still rocking and never once looking at him.

"Christ."

"Yeah," Jonas said grimly. "She's actually better than she was. We've been trying to repair her mind."

"You've done a piss-poor job of it," Wilder muttered, resuming his original kneeling position in front of her. "Castor, you may want to step outside. You walked in after."

"Right."

As soon as he'd cleared the swinging doors, the world snapped back to rights with a crackling pop and a fizz. Not dissimilar to a firecracker. Abbie flinched, and Wilder rushed to comfort her.

"She's beyond your help, Thorne," Draven said, stopping him with a hand on his shoulder.

Wilder shrugged him off and reached for her anyway. Scooping her up, he met with no resistance. "Point me to a private room."

"I'll show you," a sultry voice offered.

He shifted, meeting the single-eyed, curious stare of a redheaded woman.

"I don't know you, but I'll gladly place my trust in you if you have Abbie's best interests in mind."

"Abbie?" Her frown was fleeting, followed closely by a warm smile. "Yes, it's much more fitting than Crazy Mary."

The moniker, after finding Abbie in her current condition, made Wilder want to spit nails, but he nodded anyway. If the woman was offering them kindness, he'd take it and be grateful.

"I'm Roxanne. People 'round these parts call me Roxy, with the exception of Jonas, who prefers Red," she said as she led him upstairs.

"Wilder Thorne," he clipped out.

Her stride hitched but smoothed in an instant. Had he not been following her, he wouldn't have noticed.

"Any relation to our illustrious sheriff?" she asked politely.

"Probably. His resemblance to my cousin Alastair is strong, though we haven't had the pleasure of meeting before today."

"Yes, well, he's notoriously tight-lipped about his family." She stopped before a numbered door. "This room is usually pay-by-night, but is empty at the moment. Tomorrow, you can settle up with the hotel manager."

"The hotel is over the saloon?"

"The cheap rooms are. If you're looking for fancy, you've a longer walk ahead of you." She sailed over the threshold, straight to the window, and raised the sash. "But I don't imagine Draven Masters will let you go that far with his prized pet."

Wilder saw red, and not the businesswoman in front of him.

"Pet?"

"Your reaction speaks well of you, Wilder Thorne. Perhaps you're what this unfortunate dove needs."

"Dove makes her sound like a prostitute, and she's not," he retorted. Instantly, he regretted his attitude, realizing he sounded disparaging of her career choice. "Uh, not that there's anything wrong with—"

His attempt at a course correction met with amused laughter.

"It's fine. I understand exactly what you mean, honey." Her response suggested she'd encountered other idiots who were forced to backpedal. "And no, she's definitely not one of my girls. But I'm happy you'll be relieving Jonas of his burden."

Beneath her calm, an unnamed emotion lurked. Jealousy? But why?

"Jonas, he didn't—"

"No. He didn't. He's one of the best men you'll ever meet, honey," she replied with what appeared to be a sentimental smile for the man.

"And a finer woman never lived," the man in question stated from the doorway. The intense blue eyes locked on her spoke volumes. Sheriff Jonas Thorne considered Roxanne his mate. It remained to be seen if she returned the sentiment, though all signs pointed to yes.

"Thanks, Red," Jonas said. "If you'll have soap and water brought up, I'm sure our new friend here will be appreciative."

"Yes, ma'am, I would," Wilder agreed. "Is there another available room for Abbie's father?"

"Father?" Roxanne nodded absently as if thinking to herself. "It explains the hair."

"Yes, Alexander Castor."

"You said her name was Monroe," Draven said, entering on the heels of his comment. Suspicion weighed heavily in his voice. "Monroe and Castor aren't close. What are you not tellin' us?

We've come to the break in the story. I hope you're enjoying my version of the Wild West!

It's time to stretch your legs, *mon ami*. Might I suggest a bite or two? You're definitely going to want to dive right back in after. More of your favorites are coming up. :)

14

Wilder really didn't like the Guardian, the arrogant fucker.

"Illegitimate daughter," he bit out. "One only needs to look at them to see the truth."

Draven's lips twitched as if fighting a smile, giving the impression he was a master of the nettling game in addition to poker. He drew the coverlet back to assist Wilder.

After he laid Abbie down and attempted to stand, he halted as she refused to release his neck. Suspended in a bent position, he struggled to remove his boot, and then gasped when they disappeared altogether. Had he been expecting the magical help, he wouldn't have been surprised.

"She wasn't releasin' you any time soon, *mon ami*," Draven said dryly.

"Yeah. Thanks," he replied grudgingly. To Abbie, he said, "If you scoot to your right a little, I'll lie beside you, sweetheart."

Her hesitation spoke of her battle between trusting a complete stranger and self-preservation. Thankfully, her instincts were good, and trust won out. She shifted, making space with a tentative smile. He beamed his approval, understanding exactly how difficult her fragile faith was.

The second he was settled with his back against the bed frame, she rolled into him and wrapped an arm around his waist. Within seconds, she was asleep, and the strain of her meltdown vanished from her face.

"She knows you," Roxanne remarked upon returning.

"*Oui*," Draven agreed. "Otherwise, she'd have seared the flesh from your bones."

"I'd like to think so." Wilder stroked her hair, his heart bleeding for her suffering. "I wish I'd have known she was alive. It kills me to see her this way."

Castor paused in the entryway.

"I'm always late for the party," he quipped. His gaze locked on Abbie's damaged visage. "Someone care to explain what the hell happened to my daughter?"

"Several things," Jonas answered grimly. He crossed to the bed and stared down at her, and the fondness he displayed wasn't that of a man in love. It hinted at brotherly affection. "We ran across her two years ago. A Diné Guide had found her and tried to save her from a small band of outlaws."

"But *la dame* fell from the cliff they were climbin' to escape," Draven added. A muscle ticked in his jaw, proving the memory continued to rattle him.

Jonas nodded. "We arrived in time to prevent further harm, but the damage to her memory had already been done. My Uncle Nate and Aunt Evie helped—"

"Nate?" Castor asked sharply. "Nathanial and Evie Thorne are close by?"

Suspicion replaced the sheriff's mild-mannered expression. "I'll be asking why you want to know."

"Asking or demanding?" Wilder snorted softly. Tensions were lingering at the upper end of the scale—his among them —and needed to be defused. When the group shifted its attention to him, he shrugged. "I didn't hear a question, and based on your scowl, Jonas, it felt like more of a demand. But if I'm wrong, I apologize."

"I actually know Nate." Castor crossed to the dresser, poured water into the basin, and scrubbed his hands. "He fostered my best friend."

Snagging a small towel from the rack, Jonas crossed to him. "And that friend would be?"

They locked gazes, probably suspicious of deeper motives.

Castor broke first. "Damian Dethridge."

Other than a twitch of his brow, Jonas didn't reveal his thoughts.

"I'm assuming you know the Aether if your uncle is Nate," Castor added, accepting the towel to dry his freshly washed hands. "And if you do, why hasn't he helped Abbie?"

"What time did you say you're from, Traveler?"

With a sudden flash of white teeth, he slapped the sheriff on the back. "I didn't."

"In our time, we follow rules: the Authority, the Witches' Council. We may disagree with them, but if the magical community did whatever they wanted, chaos would reign."

"The Authority." Castor's reply was grim AF, and his grimace hinted at a bad taste in his mouth. His gaze flicked to Draven, and his expression tightened further. "They aren't known for their fair dealings in my century."

"So your century is different from ours?"

"About a hundred and forty-eight years, if Shadow gave us the correct date," he replied with a sweeping glance around.

"Why didn't you come for Mary—" Jonas began.

"Abigail."

"All right. Why didn't you come for Abigail sooner?"

"Want to take this one, boyo?" Castor tossed to Wilder.

"He wasn't aware he was a father before I told him. And I

didn't know Abbie was alive until a ghostly presence told me she saw her in the ether."

Draven and Jonas seemed to share a silent communication, perhaps attempting to determine if he was mad or serious.

"Ghostly presence?" Roxanne asked from her perch on the windowsill.

Having forgotten she was present, Wilder jerked, triggering a sleepy protest from Abbie.

"Yes. It's too long a story, but suffice it to say, my brother has a connection to the spirit world."

"Similar to Stands-in-Shadow," Jonas said, nodding as if Wilder's explanation cleared things up.

"Your Native American friend talks to the dead?" Castor asked.

"Yes, but he'd prefer that be kept quiet. Only his tribe honors his gifts. White men tend to frown on anything they can't explain."

"Okay, back to the subject at hand—Abbie," Wilder reminded them. "What's been done to heal her mind?"

"*Très peu,*" Draven replied. "We met *résistance* from the patient."

For a brief instant, humor crinkled Castor's eyes. "Your French roots are more obvious here, Masters. And there you made everyone believe you're Cajun. I'll be sure to give you hell about it when I return home."

The Guardian frowned. "I am both and neither. We're friends?"

"Colleagues fighting for the same cause, but it's not a stretch to call us friends."

"And Thorne?"

"Which one?" Castor quipped. "They're coming out of the woodwork."

Wilder shook his head. The Traveler was adroit at conversational maneuvers, and watching him was a masterclass on how to avoid answering probing questions. They all knew Draven was referring to Jonas, but rather than reveal the truth —he was long since dead in their time—Castor chose to keep the conversation light.

Switching gears, Wilder asked, "The outlaws, where are they now?"

"Two are dead, and one flipped sides," Jonas replied.

"Which one did this to my daughter?" Castor's expression became icy in a blink, leaving little doubt he'd put the man six feet under.

"The dead ones. You have these fellas to thank," Roxanne supplied. She rose from her perch, glided to Castor, and squeezed his upper arm. "I'll go air your room. My girls at the Ember need immediate supervision, but should you require company tonight—"

"Hell, no!"

They all swiveled their heads to gape at Jonas, who until that very moment had been mild-mannered.

Her seductive laughter rang out, bringing their heads back around like a tennis match. "Oh, darling, I wasn't offering myself. I've a job of it, keeping you worn out."

She winked, causing his boyish blush, then sailed out the door.

"My apologies. I, er, she…" He blew out a breath with a shake of his head. "I was taken aback for a moment, but thankfully cooler heads prevailed."

"Think nothing of it." Castor's devilish expression was a clear indicator he'd have pushed the issue with Alastair or Damian.

"I need to show my face in town for the rowdy crowd, but Draven can tell you what we've tried for Mar—er, Abbie until now." So saying, Jonas strode out.

"And then there were three," Castor quipped, shooting the

Guardian a droll look. Sobering, he asked, "What have you tried, and why wasn't Damian called?"

"Everythin', and he was, *mon ami*. But he wouldn't defy the Authority."

"That doesn't sound like the man I know." Castor met Wilder's gaze. "We'll need to find another way."

"Do you believe Isis would come if we summon her?" Wilder asked, instinctively hugging Abbie tighter.

"I couldn't say one way or the other. I might have better luck with Athena, since we share blood."

Draven straightened from his slouched position. "You're a demigod?"

"No. Just divine-blooded, thanks to Zeus's penchant for mortal women." When the Guardian frowned, Castor continued. "I'm generations removed from my demigod ancestor and from Zeus himself. But it gifted me the Traveler gene."

"Ah." Draven relaxed, assuming Roxanne's previous perch on the windowsill. "Will you be able to heal, Marie?"

"Abigail," Castor replied sharply. "And no. Not unless a miracle happens."

"I don't understand."

The tension building in Castor was visible in his squared shoulders and the muscle ticking in his jaw. With an effort to defuse the emotional bomb about to go off, Wilder said, "The journey through the portal has temporarily suspended our abilities. We suspect it's because we don't technically exist in this timeline."

"This changes things, no?"

"Indeed, it does," Castor replied heavily. "We need more Thornes and a goddess or two."

15

*A*bigail Monroe.

Mary's real name, though it didn't seem right somehow. But what *did* feel damned near perfect was the man holding her. She'd woken when the guy claiming to be her father mentioned needing the Thornes and a goddess, but remained unmoving. Over the last two years, she'd found playing possum gained her a lot of knowledge others were disinclined to share.

The door closed behind Castor and Draven with a soft click, leaving her alone with Wilder.

His voice rumbled in his chest when he said, "You can stop pretending you're asleep. Everyone's gone."

Her first instinct was to lie, but she checked it. Not only would it have been too difficult to protest aloud, but he'd likely detected the tensing of her body.

Rolling a quarter turn, she angled to see him. His handsomeness was breath-stealing, but it wasn't as if she hadn't seen gorgeous men before. The one they called the Aether came to mind. Although she'd been told they'd met, she didn't remember him prior to the shooting. But he certainly made an impression during their second meeting. Damian Dethridge, undeniably the most attractive man on earth, possessed a quality able to chill her to the bone marrow, and she feared him.

Wilder watched her in silence, and she appreciated his allowing her to set the pace. The compulsion to touch him was hard to ignore, and Mary traced his lips. They were surprisingly full for a man, but she wasn't complaining.

"Will you… tell… about her?"

His brows met. "Who?"

"Ab-bee."

His expression cleared, and he shook his head with a slight smile. "You mean *you*."

"Not… same."

"You are. She's in here," he said, stroking her forehead with gentle fingers. "We just need to wake her up."

Her throat grew thick.

He seemed to understand her predicament, and instead of pressing, he lifted her hand from his chest and wove their fingers together.

"Abbie was the light of my life," he said. His words were rough, as if torn from a throat as tight as hers. "We never spent an entire day apart since our first date. Some friends called us co-dependent, but we didn't care. We enjoyed each other's company and didn't give a shit about the outside world."

Her fingers tightened on his, and he transferred his gaze from their joined hand to meet her steady stare. "It's not to say we didn't have our arguments. We're both pig-headed." Wilder smiled, and Mary was immediately warmer.

"You," she whispered. "She… nice."

He chuckled, causing pleasurable friction between their bodies. She was swamped with the ridiculous desire to strip him bare and rub her breasts against him.

His mouth quirked, giving the sneaking suspicion he *knew*. Heat crept up her neck, but she didn't duck her head as she might've if she'd embarrassed herself in front of Draven, Jonas, or Roxanne.

Wilder's grin widened.

"Don't kid yourself, sweetheart. My Abbie—that's *you*—is as stubborn as they come. A fighter."

Other than his touch, the laid-back personality was familiar, too.

"They say"—she swallowed the pain from speaking—"I…"

Wilder placed a finger on her lips, silencing her. "Do you remember how to write?"

Did she? No one had asked her to before. Was their assumption that she couldn't?

"You haven't tried," he concluded, watching her closely.

How was he able to read her mind? The Aether-man, she understood, because they told her he possessed unlimited talents, but Wilder? Although his aura was as bright as she'd ever seen, he didn't possess the same commanding presence as Damian Dethridge, nor were his eyes as penetrating. For which she was grateful. Mary doubted she could stand it if someone knew every damned thought in her brain.

Realizing he was waiting for her answer, she shook her head, confirming his suspicion.

"We'll rectify it right away," he assured her.

He shifted, as if to sit up, and an instinctive denial arose within her. She clutched his cotton shirt.

"I'm not leaving you, Abbie. Never again." The promise in his amber eyes sparked a need in her.

Nodding, she eased away, freeing him.

"Lock the door behind me, and let no one in but those you already know," he warned. "I won't be but five minutes, okay?"

Letting him go was the hardest thing she'd done since arriving in this godforsaken place, but she nodded, turning the key behind him and sliding down onto the floor. Her tears came then. Healthy-sized sobs that wracked her body.

Somebody loved her.

He'd mourned her absence and promised never to abandon her again.

Behind her, a tap broke through her self-pitying meltdown, and she twisted around.

"It's me, Marie."

She expelled a breath, silently scolding herself for not expecting Draven's teleport. The Guardian didn't miss a trick, and would undoubtedly have known the instant Wilder stepped outside.

As he crouched beside her, his warm whiskey eyes missed nothing on their tour of her tear-stained face.

"Do I kill him?"

With a watery smile, she shook her head. "Heart... knows."

"*Oui*. It always does." His lips twisted, and the image he presented was bittersweet. "Why did he go?"

"Paper... pen."

"But of course!" He tapped the heel of his palm to his forehead. "We never asked you if you could read or write. Fools."

"Safe," she whispered.

"I believe you are, *ma chère*, but I will hang around until you are home where you belong, *oui*?"

Mary cupped his jaw, letting her gratitude and affection flow through to him. He would understand her action far better than her stilted words, anyway.

Turning his head, he kissed her palm. His voice held an aching quality when he said, "If I could remove your pain, I would."

They both knew if it came down to it, he would sacrifice his life for hers. She didn't want him to. Yet, when it boiled down to removing her scars and healing her mind completely, Draven wouldn't. Couldn't. If he were to, he must accept full Guardian status, and that he flatly refused to do.

When she was in stasis, she'd heard him apologize to her, saying he wasn't willing to cave to the Authority and the Fates' demands.

And she didn't blame him.

No one should be forced to be a slave to the whims of gods or enslaved to an organization for their skills.

"It's ok," she assured him.

The knock separated them, and he pressed a finger to his lips before voicing the spell to cloak himself.

Would she ever grow used to the effortless magic he commanded?

Climbing to her feet, she touched the key, then paused. How was she to know who was on the other side without asking?

"Abbie, it's Wilder."

His confident voice filled her with hope and warmth.

She unlocked the door and swung it wide, halting mid-smile when the gesture stretched her scarred skin.

He held up the paper in triumph. "Communication is ours!"

His happy energy was contagious, and she giggled.

"We'll start with the basics in case you for—" His gaze sharpened, and he slowly scanned the room. "Abbie, get behind me," he said in a low voice. "I feel a magical presence."

"Draven," she said.

"What?"

Her Guardian's invisibility shield fell away, and he shot her a sardonic glance. "You are terrible at keepin' a secret, *ma chère.*"

"You're gonna want to stop calling her yours, Masters," Wilder replied in a steely tone.

"Because she *est* yours?" Draven taunted.

"She's no man's. Never was. Never will be. Abbie is her own

person." He met her curious gaze. "But she gave her heart to me years ago, and I'm keeping it."

And hers melted.

Mary may not remember him, nor did she feel the name matched her, but she loved him for his sentiment alone.

Although her protectors had always treated her with respect—and here she was as lucky as could be—they hadn't understood her need to make her own decisions, however screwed up those might be.

But Wilder did.

She tore her adoring gaze from the back of his tense shoulders to meet Draven's searching look.

"Yes," she said, hoping he got what she was trying to relay.

He surprised her when he winked. "I said I would see you safely home, Marie, and I will."

What she viewed as protection, Wilder took as an affront. His body tightened, vibrating with what she suspected was the desire to strike. Pressing her palm to his back, she said, "No… Wild Man."

He froze.

His hopeful expression was painful to witness.

"You remember?"

Although she hated disappointing him, she shook her head and snatched the writing materials from his hands. Crossing to the vanity by the window, she scribbled: *Draven is no threat. He protects me.*

Wilder eyes skimmed the note, and for the longest moment, he was silent, as if processing. Finally, he placed the paper in front of her and nodded.

"Returning to our earlier conversation. What did you intend to say?"

They told me the Guide, Stands-in-Shadow, said that I came through the rock. Is this true?

"The best Castor and I can tell, yes."

What happened?

He inhaled deeply, exhaling heavily as he sat down on the bed. "You and I work together. We teach inexperienced people how to mountain climb. It consists of rope techniques, cam placement, and other safety measures for equipment." Looking out the window, Wilder shook his head. "We were on our own that day, pushing the limit to reach the peak. The adrenaline rush was what we lived for."

Pain contorted his face, and the sheer agony displayed on his visage tightened her chest, feeding her anxiety.

"The weather turned ugly and dangerous. I asked you about going back, but you wanted to continue. I knew it was a bad idea," he said gruffly. "Felt it in my soul. Then the rock you were on broke loose, tearing the cam from its mooring. I braced for impact, but the granite cut right through the rope."

"Merde!"

Mary jumped. Enthralled by Wilder's tale, she'd forgotten all about Draven.

"What happened next?" he asked, seeming as invested as she was.

"Abbie fell."

Two words, weighing as heavy as a death knell.

Is that how I ended up in the rock? She held up the paper.

"The best we can figure is that you possessed latent Traveler magic. It activated due to the high-stress situation, transporting you through time."

"You claim you didn't know Marie—"

"Abbie," Wilder stressed.

"Abbie," Draven allowed. "You claim you didn't know she was alive until you met her father."

"That's right." Ignoring him, Wilder looked straight at her. "My family and I searched for months, but we never found your body. If I'd thought for one second you were alive, I'd have come for you immediately."

Gripping the pen tighter, she wrote, *Why didn't you ask my father sooner?*

"I had never met Castor before he showed up to save my brother's girlfriend. The instant I saw him, I guessed who he was and explained the situation." He shrugged. "My brother and I tossed around the idea that you might be alive, based on something his girlfriend once said. When we got to the base of the mountain, a portal appeared. It wasn't there before. If it had been, I'd have stepped through."

"The Traveler, he triggered it?" Draven asked the question on Mary's mind.

"If he did, it wasn't on purpose. But it closed immediately, and we had to call in reinforcements to hold it open."

What reinforcements? Can they do it again? she scribbled, with Wilder looking over her shoulder.

"Your brother, Quentin, and his daughter. You haven't met them. You didn't know Castor was your father, either."

It made sense why there was no familiarity with him like she had with Wilder.

An overwhelming sense of loss struck her and, with it, the need to escape. Her cells fired as they had earlier, and she curled into a ball against the burning sensation.

"She's attempting to teleport," Draven said sharply, hurrying to her side.

Wilder waved him away and knelt in front of her. "Fight the urge, Abbie. Stay with me and focus on my voice, sweetheart."

Part of the urgency to get away eased, but her body refused to cool down.

Mary shrank back as he reached for her. "Don't touch me!"

16

Wilder recoiled at the desperation in Abbie's voice. For a brief period, she acted normally. Her current desire to run, however, superseded her sanity. Yet he wasn't unfamiliar with her type of reaction. While training others to climb, they'd encountered it on plenty of occasions. Once the fear gained a foothold, everyone reacted differently. Some refused to budge, and others scrambled back down. But a good portion had learned to power through—all under Abbie's guidance. Her calm voice and steady presence cut through their panic, breaking it down into manageable steps. In the end, they'd all had a good experience.

"I won't touch you, but I want you to focus on my voice," he said soothingly, borrowing from her special brand of training. "We're going to take this one beat at a time, okay?"

Her gaze, wild with uncertainty, locked with his.

"Good." He smiled, warm and confident. "Whenever we had a new client, you went through a process. There were a few simple tricks to success."

A tentative hope shone on her face.

"One handhold, one breath."

She scowled at the hand he offered, but accepted it anyway.

"Good, Abbie. That's good." His smile widened. "Now, one foothold, one breath."

Her expression eased into a slight frown, and she pressed her boot-clad foot onto his thigh.

"Alternate. Handhold, and breathe. Good. Foothold. That's my girl." He beamed with pride as her fear receded and her curiosity emerged. "See? You've got this."

Joining him on the floor, Abbie cradled his face within her palms and looked deeply into his eyes, as if she were trying to find her way back.

"We always promised to catch each other," he said, regret creeping in. "But I failed you. Both as your climbing partner and with my magic."

"How did your magic fail?" Draven asked softly.

"A family enemy ripped our powers away. None of us would've believed it was possible, but it went down for all of us that day. And along with it, the protection spell on our equipment." Wilder closed his eyes, hating having to recall any of it, but he would if it helped her remember. "I was a fool to rely on my abilities in such conditions. The weather, Goddess, it was brutal. Before, I'd always been able to keep us warm and redirect the worst of the winds away from us. But it turned bitterly cold. I honestly worried we'd freeze before reaching the summit."

"Arrogance," Draven replied, not unkindly. "We all possess it, *mon ami.*"

"Yes. I suppose we do." It hurt to swallow past the grief his own had caused. "But when you're special from birth, you don't view the world as a dangerous place. You push past what mortals would be wary of."

"This is true. And Abigail, her faith in you would be unfailin', *oui?*"

"Yes," he said roughly, his voice breaking when he added, "I'm so fucking sorry, Abbie."

She surprised him when she pressed her mouth to his in a tender kiss. "It's... oh-kay."

His throat tightened, and a sob lodged in his chest, feeling like a fucking heart attack as the pressure built. But he wouldn't cry in front of her. Wouldn't add to her trauma or risk sending her into another panic attack, not if he could help it.

"The Traveler, he said your *magie* is gone." Draven moved to the window and looked out at the blackened night. Not waiting for confirmation, he said, "You are *très vulnérable* here, I think."

"We have our weapons and a good idea how to use them, but yes," Wilder replied, standing and helping Abbie to her feet. "I don't know what Castor has in mind, but I suspect he'll want to gather whatever family I have here to help."

The Guardian shifted to study him, and Wilder returned his open stare. Finally, Draven nodded. "Jonas is a *sincère* man with a good heart. He is my dearest *ami*. He will help you."

Relief eased Wilder's tension. "It's more than we dared hope."

Abbie surprised him again when she interlaced her fingers with his and gave a gentle squeeze.

"But the first order of business tomorrow is to restore Abbie's memories," he said.

"Very well. I will see her home. Come, Mai—Abbie."

They protested. Wilder with words, and she by clinging to his arm.

Draven chuckled. "Ah, *l'amour*. It is hard to separate lovers. *Son cœur*, it knows you."

"*Oui, nos cœurs sont deux moitiés d'un même tout*," Wilder replied as he looked down at her with all the love he felt.

"You know my native tongue. I like you more." Crossing to

Abbie, Draven sketched a half bow. "If you need me, *chère*, I will be there. Until then, I bid you *bonne nuit.*"

"Good night," Wilder returned.

"Lock the door behind me. This town is rowdy after sundown."

"Understood."

After Draven left, a wave of shyness overcame Mary.

No. Abigail. Abbie, as Wilder called her.

Would the name ever feel right?

She pulled away and, turning her back to him, hugged herself.

"Are you okay, sweetheart?" he asked. His concern for her emotional state was at the forefront of every conversation, and she appreciated his consideration. But part of her wished he couldn't see through her as easily as he did. It made her want to escape his attention.

Her bracelet warmed.

One handhold. Breathe. One foothold. Breathe again.

Oddly, those words *did* feel familiar.

The silver cuff cooled.

"Why don't you remove it?"

She spun to face him and followed the direction of his gaze. Crossing to the desk, she wrote, *It's charmed. Draven must unlock its spell.*

"You're tethered to him?" Wilder asked with a dark scowl.

Only to protect me, he said. My panic attacks would take me back to the place they found me.

His expression cleared, and he shook his head with a wry smile, giving her the impression he believed his gut reaction was silly. He perched on the desk's edge, crossed his arms, and leaned on his bent leg. The casual position wasn't threatening, and the building trepidation she experienced at being alone with him lessened.

"You have no control in that state?"

No. Or I hadn't until you talked me down earlier.

"It was lighting up again less than a minute ago. Does it scare you to be alone with me? Because I can—"

She touched his arm, shaking her head. Wishing she could speak properly, she huffed out a sigh and turned the paper over to write more.

With you, I'm at peace. Mostly. Until a minute ago, I was unable to get a handle on the emotion. You've provided a coping tool. Thank you.

"Have you reacted this way the entire time you've been here?"

No. Or at least, Jonas said I haven't. It began after the bank robbery when Harlan shot me in the face.

Wilder paled. "Jesus!"

He was a cornered animal and recognized Draven's promise of death.

Pain flashed in his eyes, and he lowered his gaze to the paper as he straightened his upper body. She couldn't say how, but she felt his emotional strain.

"You and Draven… Are you…? Have you…?" He closed his eyes and expelled a breath. "Are you lovers? Is that why he claims you as his?"

She sensed the hint of jealousy resulted from his worry that she'd moved on. And when he lifted his lids, his amber irises appeared darker.

"No," she said, as clearly and firmly as she could.

His relief was so strong it reached out and touched her.

If we were, would you—

Wilder grabbed the paper and crumpled it. *"Kill him for taking advantage of your vulnerable state."*

The words were crystal clear, but he never spoke aloud.

She gasped.

Was this some fresh new hell associated with her broken brain? Was she hearing things? Imagining responses where there were none?

He appeared nonplussed, but his shock gave way to curiosity.

"Abbie, can you hear me? Inside your head?"

Oh god! His lips hadn't moved!

Her skin burned under the bracelet as panic consumed her.

"Don't freak out!" He reached for her.

Perhaps it was the fear of losing her mind, but her body decided electrocuting him would be appropriate. The bolt wasn't as forceful as with most, but it was enough to slap him away. Wilder drew back with a hiss as she scurried across the room.

"Fuck!" He waved his hand, then covered his burnt skin. "Shit. Sorry. I didn't mean to grab you." Wilder didn't move, despite her bolting for the door. "Abbie, please, sweetheart. Please don't leave."

Her hand was on the knob, and she was halfway to fleeing, when his quiet plea stopped her.

"I don't know how to do this," she wanted to cry.

"That's okay. We'll do it together," he replied.

She froze, her body going cold. Ever so slowly, she pivoted to face him.

"You heard me?" she asked inside the confines of her mind.

"Yes."

"How?"

His mouth curled.

"Fated mates who are miles above regular witches with the magic they possess," he said aloud.

"I don't understand."

"Well, it isn't me. I don't have the type of power it takes. So it must be what you inherited from Castor."

"Traveler's child. Stands-in-Shadow calls me that."

"Yes. Castor is a Traveler. He has—or had—the ability to move throughout his lifetime. We guessed you had a similar gift after we realized he was your biological father. Somehow you opened a portal and teleported yourself into the past." Wilder rose but didn't approach her. "And those gifts from the deities, they make you one badass mofo."

"All I can do is shock people," she replied in disgust.

He huffed out a laugh as he held up his blistered arm. "Yeah, well, it's one helluva burn, baby."

She cried out and rushed to him. *"I'm so sorry. Wilder."*

"None of that, okay? You've been through too much to apologize for an accident."

How he could be calm and sweet to her after she'd hurt him was a mystery.

"You spoke of healing before. Is repairing the damage something I can do?"

"Do you want to try?"

His eyes were dull with the pain he felt, and Abbie wanted them to be bright, filled with love, as they were before. She nodded, willing to do whatever it took to soothe the angry skin and rid him of his suffering.

"Okay." When they were seated on the bed, he held out his arm. "You were never squeamish before, but there might be a first time for everything. So stay as focused as you can and place your palm over the wound."

She grimaced but nodded, then fought the urge to pull back when he sucked air through his teeth.

"Good," he grunted. "Visualize healthy skin, like this." He pointed to his uninjured forearm. "Pull from a cellular level, where you felt the warming as you tried to teleport."

She considered how her body heated when the need to escape threatened, and broke it down, tracing the source.

"Good! Yes! The nucleus of your cells is where magic lives.

It's the control center, and branches out through threads to the membrane. From there, you can push it to your extremities, and in this case, your hand. Visualize the blisters smoothing out and the skin returning to normal."

"This seems advanced. Should I get Draven?"

"Try. If you can't repair the damage, we'll get him."

A sharp rap sounded.

"It's Jonas," came a muffled voice.

Wilder cursed himself for not locking up earlier when Draven encouraged it, but he wouldn't deny the man entry. "Come in."

The sheriff entered, followed by a woman Wilder would recognize anywhere. Her portrait hung in his father's home.

"Evie," he whispered. Never in a million years would he have expected to see his great-great-grandmother step through the door.

17

"Step away from him, my dear," Evie urged Abbie. "You're not to heal him."

Anger crackled beneath Abbie's surface, and defiance rose up. Who the hell were they to tell her what she could and couldn't do to help Wilder?

"She'll have her reasons, sweetheart," he told her through their new mental link. Aloud, he said, "Do as she says."

She jerked, having momentarily forgotten he could read her mind. With a short nod, she rose and went to her precious paper supply.

After writing, she held it up.

Why?

"Well, I'll be! None of us thought to ask about the poor dear's education," Evie exclaimed.

"Most everyone, from every class, possesses the fundamentals in my time," Wilder replied. "Abbie actually went to college."

Evie studied him as she moved closer. "You have the look of my son's wife, Josephine."

"Josephine Crandall-Thorne." He cast her a half smile. "From all accounts, she had dark hair and eyes. My siblings always believed our exotic coloring was from our Egyptian ancestors, but it's more likely from our great-grandmother, Jo."

Wordlessly, she gripped his arm and pressed her palm over his burnt skin. Purple light seeped from whatever space existed between them.

Abbie gasped. She hadn't witnessed anything like it, and her curiosity propelled her forward. *"She's healing you? Like you planned for me to do?"*

"Yes," Wilder replied, grinning at her excitement. "For some of our kind, it's effortless. Eventually, it will be for you, too."

"I see you have a connection," Evie said mildly, glancing between them before returning her attention to her chore. "It's rare to be able to communicate the way you do."

"It's new for us." When he offered his hand to Abbie, it felt natural for her to clasp it. The warmth of his approval flowed through her, fueling her desire to bask in his light.

"She trusts you. Jonas told me it was immediate, but I wished to meet you for myself," Evie said.

"I didn't get to know you while you were around, but Cousin Alastair told me you were a wily one," Wilder replied with a chuckle. "'Evie saw through any BS disguised as charm,' he once told me."

"Alastair?" She sent a sharp glance at Jonas, then looked at Abbie. "You once called my husband Alastair."

Had she? Abbie couldn't remember.

"She doesn't recall," Wilder replied for her.

"Naturally. It was before that ugly bank business." Evie dropped her hands with a satisfied nod. "You're as good as new, young man."

"Thank you."

Hoping to inspect his skin for herself, Abbie touched his arm. Dutifully, he lifted it for her to stroke. As her fingers trailed across the pinkened flesh, it darkened to its natural tan. Her mouth dropped open, and unable to contain her excitement, she hugged him. He laughed as he tightened his embrace.

"Welcome to the world of witchcraft, sweetheart."

Drawing back, she smiled at him. Or tried to. The painful tug on her cheek stopped the movement.

It's truly amazing. I wish she could fix me.

Wilder sobered, and she mourned the loss of his good humor.

"We'll find the Aether. He can do it," he assured her.

"Damian has already said he won't get involved," Evie said. Regret hung in her voice. "I'm sorry."

Anger flashed across Wilder's face as he set Abbie away from him and stood. "Did he say why not?"

"The Authority. He won't fight them for a few scars."

"A few scars? What about her memory? Her inability to speak?" he snapped back.

Jonas stepped around his aunt, his hands dropping to his gun belt. "Calm down, Wilder, and show her respect."

"I'm not annoyed with her. I'm angry because Damian's calling is to assist our magical community, not ignore those in need," he retorted. "For two years, he left Abbie to suffer. What kind of man is he in this world?"

Their hostility knotted Abbie's insides, and the desire to flee sparked. Instinctively, she ripped at the bracelet chaining her in place.

"One handhold. One breath," Wilder said, reaching out, palm up.

Fearing she'd burn him, she stepped backward and tucked her arms behind her.

Disappointment clouded his eyes, but on its heels was understanding.

"I'm not scared," he assured her. "I'll take a hundred strikes if it helps you stay grounded." Extending his hand farther, he repeated, "One handhold. One breath."

She grabbed on for dear life. Within two short hours, he'd become her anchor. A beacon in a storm of chaos.

"I'm beginning to suspect you're an empath, Abbie," he said in a tone used to gentle wild creatures. "We need to teach you to build walls against stronger emotions. It will help with your panic attacks."

"Christ. That explains so much." Jonas grimaced. "Why didn't any of us see it before?"

"I'm sure you had other things to contend with. But Alastair and a few of my other cousins possess the same gift. Even knowing how to handle a tsunami of emotions, they can get overwhelmed." Wilder led her to the chair and offered the pen. "Write what you feel, sweetheart. And if you can't find the words, sketch what's in your head."

"She can draw?" Evie asked curiously, joining them at the desk.

"Yes. She's a remarkable charcoal artist. Mostly views from the summit, but her work hangs—hung—all over our apartment."

A vague recollection of charcoal pencils filled Abbie's mind, of her fingers flying as they recreated whatever she saw.

Wilder's excitement hummed through her veins. "You remembered something."

With a small shake of her head, she said, *"A fragment. But you took the pictures down? Why?"*

"They were too painful," he confessed. "A reminder of what I'd lost." He stroked a finger along her blemished cheek. "The love I failed to save."

She had a sudden urge to sketch him in his current state, staring down at her with such longing and pain, yet she worried something so personal might offend him. He might not wish those emotions displayed for others to see.

A wicked gleam caused his eyes to sparkle. *"You've sketched me nude. What's a little stark emotion?"*

The idea of sketching him nude held great appeal, and in her mind's eye, she constructed a vision of how she'd model him.

"I'm growing uncomfortably aroused. You might want to think about something else, or you'll embarrass me," he telegraphed.

Her face warmed under his steady regard, and she compressed her lips to hold back an unexpected giggle.

Wilder wished his relatives were anywhere but there. Yet he wouldn't make advances on Abbie. Until she one hundred percent bought into the idea she was truly who he claimed, he wouldn't press for anything but recognition, if it were at all possible for her. She should be comfortable, seeking confirmation rather than him pushing the past on her and expecting her to accept whatever he fed her.

"I do believe you, Wilder. I don't know why, but I do."

Her faith humbled him, and he blinked against the sting of moisture in his eyes. *"It means more to me than you'll ever know, sweetheart."*

Evie cleared her throat to get their attention, and when she had it, she said, "Damian might not be willing to disobey the Authority, but the rest of your family are."

For a couple of heartbeats, he stared, unable to comprehend. When her meaning eventually sank in, he whooped and hugged her.

"Thank you, Evie. *Thank you!*"

"It's the least I can do for my great-great-grandson and our lost lamb."

"You and Nate were always the backbone of our family. Your values and teachings resonate through all the generations after you," he told her. "I didn't have the pleasure of meeting you before you chose to move on, but I'm so damned happy I got to now."

She patted his cheek. "Clearly, my 'don't swear in mixed company' didn't stick."

He laughed and hugged her again.

"Dare I ask about the future, and if Isolde becomes even more of a problem?" Evie tilted her head, and a mischievous smile curled her lips.

Wilder didn't take the bait.

"I wish I could tell you, but Castor has threatened me with penalty of death should I talk."

Her brows shot up. "Hmm, your avoidance tells me she does."

"My lips are sealed, Evelyn Thorne. You'll not get any secrets out of me." He mimed zipping his lips.

"Cheeky boy."

A tug at his sleeve turned his attention to Abbie's newest question.

Who's Isolde?

Her pursed lips hinted at displeasure, as if jealousy had gotten the better of her. And because they had always teased each other in the past, he saw no reason not to rib her now.

"The Enchantress." He sighed. "Rumor has it she's the most beautiful woman in the world, able to—"

She kicked him.

Exactly as his Abbie would've.

Applying pen to paper, she wrote, *Jerk.*

Dropping to his knees before her and placing his hand over his heart, he dipped his head. "You, my queen, will always be held in my highest regard."

She snorted, and when he glanced up, amusement crinkled her undamaged eye.

"But it's getting late, and I'm starving. It's possible my judgment is impaired," he added.

Evie smacked him upside the head. "That's no way to court a woman. You and Jonas could take lessons from Nathanial."

Wilder was pleased Abbie had understood his jest and didn't take offense.

"What does this town offer for takeout?"

"Takeout?"

"A meal I can box up and bring back here to share with Abbie," he explained.

"Jonas or I can conjure whatever you need, my dear."

Abbie's sudden stillness bothered him.

"What's wrong?" he asked, tipping up her chin so she'd meet his eyes. "You know I was kidding about impaired judgment, right?"

She nodded, glancing down again.

"You don't believe me?"

Jonas stepped forward, inserting himself into their conversation. "I suspect she's worried you might be embarrassed to be seen dining with her."

"*What?*" Wilder looked between them, and sure enough, she flushed and ducked her head. "My god, Abbie, no. I'll march through town, declaring my love for you every hour on the hour to any who'll listen."

A single tear escaped to track down her cheek. Her insecurity was understandable, but he hated that she'd ever believe him so shallow.

"I mean it," he said, angling to peer into her face, hoping she would recognize his sincerity.

She nodded, but her hurt lingered.

Picking up her hand, he kissed her knuckles. "Abigail Monroe, would you do me the honor of dining with me tonight? In any establishment of your choosing?"

"*Don't pity me!*"

Her fierce anger echoed loudly inside his mind, and he winced.

"Don't mistake my desire to be with you as pity, because it isn't." He dropped her hand and stood. "You have a few scars, so damned what?"

Her expression turned wary in the face of his annoyance, and he worked to stay calm.

"I get you don't remember me, Abbie, so you can't know if I'm being honest. But let me state for the record, your injuries don't make you any less of a person in my eyes." Lifting the pen and selecting a clean sheet of paper, he drew a heart and wrote her name at its center. Then he folded it and put it in his left shirt pocket. "I'm heading out for food, and if you care to join me, I'd welcome it. But if not, I'll flash this note and show everyone who my love belongs to."

Pivoting on his heel, he stalked to the door.

"Wilder!"

He glanced back and held out a hand.

"Come with me, sweetheart."

She rushed forward and placed her palm in his.

18

Abbie's transformation gobsmacked Jonas. It was as if the moment Wilder spoke to her, she came alive. For three months after she woke from her stasis, they'd tried to bring her out of her shell and help her participate in life again. Yet she'd been resistant, muttering about curses and wanting to go home. When asked, she could never recall.

Tonight was the first time she ventured out of the house, and he'd been surprised when she tagged along behind him. If he didn't know better, he'd believe she had anticipated her mate's arrival. She went from curled in a corner, picking at the wood slats, to interacting with the guy. When she'd caressed his face, Jonas's jaw hit the floor, and with unheard-of clumsiness, Draven had fumbled his cards.

Granted, Wilder had an easy charm and worked on the assumption she'd recognized him on a cellular level. And perhaps she had. Her trust wasn't easily given, and he was the only stranger who hadn't been tossed across the room when he touched her without permission.

The man's brass balls were admirable, and bystanders

would make his challenge legendary soon. Rarely did anyone stand up to a creature like Draven. Most sensed his underlying strength. Mortals wrote it off to a deadly gunslinger, but those in the magical community knew what he was and who he was destined to become. Only Draven refused to fall in with the Fates' plan for him.

"I've been around for a long time and never heard of a Traveler until our girl," Evie said as the door closed behind the couple. "Now we have two. Father and daughter."

"Yes. We should reach out to Damian, or at the very least to Isis, to learn more. If there are other magical entities out there like these, I want to know."

"It stands to reason there are." Absently, she waved her hand, setting the room to rights as if by habit rather than intentionally. Evie loved a tidy house.

"Right," he replied. "And I suspect the Authority has a long list of those individuals at its disposal. Makes you wonder why they're trying so hard to get Draven to accept his responsibility as a Guardian."

"In my experience, the Witches' Council and Authority only assign one Guardian at a time. They wouldn't dare grant that type of power to more in case the supercharged banded together to overthrow the establishment."

Jonas nodded. "Makes sense. They aren't as confident as they'd like everyone to believe. So who is the current Guardian?"

"As far as I know, they don't have one. It's why they're pushing hard for Draven. Soon, they'll take away his freedom and force him if he doesn't conform."

"But he refuses to guard a 'dusty old tomb.'" He chuckled when she lifted an inquiring brow. "His words for the Enchantress's garden. He'd rather gamble and waste his life here in The Devil's Backbone."

"I'd love to know his history." Patting his arm, Evie said, "But for now, I need to speak with Nate and Damian."

"Why?"

"Wilder was right. That poor dear should be healed without delay."

"You know, *you* would make an excellent Guardian, Aunt Evie. I'm surprised they haven't recruited you for the job."

"They have. I told them after my boys were settled, and only with Nathanial by my side."

"It sure doesn't hurt that the garden is beside your favorite son's estate," he teased, wishing his own parents had been as loving as his aunt and uncle were.

"I don't have favorites. I can't say the same about my husband. He's always had a soft spot for Damian."

"Do you think you can convince him to help Mary—uh, Abbie?"

"He's going through a stage where he believes he knows best. But Damian will come around after a good talking to," she assured him.

<hr>

The only place to find a meal was run by a man named Cookie, who was sweeping up when Wilder and Abbie arrived.

"Kitchen's closed."

"Even for a weary traveler and his lady love?" Wilder asked.

"Don't play favorites," Cookie said, not bothering to look up from his chore.

"We'll take whatever you have leftover. It doesn't matter if it's not hot."

The owner finally glanced up, eyeing him before Abbie. His expression softened. "Was in the bank that day. It's sorry I was for what that good fer nothin' Harlan did to ya, gal."

Abbie nodded her understanding.

"It's good to see ya up and around. Don't hold with harmin' women or children."

Sensing her discomfort over the topic, Wilder wrapped an arm around her. "Abbie and I would really love a meal, sir. We're happy to pay extra."

Cookie gestured with his chin to a table by the window. "Have a seat. I've got extra stew and biscuits I've been saving for Gus. Boy's a reed."

Gus.

He'd heard the name earlier as one of the gang members who'd initially found Abbie.

"He's a good boy, Wilder." She covered his hand with hers. *"Really."*

"Has he already eaten? I wouldn't want to take his food."

Cookie barked a laugh as he set his broom aside. "That boy had four meals today alone, and none of them small."

"Fair enough."

Wilder drew out a chair and assisted Abbie into it, then immediately sat beside her.

Within minutes, two steaming bowls were placed on the table, accompanied by a plate of biscuits and a beer for each of them. With one bite of the savory dish, Wilder's taste buds were transformed.

"Good lord! Are you a wizard?"

Cookie chuckled and continued his closing procedure.

Abbie watched Wilder with a fascination new to him. Even in their early days, she wasn't as enthralled. The disturbing sensation caused him to look away.

Across the street, a light burned in the apartment above the mercantile, outlining Bart's distinctive figure. Wilder couldn't shake the feeling he was watching them specifically, and his skin crawled. He barely suppressed the urge to draw Abbie back into the shadows of the restaurant.

"Tell me about Bart," he said softly.

She looked up from the biscuit she was buttering. *"Why?"*

"He gives me the creeps. I can't put my finger on it, but I didn't appreciate the way he talked about you earlier."

Slowly, she turned her head toward the street.

"I've overheard Red say he's the type who thinks to control women. Routinely tries to buy her girls."

He clamped his jaw to hold back what he wished he could say.

Abbie gasped. *"He offered money to Draven for me?"*

"I was trying to hide that little factoid from you," he replied with a healthy sigh. "But yes, and Shadow had to hold me back from killing him on the spot."

"He should've let you."

Her thought was matter-of-fact, bordering on uncaring, and Wilder couldn't help but wonder if the callousness was from her experiences here.

"Yes," she answered aloud, after a sip of her beer.

"God, Abbie. I should've realized when we couldn't find your body..." Choking back the regret, he clamped his lips together and shook his head. "I'm so fucking sorry."

"Not... your... fault," she stressed, despite the effort to speak. "Not."

"Our enemies—"

Slapping her palm over his mouth, she glared. "Not."

Her reaction was so much like her old self, he had to laugh. Before she could draw away, he kissed her palm.

"Fine. If you say so."

With a decisive nod, she bit into her biscuit, not at all hiding her smile behind the gesture.

He grinned in response.

Goddess, he missed this. Their easy camaraderie and willingness to understand. The way they had always sought to ease each other's hurts or fears.

"As my date for the night, would you like to go to a dancing hall or the saloon after?"

"Both are for the so-called soiled doves hereabouts," Cookie said, sliding the last chair onto the table next to them. "Good girls don't frequent those places, my boy."

"Oh. I didn't know." Feeling foolish, Wilder finished the last of his beer. "Is there somewhere else?"

"During the daylight hours, I'd say a walk along the boards or a drive outside of town. But this late?" Their host scrunched his nose. "I wouldn't recommend hangin' out after dark. The bad elements come a'callin', seekin' trouble."

"Understood. Thank you, Mr. Cookie."

"Just Cookie. And you watch old Bart, yeah? He's a predator, that one."

Wilder hadn't realized the restaurateur had overheard their conversation.

"I know what you are," the man said, eyes narrowed in shrewd study of him. "The others 'round here, they don't, but I've been around a long time. The Devil's Backbone is where they all come to test their skills."

"And Sheriff Jonas? He always able to put them down?"

Cookie's focus shifted to Abbie. "Mostly. One or two remain to cause trouble, but eventually they go the way of the others. It helps having the Guardian around."

"You know what Draven is?" he asked, surprised the old man knew so much.

His rheumy eyes twinkled, and a ghost of a smile curled his lips. "Your meal's on the house, son. Any friend of our Mary's is a friend of mine."

"No! You stayed open and—"

"You refusin' my hospitality, Thorne?"

Wilder went cold. "I don't believe I mentioned my name."

"You didn't. But that don't mean I'm ignorant of who you are."

"Care to share?"

"Let's just say, you're a descendant of mine, child." The voice was distinctly feminine, and a shimmering image of the Goddess appeared in place of Cookie before it disappeared.

"Isis," he breathed, bowing his head. "Exhalted One. Forgive me."

"Think nothing of it, Beloved." Drawing out a chair, the Goddess, disguised as Cookie, sat at their table. "But if you would keep this between us, I would look favorably upon you."

"Why are you here?"

"Two of the world's four Travelers are stuck here. Their presence has offset the balance, and it must be maintained in all things."

"How do we get home? Castor and I are powerless, and Abbie doesn't even remember who she is."

It struck him that she was particularly quiet upon discovering Isis was masquerading as Cookie in the Wild West. He swiveled to look at her, then jumped into action.

"Oh, shit! Abbie!"

"She's merely asleep, child. Sit back down while there's time."

Heart racing, he did as Isis bade.

"Why hasn't anyone restored her mind and body? Why allow her suffering?" he demanded. "Damian—"

"Damian does as he's told. As for healing her, do you think her stunning beauty would go unnoticed in this place? She's safer under the guise of a crazy, scarred spinster."

"That's bullshit," he snapped.

Isis's cold stare recalled his manners.

"Apologies, Exhalted One," Wilder muttered. "I only meant that she might've found a way home sooner."

"The Fates want her here. For Draven."

His stomach dropped.

19

"What do you mean?" Wilder asked, feeling shaky and on the verge of losing his biscuits. "They want her to be Draven's mate? Because it'll be over my dead body."

"Nothing so dire," Isis assured him. "They're hoping to give him a shove in the proper direction. Draven Masters is protective of Abigail. She reminds him of a woman he met when he was young, though he doesn't recall who."

"It's not as if he's old. At best, he's in his late twenties, but I'd venture to say he's closer to twenty-three or four."

She waved a hand. "People mature faster in this century due to hardships."

Why was she so blasé? What was he missing?

"What hardship did he face?" he asked.

Her eyes held approval, or rather, Cookie's did. The Goddess superimposed on the elderly man's visage was disconcerting.

"His love was married off to another, thanks to the Fates. A man very much like Bartholomew Mercer."

Curbing the urge to swear, he asked, "Was it a youthful crush or true love?"

"You are wise to ask." Her eyes grew sad. It was well known Isis was a romantic at heart and had a weakness for star-crossed lovers. "It was a true love match, and now, she suffers abuse at the hand of a husband she'll never love."

"Dear God! Couldn't Draven save her?"

"The Fates wiped his mind immediately upon her betrothal, much like they did your Abbie's."

Rage boiled in his veins, and the desire to retaliate against those meddlesome witches burned him up inside. "Let me get this straight. He doesn't know about his life at all? Or is it just of the girl?"

"He knows one of the Sisters of Fate is his mother. She hasn't hidden it from him, but other than his French heritage and an aching sense of loss, he has no recollection of anything before coming to Perdition Ridge."

Draven's protective feelings for Abbie made a helluva lot more sense.

"Has he tried to recover those memories?"

"He knows there's no point. His mother has made no secret of holding the key hostage until he agrees to his destiny. Only then will they restore his mind."

Wilder considered what she'd told him. "Who is she? Can she be saved?"

"She can."

"But you won't tell him," he said flatly.

"The young woman is inclined to believe Draven is faithless and has abandoned her. But I'll not anger the Fates by telling him, no."

"And will you reveal her name to me?" It was a long shot, but maybe with her soft heart, she would provide contact details. "Granted, it's a technicality, but you aren't breaking your promise to keep it a secret from him."

"Wait until the time is right. You'll know."

"That's cryptic as fuck," he muttered. "But okay."

She laughed, and Wilder would swear the room lit with her merriment.

"Her name is Céleste Duval, and she's from a wealthy French Creole family in the place you call Louisiana." Isis stood and circled him to touch the crown of Abbie's head. "Cookie is getting impatient, and I must go or upset the balance further."

"Wait!" He jumped up. "What about Abbie? How do I heal her and get home if I'm battling the Fates to do it?"

"Trust her."

He frowned. "I do."

"Hm, perhaps. But have a care, Beloved. Someone covets your prize."

With those puzzling words, she shimmered away, leaving a dizzy Cookie in her place. Wilder helped him to the chair, taking his place just as Abbie returned to consciousness.

"I have to see her home. Will you be all right, sir?"

"Get on with ya. The day I need someone to wipe my behind is the day they can put me in the ground," the man grumbled.

Wilder drew out a one-ounce gold nugget and pushed it toward him. "I know you said no charge, but I can't thank you enough for your hospitality. And if you have more of that stew and biscuits, I'm happy to take some off your hands for Abbie's father."

Five minutes later, they were on the boardwalk, heading back to the hotel.

"Your thoughts are churning," Abbie said.

"I've got a lot to proc—" He stopped and stared.

When she realized he wasn't beside her, she returned. "What's wrong?"

"Abbie, you spoke! Twice!" His elation echoed in the street, turning the heads of those close by.

Her expression was pure shock as she pressed her hand to her throat.

"I did. Oh my god, Wilder. I did!"

Laughing, he scooped her up and swung her around.

"One healing down, two more to go," he said, grinning with happiness.

"Two?"

"Your memories and restoring sight to your eye. Later, if you want the scars removed, we can do that too, but those are the least of our concerns."

"Do you think it's possible?" Her tone indicated she feared it ever happening.

"Better. It's probable."

Hand in hand, they crossed the street, lost in their happiness. The footfalls behind them registered too late.

The impact of the bullet in Wilder's back coincided with Abbie's bloodcurdling scream. He wanted to assure her he would be fine, but darkness encroached on his vision, and his knees gave out. Only after he was facedown on the wooden slats did the lack of feeling in his legs register.

Recalling his weapon, he fumbled for the revolver, earning himself a heel stomp on his fingers and a wicked kick to the ribs.

Thank Christ Abbie had the presence of mind to run.

"Grab her!"

Energy crackled in the air around them, and simultaneous shouts rang out.

"Gotta do everythin' myself," a man growled.

The thud of Abbie's body hitting the ground caused Wilder to cry out.

"Abbie, get up," he shouted, using his upper body to drag himself toward her. "Abbie!"

Booted feet blocked the sight of two men picking her up and dragging her toward the alley.

"Don't look for her. You'll be contacted where to drop the gold." Fleshy hands patted his pockets, stripping him of his valuables. "Stupid, Easterners!"

Bartholomew Mercer.

With his disdain and distinguishable voice, he gave himself away. And if Wilder didn't bleed out before Castor or the others found him, he'd be able to get help for her.

His magic was tied to the earth, and he prayed Isis was still around to hear.

"Goddess, hear my plea,
Assist me in this time of need.
Gift my powers back to me,
So that I might save my love, Abbie."

Although his cells warmed, he wasn't able to manipulate the wooden planks or the ground to slow their escape. The heating of his body gave him hope. If he could teleport, he might get help to save her. Closing his eyes, he envisioned the restaurant as they'd left it, but when he lifted his lids, he was still on the boardwalk where he'd been left to bleed out.

He reached back with his uninjured hand, feeling for the wound. The pain was minimal, but when he drew back his hand, it was drenched in blood. He was losing too much, too fast.

"Grant her power, Exalted One. Please," he whispered, and he drifted into unconsciousness.

Soft hands stroked his brow. For a moment, Wilder pretended it was Abbie and imagined this was all a horrible dream. He cracked a lid, only to find himself alone. Witnesses remained at a distance, as if fearing to come to his aid. What had he expected? They'd landed in the Wild West, lawless except for a brave few.

———

Gus Green's self-appointed job was to watch over Crazy Mary when Sheriff Thorne couldn't.

He'd never seen the dark-haired man before today, but Mary seemed at ease with him in a way she'd never been with anyone else. Although it caused his heart to ache, he wasn't fool enough to believe she'd ever fancy someone as young, as stupid, or as lowborn as him, to say nothing of his criminal background. She was a true lady despite her bad luck.

Still, Gus intended to be her protector whenever the others couldn't. Hadn't he confronted Pa, even at the risk of getting beat, hoping to stop him from hurting her in the alley a little over a year ago? He'd failed to get her away, but thankfully, Draven had arrived to prevent any real harm. Then, learning from his mistake and knowing he wasn't so strong as to confront Harlan during the bank heist, Gus had fetched Jonas and Draven. Although she was alive, Mary suffered from him butting his nose in. She might still be mostly whole had he kept his mouth shut.

Right now, he faced another such moment. If he got the gambler and the Sheriff, she might be injured again. But if he waited, biding his time, he might be able to sneak in and free her.

No one interfered as Bart shot Mary's dark-haired suitor in the back, nor when he robbed the guy and left him on the wooden planks for dead.

Gus had a split second to make a choice.

Turning away from the man's suffering, he darted down the neighboring alley in the same direction as Bart and his hench-men. When he got to the end, he stayed at the opening, letting the darkness hide him. Seemed his whole life had been spent hiding. From his Ma's gentlemen friends, then Pa, when he'd become useful as a warm body to point a barrel at.

Only Sheriff Thorne treated him with any respect. Ruffling his hair instead of boxing his ears when he did wrong. The gambler was never mean, but he tended to look straight through Gus, as if he didn't see him at all.

Peering closer, Gus saw one man binding Mary's hands as the other stuffed a kerchief into her mouth. Her feet were next before they tossed her onto the buckboard like a sack of grain. Their only attempt to hide her was a canvas tarp.

"Well done, gents. And now for your payment."

Two shots were fired. The back of the head for the closest and the heart of the second as he turned from the tailgate.

The buckboard strained under Bart's weight as he climbed onto the seat and flicked the reins. Gus hugged the wall as he passed by, not giving chase. He had a good idea where the merchant was headed. The caves west of town were notorious hiding spots for bandits and killers on the run. He'd follow at a safe distance, then circle back to tell Jonas of the location if he couldn't save Mary himself.

Fairly positive his plan was a good one, Gus ran for the stables to saddle a ride. Thankfully, Sheriff Thorne had posse horses at their disposal.

20

"Damned drunks out there firin' shots again." Dwight King, Draven's current poker adversary, squinted at his dwindling pile of money. "And where's Sheriff Thorne when ya need him, eh?"

Unease rippled along Draven's nerve endings as the crowd noise increased, and he gave serious consideration to checking out the commotion.

"Shot him right in the back and left 'em for dead, they did! Took his gold *and* Crazy Mary," someone left of him exclaimed.

"Merde!" Shoving back his chair, he stood and ordered, "Find Jonas."

"Sure thing, Masters. We can pause—"

"No need, *mon ami*. The hand is yours."

He didn't wait for a response. Alexander Castor appeared right on his heels.

Less than a minute later, they were kneeling beside Wilder, staring down at his gray face and agony-filled eyes.

"It was Mercer," Wilder said between gritted teeth. "Forget about me. Please, save Abbie."

"*Oui*. But we will get you patched up first, yes?" Draven's driving need to get to Abbie was anxiety-producing, and when he found Bart, the bastard would meet his maker. However, Wilder's situation was grave, and he required divine intervention to survive. Yet, it couldn't be Draven, which meant he had to go for Jonas.

"If I don't make it—"

"There'll be no talk of that, Thorne." Castor bent to examine the wound. He swore. "Spine." Quick on his feet, he managed the onlookers like a professional. "Back up, folks. Nothing more to see here." Then, under his breath, he said, "Freeze time and heal him, Masters. He's not long for this world if you don't."

"I'm not able to fix him. But I know someone who is." Pressing his palm flat on Wilder's wound, Draven lowered his voice and said,

"His blood be stilled,
Flow bound until willed."

Only the barest hint of light emerged from beneath his hand. Not enough to raise questions, but if asked, they could say Castor had struck a match for them to see better.

"He can be carried now. Assist me."

Wilder grunted. "I'm still awake here, fellas. Just prop me up and go after Abbie."

"We'll find her. But your life is at risk, son." Castor gripped him by the arm and flung it around his neck, waiting for Draven to do the same. When they had him supported, they set off for the hotel.

"Mercer had two others with him, and there were shots

from that direction," Wilder said between pants. "They knocked Abbie out. What if she woke and—"

He was working himself into a state, and the only way for Draven to calm him was to knock him out.

"Dors!" he snapped, forgetting to lower his voice with the spell.

No less than three people rushed forward to open the actual door, earning a huff of approval from Castor.

"Two for one."

They managed the stairs with ease, thanks to another boost of Draven's magic, and settled Wilder facedown on the bed. "I will find Jonas. You go for Roxanne," he ordered.

Castor's brows shot up. "They aren't together?"

"C'est douteux. It's a Friday night. She has business to manage."

"Does she have abilities?"

"Non, but she receives visions. She could give us a location on Mercer."

Without another word, Castor strode out the door.

Leaving a fatally injured man defenseless didn't sit well with Draven, but he didn't have much of a choice. Abbie was in peril.

Bart had offered to pay for her "services" in the past, refusing to take no for an answer. Over time, he'd become more obsessed with the prize he couldn't have. Men like Bartholomew Mercer didn't care to be denied and found ways to gain what they wanted, regardless of objection or morality.

The secondary problem was the sonofabitch's greed. If he decided her bracelet was valuable, he might try to take it, unaware of the danger they all faced if her magic was unleashed. Abbie couldn't remove it until she was of sound mind, but Draven had stupidly failed to add a contingency in case someone else stole it off her person. He planned to rectify the situation once they found her.

Closing his eyes, he envisioned the Thorne homestead at the edge of town. Pulling from his third eye, he sent a thread of energy to scope out the place ahead of his teleport. When the way appeared clear, he visualized himself in Jonas's front yard. Before his cells warmed to burning, he'd arrived.

Draven took the steps three at a time and banged on the door.

"Masters? What's wrong?" Jonas's expression altered, becoming alarmed. "Christ! Where did all that blood come from? Are you hurt?"

Unfortunately, Draven had given little regard to his appearance, failing to notice the bloodstains. "Not me. The other Thorne."

Evie sailed through the door, little black bag in hand. "Take me to him."

"Aunt Evie—"

"I won't hear another word of objection, Jonas." She waved her nephew off, much to Draven's silent amusement.

"There's another *problème. Marie—er, Abbie—she* is gone."

"Gone?"

"Bart Mercer abducted her." Draven's rage for the man was building, and if he didn't get it under control, it could be catastrophic. His unleashed power could rival Abbie's.

Jonas shrugged into his duster and strapped on his belt. "Which way did he go?"

"I do not know, but if I had to guess, the caves where we found her."

Evie touched his arm, halting him from leaving. "Let's use our heads, Jonas. First, we heal Abbie's young man. Then we find her."

"You don't know the kind of man Bart is, Aunt Evie."

"I've been around a great many years, my dear. Trust me, I've seen his type before. But remember, our girl has a built-in defense mechanism."

"If that's true, how did he abduct her in the first place?" Jonas countered.

"Wilder said she was knocked unconscious. It could explain why she was easily taken, *oui?*"

"Where is he now?" Evie asked.

"His room at the hotel. Alone."

"Follow me, fellas." Without waiting for them, she blinked away.

"Uncle Nate is going to kill me if she gets hurt," Jonas muttered.

"Then we must make sure *ta tante est* safe, *mon ami.* Let us go."

Within minutes of everyone leaving Wilder, they'd reconvened in his room with reinforcements. Castor, the first to arrive, told him Roxanne hadn't gotten a clear vision of Abbie's abduction.

Jonas grimaced. "Sometimes it happens that way for her if she is too busy. Apparently, her mind needs to be calm to receive messages."

"All right, let's get to this." Evie clapped her hands before pointing everyone to a corner of the bed. "Don't let him move. And Draven, please remove whatever incantation you used to stop the bleeding for me to work."

Castor, Jonas, and Draven each braced their weight on Wilder for the bullet extraction. Despite the numbness from his waist down, the point of entry still hurt like a bitch as she gently probed the opening to find the slug. Evie was remarkably skilled, performing the task with the expertise of a neurosurgeon.

Wilder held back as best he could by biting on the leather strap Jonas provided, only crying out once during the procedure. Although the pain was the greatest he'd experienced, it was nothing next to the loss of Abbie on the mountain that day. If he had to face the same type of torment again, he'd not survive it. Hell, he wouldn't want to.

"Okay, that's got it," Evie announced. "Now, to stitch him up. I don't need you fellas for this. Go bring our girl home."

"Yes, ma'am." Jonas dropped to one knee and twisted his torso so Wilder could see him. "I won't rest until she's safe. You have my word."

"Thank you," he said gruffly. "If you leave me a horse, I'll follow as soon as I can."

Castor pressed a hand to his shoulder. "You can be sure I'll do what's necessary to find my daughter."

"Rest up. We intend to have her home before dawn," the sheriff promised.

In a flash, they were gone, leaving Wilder alone with his great-great-grandmother.

"I can't thank you enough, Evie."

"There's no need, though I do admire your pretty manners. Nathanial would be especially proud if he were here."

She laid a hand on the back of his head, and he'd have sworn he could feel her love flow through him. The urge to cry was strong, and he barely suppressed a sob.

"Trust Jonas and Draven, my dear. They won't let you down. And Abbie's father has added incentive to find her."

"I know, but I despise feeling helpless."

"Why don't you tell me about your time with her before she landed here while I seal your wound?" she suggested kindly.

"She's my world," he began. "From the moment I met her, I wanted nothing and no one else."

"And she felt the same?"

The warmth from her hands on his back felt encouraging, as if maybe he'd heal completely.

"Not immediately, but eventually, yes. Thank the Goddess."

He recalled the day they'd met. "We were both attending the same college, and there she was, across the courtyard, laughing at something a friend of hers was saying. It was an arrow straight through the heart. Or as some would say, love at first sight."

"I find it gratifying that men and women attend the same school in your time. Equality is important."

"I've always believed so," he agreed with a grunt as the heat turned up, entering the spinal cord. "We were introduced by mutual friends, but she was already dating another guy."

"Did she leave him for you?" Evie asked, in what he assumed was a distraction maneuver.

"No. She married him."

"Foolish girl."

Wilder curbed the desire to laugh. "I won't argue. He was a controlling ass, and she divorced him a few years later. But it made her gun-shy."

"In what way? She doesn't want to marry you?" Evie's indignant tone was gratifying.

His and Abbie's relationship had been defined early, but she'd eventually come around in the year before she disappeared. She'd stated she wanted to tie the knot and start a family if he was willing.

"It wasn't just me. It was anyone at the time. Marriage isn't the be-all, end-all anymore. Many people remain single their entire lives." He sucked in a breath as a particularly painful burst of magic rocked him.

"I apologize for the discomfort, my dear. This particular section requires a lot of attention and finesse."

"It's all good," he assured her, through gritted teeth. And it was. He'd take whatever she handed out if it meant restoring his spine to its pre-gunshot state and allowing him to walk again. "But to answer your question, she changed her mind and actually proposed to me." He wiggled his pinky, displaying the promise ring Bart had overlooked. Over the last two years, he'd considered removing it, but doing so would feel like a broken vow. "Right before our last climb, she arranged an intimate dinner. In the center of my plate was a jewelry box."

"How romantic!" Evie chuckled, then stepped away to wash the blood from her hands. After drying them, she poured more water into another bowl, dipped a cloth into it, and wrung it out. "All that's left is to clean up your back," she said. "But you'll need to rest and mend."

"Will I walk?" he choked out.

Before that instant, he hadn't considered what it meant for him to be paralyzed. He hadn't climbed since Abbie's fateful day, but he didn't want the ability taken away from him. His entire way of life would change, and what did it mean when it came to making love? They'd always had a healthy sex life. Could he give her what she needed?

"We'll make sure of it," she promised. "Now here, drink some water."

He tilted his head back, but then recalled history class. "Um, is it purified?"

"Purified?"

"Yeah, boiled or whatever to remove the bacteria. Dysentery was a real issue in the West."

"My boy, you're a magical being. We don't suffer the same diseases as mortals." And damned if she didn't sound remarkably like Alastair. Maybe she was where he'd gotten his droll tone. "Now, drink up."

"Yes, ma'am."

$\mathcal{A}$bbie woke with a raging headache and an even angrier temperament. Following her initial fury came terror. Wilder had been shot in the back by that low-life bastard, Bart Mercer, and she had no idea if he was dead or alive. He'd come all this way for her, from their timeline. And if his actions didn't make her love him more than she already did, she would've fallen hard because of his kindness to an injured outcast.

She gasped, nearly choking to death on the stinky material in her mouth as she angled to remove it.

"I remember," she whispered. "Oh my God, Wilder, I remember."

Could he read her mind from whatever distance separated them? She prayed his silence was only their parting and not the more dire explanation of his death.

Her good eye burned from the sudden onslaught of moisture.

For two solid years, she'd been in the dark, and for the last three months of it, her brain was little better than Swiss cheese. How had it repaired itself? Certainly not the knockout, right? Had it shaken a bone fragment loose?

And Wilder hadn't moved on. He'd been steadfast in his love, and adding to his dedication, he'd traveled to this godforsaken place to save her.

Along with a man claiming to be her father.

She and Castor were related. There was no denying their hair color and eye shape. But her mother had said Abbie's father was a man named Alex Collins. Why lie? Who had she been protecting? And if Mama had told the truth as she knew it, then it meant he'd fed her false information from the start. Again, why?

Movement beneath her sank into Abbie's consciousness, as did the oppressive air under the thick cover brushing her face with every sway of her transportation. Turning on her side, she felt around in the dark: wood, dirt, or grain—hard to tell— and a fuzzy item as large as her foot.

It squeaked when she touched it, and she choked back a scream.

Dear Goddess, don't let it be a rat!

Another something, long and skinny, dragged over her wrist as the creature scurried away.

A tail. Definitely a tail!

She added horror to her list of uncontrolled emotions. Did rats in the late 1800s carry plague? At the very least, they'd have a nasty bite.

If only she had Wilder's cousin's ability to talk to animals, then maybe she could have it gnaw through her bindings.

Wait! According to him, she was now a witch, possessing potent powers, like a Traveler. Even the term seemed badass. The ability to manipulate time? Her? It didn't seem real. Perhaps it wasn't. Maybe her mind hadn't survived all the traumas she'd suffered during her stay in Perdition Ridge.

The Devil's Backbone.

It certainly was.

Not a day went by when some lowlife didn't try to harm her. If it hadn't been for the kindness of Draven, Jonas, Red, and Gus, she would likely be dead or bartering sex for food and lodging.

She shuddered.

No one had touched her in a romantic way since her last night with Wilder. He'd been tender, yet fierce, as if he couldn't get enough. And she'd reciprocated, giving him her all as she drank in his passion.

The wagon drew to a halt, and her fear returned, doubling. Bart had one intention, and it wasn't good.

Abbie redoubled her efforts to free herself, working the knots at her wrists with her teeth, but they held, much to her frustration. It stood to reason a shopkeeper would know how to tie his merchandise.

Her fingers brushed Draven's bracelet.

Could she teleport if she removed it? In the past, she couldn't, but she'd been frantic, blinded by panic. Examining it by feel, she searched for a clasp.

Nothing but smooth silver.

Her memory was of the sides coming together and fusing into a single band. But it was once hinged, which meant it could be opened again. What would it take? A calm mind? The trick seemed right up Draven's alley, the wily fox.

She struggled to remember the day he clamped it on her arm.

"It's for your protection, *ma chère*. Your well-being is your key. When your mind *est guéri*, I will know, and the lock, it will open."

Her healed mind.

That's it!

Somehow, she had to convince this chunk of metal she was

well. The question was, how did one go about making an inanimate object understand?

"Please," she whispered, lightly caressing metal. "My mind is whole."

It warmed but remained solid, indicating she was riding the right trail, even if it forked.

"Draven Masters, you remove this shackle immediately," she hissed.

Nothing. Nada. Not even a fizzle.

Damn him!

Teleporting was out, which was probably a good thing since she didn't know how to do it properly anyway. What was she left with? Could she shock Bart if he touched her? Perhaps she was a human defibrillator, capable of stopping his heart? Wouldn't that be a bonus!

Thirty minutes later, the tarp was pulled back, and her rat friend bolted, scaring a curse from him. His shout fed the evil part of her soul, wishing him to the real Perdition.

"Those good-for-nothings! They were supposed to clean this wagon bed," he grumbled, holding his lantern higher and presumably checking the buckboard for additional critters before snuffing out the flame. The dusky light was fading as the sun crested the horizon, but they still rested in the shadow of a canyon.

"Just can't get good help these days," Abbie replied in a chipper tone she didn't feel. Her throat, though tight, didn't pain her as it had before when speaking. A fact she'd discovered earlier with Wilder.

Other than to stare at her with suspicion, Bart remained unmoving.

"Cat got your tongue?" she sneered, rolling to a sitting position.

"Were you fakin' the whole time, girl?"

She grinned, and despite the painful tug of skin, she maintained it. The grotesque mask would give him a nice chill. Let him believe she was capable of anything.

"Get on out of there. We're walkin' the rest of the way."

Remaining stationary, Abbie glanced around. The landscape she could see wasn't familiar in the least.

"What about the horses? Won't they die without water?" she asked with faux innocence.

Perhaps, if he intended to take them, she could steal one and get away. Though she didn't know which way they'd come or what direction she should head if she did manage an escape, she would take her chances.

"They'll head back to town."

Good to know. It meant if she gave the beast its head, it might take her straight back to Wilder.

"I said, get down from there, girl. Are ya hard of hearin' as well as dumb?"

"Watch your tone, Bartholomew. I've had about enough of asshole men." Her frigid tone left little doubt the needle on her bullshit meter had reached the red.

He drew his pistol and aimed.

Okay, bluff called, and all chips were firmly on his side of the table.

Gus knew the route to the caves by heart, and with the moon as bright as it was, his horse was able to effortlessly pick its way across the desert terrain. Ahead, the steady golden glow disappeared, suggesting Bart snuffed out the lantern due to the rising sun. Likely, they'd need to walk the rest of the way since only horses could manage the narrow trail head. But if Mary was still unconscious, Bart wouldn't be moving her any time soon.

Their slowdown worked in Gus's favor.

Only when he was three-quarters of the way did second thoughts intrude. He wasn't fast in a gunfight, and it might see him dead. Regret for leaving Mary's man to suffer was also weighing heavy. He prayed a kind soul saw their way to helping him and didn't leave him to bleed out on the boardwalk. If Gus managed to rescue her, would she be sore at him for not saving her guy?

He hoped not. She was the reason he tried to be better. Not just to impress her, but to earn her respect. Deep down, in the far reaches of her broken mind, she remembered all he'd done to help her. He was sure of it.

"I'm comin' for ya, Mary," he promised.

As Gus drew closer, he could make out the outline of Bart and Mary. Should he shoot the merchant in the back? He risked hitting her from here. Anxiety caused his heart to hammer and him to miss the pounding hooves of the Silver City Gang until they were upon him.

Five riders circled him, leaving no doubt as to the trouble they were about to heap on his head.

"What do we have here, fellas?" drawled Silas Hastings as he drew up. He shifted in the saddle, resting his forearms on the pommel and loosely holding the reins in his gloved hands.

"Looks like Harlan's kid, boss," Jennings replied uselessly.

Gus was as familiar with these outlaws as they were with his pa. They'd all colluded at some point.

"Heard you went straight, Green," Silas said, ignoring his main henchman and pinning Gus with a snakelike stare. "Working for Sheriff Thorne. Ain't that right, boys?"

A chorus of confirmation chilled Gus's blood. No way was he getting out alive. He was doubly sad he hadn't saved Mary's man for her. Without him around, she would need someone else to look after her.

"Nobody likes a rat, Green," Silas stated coldly. "And I'll be damned if you ain't the biggest one around."

"I ain't never told on you or did you no harm, Mr. Hastings. You know that."

"What do we do with rats, fellas?"

"We shoot them in the head," Royal Hastings supplied, as if bored to be there. "But the boy's right, Si. He's never harmed any of us. And pulling the wings off butterflies ain't sporting when we have a job to do."

Silas's considering gaze shifted from Gus to Royal and back again. "Seems my brother likes you, Green. What do you say to that?"

"Mr. Royal is a fine man," he said, unknowing if it was true or not. He lifted his chin. "But maybe I can help you. About that job and all."

Though his mouth curled, Silas's eyes were void of humor. "Is that right?"

Gus shot a glance at Royal. His heavy sigh and eye roll said Gus just stepped in it. Seems he screwed up right proper by offering his services.

"Well, sure. Maybe." He did his damnedest to hold back a stammer. "If I can, that is."

To Silas's right, Jennings smirked, probably already knowing how this confrontation would go.

"What are you doing out here, Green?" Royal asked. "Aren't you far from home?"

No way was he going to give Mary away. Dealing with Bart was dangerous enough. These men would use her poorly and, when done, shoot her full of holes for the fun of it.

"I'm looking for the sheriff's injun friend," he lied.

But his flush gave him away, and the pity in Royal's eyes was uncomfortable.

"Hear that, boss? We got us a two-fer-one this fine mornin'!" Jennings crowed.

"I'm not deaf, you half-wit," Silas growled.

Although Jenning's cheeks reddened, he wisely held his

tongue, making him more of a three-quarter-wit to Gus's way of thinking.

"If you don't mind, Mr. Hastings, I'll be goin', sir." Gus gestured to the canyon. "Gonna see if Stands-in-Shadow is hangin' around and tell him Sheriff Thorne's lookin' for him, if he is."

"Don't let us stop you, Green." Silas straightened, tightening his rein and spinning his horse in the direction Gus had pointed. "As a matter of fact, why don't we help with your search?"

"It's not that I don't appreciate your help, Mr. Hastings, but I wouldn't wanna take you away from your job, and all."

"It's no trouble. We noticed the merchant has new goods to sell, and my friend Morcant here is feeling peckish."

Gus turned his attention to the thin man on Silas's left.

A thin, cruel mouth worked in conjunction with the sharp, beak-like nose, thin-set eyes, and pallid skin, giving him a gruesome appearance. If vicious had a look, it belonged to Morcant. Though the man couldn't have been more than a few years older than Gus, he had an aged quality, as if he knew too much. And it seemed the more nervous Gus grew, almost certain of death, the man's eyes glowed with an unholy glee. As hard as he tried, he couldn't break the mesmerizing hold.

"Lead on, Green," Royal barked, causing Gus to blink and return to himself.

Why did he suddenly feel sweatier and weaker? "I'm not so great. Maybe I'll head on back to town and talk to Doc."

"You'll ride toward that canyon if you know what's good for you, boy," Silas replied, unmistakable menace in his voice. "Start moving."

bbie's feet ached almost as much as her back, and she thanked the Goddess she ditched the bustle in her early Perdition days. Sweat pooled in her pits and other unmentionable places despite the lack of proper underwear. If she ever got out of this, she was never wearing another dress as long as she lived. The restrictions put women at a disadvantage.

All along the way, Bart huffed and puffed in a surprisingly good impression of the Big Bad Wolf, but she put it down to his girth. The man was built like a Sherman tank, with meaty fists to match. About five minutes into their trek, he holstered his weapon, relying on his hands to push her when she slowed. She was faster than he was, so she put down the pinches and shoves to basic cruelty. It was too much to hope he'd keel over from a heart attack in this infernal desert.

Glancing up, she noticed the canyon walls narrowing, providing more shelter in the mid-morning sun.

"Stop here," Bart ordered.

Because she needed the rest, she saw no reason to rebel. At least not yet.

He uncapped his canteen and guzzled water, then replaced the lid.

"I don't get any?" she asked, already guessing his game.

A sly smile curled his mouth. "You gotta work for your rewards, gal. What are ya willing to offer?"

"Fuck off."

Her head snapped back under the force of his open-hand slap. The burn was instant, creating a fiery throbbing in her cheek. Inside her mouth, the metallic taste of blood indicated she'd cut the flesh on her molars.

"You'll show me respect, or I'll beat it into ya!" he shouted into her face.

With deliberate slowness, she wiped his spittle away, grimaced at the fluid on her palm, and casually rubbed it on her dress's skirt. "Well, *that* was disgusting."

His rage flared, turning his already ruddy complexion an apoplectic red.

"Simmer down, Barty Boy, or you're likely to have a stroke. Fantastic for me, but a horrible outcome for you," she taunted.

He grabbed a fistful of her hair before she could dodge away. Abbie had to hand it to him; the man possessed rabbit-fast reflexes.

"You got a death wish, girl?" he demanded, shaking her hard enough to jar her bones from their sockets.

Clearly she did, but she remained silent.

"You'll get no water for your insolence. Now, get movin'."

The hard nudge sent her to her hands and knees. She hissed from the pain of the rocks on her tender skin.

"You look good down there. Maybe I'll throw them skirts over your head and show you what a real man can do."

As difficult as the movement was, she scrambled up to her feet, tripping over the hem and righting herself again.

"Real man? Oh, Barty Boy, don't kid yourself," she scoffed. "Odds are you got nothing but a broken candy stick where your cock should be."

She anticipated the charge, dancing to the side and sticking her leg out. What she hadn't counted on was her good fortune.

His large frame worked against him, propelling him toward the stony outcrop. His footing was precarious, and the momentum too great. The sickening sight of his head wound shouldn't have gratified her as much as it did, but after all the abuses she'd suffered by men, she couldn't drum up the concern.

He lay unmoving.

Abbie didn't love the idea of checking for a pulse, but his sightless eyes told the tale. Bartholomew Mercer had met his demise at the hand—or rather booted foot—of a woman.

She slumped down onto her knees and offered up a prayer of thanks, then waited another minute to make sure he wasn't playing possum. His chest showed no signs of breathing, so she threw a rock.

Nothing.

No flinching of any kind.

With a heavy dose of caution, she inched forward and flicked his nose.

Not even a blink.

She punched him between the eyes before placing two fingers against his neck.

Still dead. Good.

Satisfied, she unbuckled his gun belt, withdrew the knife from his waistband, and dragged the strap of the canteen down his fleshy arm. The first sip was pure heaven despite the tinny taste. She allowed herself another swallow before capping it. If she didn't ration her water, she'd die.

After looping the strap over her shoulder, she rose and kicked Bart in the face.

"Rot in hell, motherfucker!"

Vicious, yes, but she doubted she was the first person the pig fucker had assaulted.

It took her a solid second to register the dust in the canyon seemed thicker. Right before she turned, an ugly foreboding washed over her. She froze, her reaction similar to a wild animal's as a hunter took aim. Goosebumps accompanied the rising hair on the back of her neck.

"Bloodthirsty. I love it," approved a deep voice.

A horse blew out its breath, confirming she had company. With a sense of the inevitable, she spun toward the canyon's opening.

Seven men on horses spanned the trail's width, identities hidden in shadow.

Lifting the pistol, she drew back the hammer.

"Can't get us all, woman," a different guy's voice taunted menacingly, as if trying to invoke fear.

"Maybe not, but I can hit a few of you," she retorted.

His chuckle was akin to an evil spirit slithering across her soul.

"Green, fetch her to me," another man ordered.

Saints alive, this was all too familiar. Was this particular stretch of land cursed? She only needed to look up and see Stands-in-Shadow's horror for it to be a shitshow homecoming. Although, to be honest, she'd welcome a friendly face.

As "Green" drew closer, a sunbeam revealed Gus's tortured visage. As his mount galloped nearer, their gazes locked, and in his lived apology. Participating in their games went against every fiber of his being, and if he was with the motley crew, it wasn't willingly.

"It's okay, Gus," she said softly as he reached her.

He swung down, using his body to block the others who progressed at a leisurely pace. "I'm gonna swing you up in the saddle, Miss Mary, and you're gonna ride out of the canyon, then straight east. Ya got it?"

"I don't know—"

"What's taking so long, boy?" snapped the obvious leader.

"Just helpin' her up, Mr. Hastings," Gus called over his shoulder. When he looked at her, his doleful eyes held a warning. "Don't run full out, but keep him at a trot—"

A pistol's report cut him off, and for one heart-stopping moment, she thought maybe they hadn't shot him. But the light faded from his eyes, and with his last, gasping breath, he said, "I'm sorry I failed ya."

Acting on instinct, she lunged for the reins, but the contrary beast side-stepped, leaving her exposed. Blindly, she fired in the group's direction, grunting her satisfaction as they split up. Wasting precious seconds, she bent to claim Gus's revolver, then dashed for his horse. The perverse creature bucked and reared, screeching as bullets flew their way.

Pumped full of adrenaline, she failed to initially notice the burning in her thigh, but as she spun to flee, her leg gave out. Abbie refused to go down without a fight. Rolling onto her back, she leveled the pistol at the man striding toward her. The warning in his moss-green eyes gave her pause. Squatting, he ripped the gun from her hand.

"Play along, Fire Cat," he murmured. Raising his voice, he said, "I'm claiming her as mine."

"What?" hollered the unkempt outlaw arriving behind him. "Ain't no call to keep a woman to yerself, Royal!" His outrage was almost laughable. "Tell him, Silas. Me and the boys want a turn."

"I said, she's mine," Royal snarled, standing and delivering a vicious kick to the man's balls.

Jennings dropped. Gray-faced, he cupped his sack and curled into himself.

In a tone cold enough to freeze Abbie's bones, Royal added,

"Don't ever question me again, Jennings, or next time I cut them off."

When he glanced down, her heart stopped. His were the eyes of a stone-cold killer. They softened only slightly as he reached for her. After hauling her up and into his arms, he strode straight for a nearby crack in the canyon wall.

"I have people who are coming for me," she bluffed. His skeptical expression prompted her to add, "Ones you don't want to cross."

"Is that right?" he drawled. "Can you feel me quaking in my boots, Fire Cat?"

"A little," she replied with a bravery she didn't feel.

His grin revealed surprisingly straight, white teeth that made him downright handsome. But she wasn't fool enough to associate a good-looking guy with a great personality.

The remainder of his gang meandered into the cavern, leading their horses along with Royal's and Gus's.

Even knowing panic would cloud her mind and judgment, she couldn't suppress it.

"I can't tell you why, but it's important you stay calm," he said in a low voice. "These men fear me almost as much as my brother, love. You're safe enough unless he or Morcant gets it into their heads to claim you."

"And if they do?" She hated the tremble in her voice.

He met her worried gaze, and she imagined she saw compassion. "It won't get that far. Morcant hasn't shown interest in women other than to instill fear." He cast a glance at the vampire-looking dickhead with the dead eyes, then looked at the guy stripping a bedroll from his saddle. They shared a nod. "Silas won't fight me on this. I never take part in their games, so he'll consider you fair payment for my loyalty."

She shivered, drawing his notice.

"Are you cold?"

"A little." She grimaced. "I think it's shock setting in. I was shot in the fray."

Royal stilled, glancing down at her body and finally noticing the blood soaking her clothing. He laid her gently on the ground and eased her skirt up her injured leg, but only a few inches higher than her wound, preserving her modesty. She could've kissed him for his thoughtfulness.

He swore.

"Yeah, no kidding," she replied faintly, fearing unconsciousness. Goddess only knew what this band of outlaws would do to her.

"Please, don't let me black out," she prayed, as if the deities gave a crap about her, which they didn't.

"Sleep if you've a mind to," he said.

"As if."

He frowned. "You're safe. You're mine, and no one touches what's mine."

Abbie's lids grew too heavy to keep open. "Why do men keep saying that to me?"

"Maybe because they recognize your indomitable spirit and want a piece of it for themselves?" he suggested lightly.

"Sure, that's it," she replied dryly.

"What's your name, Fire Cat?"

"Abigail. Abbie."

"Well, Abigail-Abbie, I need to remove that bullet. And I won't lie. It'll be painful as hell."

She opened her eye and met his concerned gaze. Pointing to her face, she said, "Not sure anything could be as bad as this was."

"Who hurt you?" His question held demand, as if it truly mattered to him.

"They're long dead."

"Names?" he gritted.

"Harlan Green and his sidekick, Eustace," she revealed on a tired sigh. "Must sleep. Don't let them rape me."

"Rest, Fire Cat. I'll treat your leg and watch over you," he assured her.

"You'd make an excellent Guardian," she murmured as blackness descended.

As Royal plotted the best course to save the woman's leg, he shoved down his rage. Jennings had thought nothing of firing at her, then deciding to assault her further as she bled out, the horse's ass!

Under Royal's direction, Frank and Wendall built a fire out of sight of the entrance, where the rock funneled up into a natural chimney. Though it was only midafternoon, they would need the heat come sundown, and based on Abbie's blood flow, Royal suspected he'd have to cauterize her wound.

"Put pressure here," he instructed, applying his own over Frank's hands to show the amount needed. "Don't let up."

"Yessir, Royal."

"Bring me a soap, a cloth, and a cup," he called out to Wendall. The idiot walked like he was an old-timer on his deathbed. "Move!" he shouted, about two seconds from gifting the pokey fucker with a swift kick to his backside.

As soon as Wendall brought him the items, Royal dipped the cup in the grotto water, wet his hands, then handed it off to him. "Give me the soap and refill this."

After gaining a small measure of lather, he nodded at Wendall. "Slowly pour that and rinse all the soap off."

Satisfied he was as clean as he'd get, he elbowed Frank out of the way and stuck his finger into the bullet hole, feeling around for the lead. His relief was profound when he found it lodged in the meat of her muscle, and not the bone.

"Frank, wash and heat your blade. Wendall, fetch the whiskey."

"Whisky? You ain't—"

Royal's glare promised death.

"Sure, I'll fetch it fer ya, Royal."

"And get a needle and thread. Be quick about it."

In their line of work, one of them always needed stitches. It only made sense to keep the necessities handy. He didn't allow himself to falter when they returned, and he poured the alcohol into the opening, then used more on the knife. After the sizzling stopped, he eased the end into the muscle, getting underneath the ball. Next, he gave it back to Frank.

"Heat it again. Make it red." To Wendall, he said, "Thread the needle."

If there was one thing Wendall did well, it was sewing.

Using the booze, Royal doused his tools and began stitching the muscle. As soon as he was finished, he gestured to Frank.

"Give the knife to me." Once in hand, he said, "Press the sides of the wound together, but keep your fingers out of the way."

Abbie woke, screaming, the instant he seared her flesh.

On her wrist, an ornate silver bracelet lit up, drawing gasps from Frank and Wendall.

Shit! Why hadn't he guessed she was a witch?

ilder was champing at the bit.

Morning had come and gone without any word from Castor or the Perdition Ridge duo. His worry for Abbie was so high it was stratospheric. Evie had done her best to entertain him, but even she couldn't contain her concern for the others.

"Will you find Nate, Evie?" he asked as she examined his back. "And Damian. We need their firepower."

"I will if you remain here and don't do anything foolish." She pressed her fingers to the wound and grunted her satisfaction. "This is healing neatly. How is your pain level?"

"Manageable. And I'm regaining sensation in my legs."

"Good. Two or three more magical infusions and you should be fully recovered."

"I can't thank you enough for all you've done," he said as she helped him to roll over.

"It's no bother. I'd have done it for any of my great-great-grandchildren," she replied with a cheeky smile.

He laughed. Her humor was as expected, considering the

story of the "big dill" socks his cousin Mackenzie told at a family get-together. The idea of this lovely lady posing as Sebastian Drake's dotty old aunt was hilarious.

Wilder touched her arm as she straightened his coverlet.

Her brows shot up as she sank onto the mattress. "What is it, my dear?"

"You are better than I ever could've imagined. I'm honored to have gotten to know you during my stay here."

When she smiled, it lit the room. "And I you, Wilder. I'm glad Abbie has you to care for her."

"What was she like before the bank robbery?"

"Fun. Refreshingly happy, despite the memory loss." Evie glanced down at their joined hands. "But underneath, she had a longing Nate felt and I saw. When she woke the first time, she called your name."

"She did?" His heart hammered, pounding so hard it felt as if it were trying to escape his chest. "She actually said Wilder?"

"Indeed, she did. My heart was broken for the poor thing."

"I only wish I'd have known she was alive earlier. If I suspected for one minute—"

Evie pressed her index finger over his lips. "Shelve the regrets. The Fates had a plan for her, though it's unclear what that is right now."

"Actually, I know," he confessed.

Her expression arrested, and her mouth dropped open.

Wilder chuckled, getting the impression she wasn't easily shocked.

"Well, out with it," she ordered.

He wasn't sure why he felt the sudden urge for privacy since there were only the two of them. But he couldn't shake the feeling they should be discreet when discussing the Fates.

"Can you ward the room against eavesdroppers?"

Although she narrowed her eyes, she nodded, then used an

effective incantation the Thornes would eventually call "Granny Thorne's cloaking spell."

"Please, continue, my dear," she urged.

"Okay, so Isis possessed Cookie's body at the restaurant and gave me the scoop. It seems Abbie was brought here to spark Draven's instincts and trigger his Guardian powers."

"I don't quite understand. Why her?"

"He is in love with a woman named Céleste Duval, but she was married off to another, and on the night he would've saved her, the Fates stripped him of his memories."

"Dear lord!"

"Yes, it gets worse. Apparently, she's married to an abusive bastard like Bart Mercer," he said grimly.

"We must tell him!"

"The Goddess indicated I should wait for the right time, but I don't know when that is."

Wilder could almost see Evie weighing the pros and cons of revealing what she knew to Draven.

"He doesn't remember his past," she eventually said, as if seeking clarification.

"No. It explains why he's so protective of Abbie in her state."

"Yes." She rose and patted his hand. "Trust Isis. She's always seen our family through the tough times. She will again."

"I know. But as someone who has missed his fiancée unbearably, I hurt for him."

"Your empathy speaks well of you, my dear." Evie brushed the hair back from his forehead, following it with a feather-light kiss. "I'll find Nathanial and Damian, but you must remain here. Don't go charging off alone."

Although it killed him to agree, he did. It wouldn't be smart to gad about when he could hardly walk and didn't know where the hell to start.

"Is it like Jonas not to check in with you?" he asked.

"We've never been in this particular situation before."

Wilder didn't fail to note she avoided a straight answer. "So like Alastair."

"I can't wait to meet him," she replied with a twinkle.

"Look at your husband and imagine your personality."

Evie grinned. "That's a terrifying thought."

"Isn't it, though? Al's formidable and well-respected, if not feared."

"Good. Now, is there anything I can conjure for you before I go?"

"I'm fine. Please bring Nate and Damian here, and tell the Aether it's imperative he help Castor. He'll regret it if he doesn't."

"He won't like an idle threat," she warned with a stern look.

"It wasn't meant as one. Castor and Alastair turn out to be his best friends. He wouldn't want anything to happen to him."

"I see. In that case, I'll make sure he joins our search party."

In a flash, she was gone, and Wilder was left to stress out until someone returned. His inactivity lasted three whole minutes.

Throwing back the covers, he eased his legs over the mattress edge and used the side dresser to haul himself up. His body shook from the effort, and sweat pooled at his lower back as he straightened into a standing position.

"One step in front of the other," he urged himself. Shuffling forward at a hundred-year-old tortoise's pace, he reached the end of the bed. Thank the Goddess for the scrolling metal frame, because of a certain, he'd have been face down without it.

"For Abbie," he chanted whenever his body wanted to quit. "For Abbie!"

He was halfway to the window when the door swung open.

There was no mistaking the black-haired man, despite his oddly arrogant attitude.

The Aether had finally arrived.

"Tell me about this Castor."

Abbie was burning up. Her leg was on fire, and she felt suffocated by the heated weight encircling her. The instant she realized an unfamiliar man held her, she freaked, and her body's electrical force field flared, but fizzled.

Royal swore softly, but didn't release her. "Pull it back, Fire Cat. You have a fever and need the warmth."

"Well, I'm hot, so get off me," she snapped, shoving at his broad chest.

"Doesn't mean your fever's gone," he replied dryly. "And I'm comfortable at the moment, so indulge me."

"The hell I will!"

She wiggled to escape, only to have his arms tighten.

"Calm down," he ordered in a low, urgent voice. "I have no intention of hurting you. But your heightened fear is feeding Morcant, and you need to simmer down. My holding you is for show."

"You could've started with that last bit." She followed Royal's cold stare to the man tucked in the corner.

The creepy fucker was half in shadow, with his glowing eyes. The gleam of his smile sent a ripple along her nerve endings and made her want to puke.

"What is he doing?" she whispered, striving for the calm Royal encouraged.

"He's an Arcane Devourer and lives off strife. The best we can figure is he absorbs the heightened energy," he said in a hushed tone. "I try never to give him what he wants."

"That's some remarkable self-control you have there, buddy." She shifted her head to see his face. "Thank you."

"Life is all about control, Fire Cat." He watched her closely as he said, "As a witch, you should know that."

Her face might not give her away, but she was sure the tensing of her body did.

"What elemental are you?" he asked, loosening his steely arms to give her a little freedom.

"I don't know."

His brows dipped. "How can that be?"

"Whatever magic I was gifted didn't manifest until I fell off a mountain." She hesitated to tell him she was a Traveler's daughter. There was no telling what an outlaw might do with the information. "And how do you know about witches? Most mortals don't unless they get involved with one."

"That's not important."

His tone indicated further discussion was closed on that end, and she waited him out. Eventually he said, "We fell in with some a year back. It's how Morcant became part of our gang. Jennings is twisted, and Morcant enjoys feeding on the chaos he causes."

"Is that why Jennings shot Gus?"

"Yes. He's a sick fuck."

She blinked at his modern speech. "What year were you born?"

He stilled.

"Not this century, I'd venture," she said.

"Don't go there."

"Why?"

"Because I'm tired and want to sleep," he retorted without heat.

"How are we supposed to do that with Creepy McCreeperson hanging about like a fucking spider waiting for a fly?"

Royal's white grin flashed in the low light. "You rest, Fire Cat, and dream delicious thoughts of me. That'll keep him from feasting."

Her stomach flipped. Whether from the suggestion of delicious thoughts of the man holding her or from the horrid image of Morcant tapping into her dreams, she couldn't begin to say. There was no way she was sleeping now. Besides, her leg ached too fucking bad.

"Did you fall through a portal, too?"

Royal's surprised jerk gave him away.

She gasped. "You did!"

"Shh. Keep your voice down. The others may be on the other side of the fire, but noise carries in these caverns."

"Tell me."

"No," he replied succinctly. "Go to sleep."

"I can't. My thigh hurts too badly."

"Want to lift your skirts for me to take a look?" His offer was jam-packed with sexual innuendo, and Abbie's entire body grew warm.

"Stop it," she warned. "I'm engaged, and I love Wilder."

"Is he one of those people searching for you who I'm supposed to fear?" he taunted softly.

An unexpected sob caught in her throat. Brought on by the burgeoning emotions of worry and sorrow. Had she and Wilder suffered two years apart only to meet an end like this? Her to die at the hands of renegades while he bled out on a sidewalk in The Devil's Backbone? The fucking place should've been called The Devil's Armpit!

"Rein it in, Fire Cat. Grief is just as good as fear for our resident energy vampire." He cradled her against his chest, rubbing small circles on her back. His actions were at odds with his gruff warning to get it together and encouraged her to cry. "Shhh, Abbie, it will all be okay," he promised.

The urge to rail at him was severe, to tell him she'd be back in Perdition Ridge, finding out Wilder's fate by now, if they hadn't accosted her. Yet after learning what the Freakazoid in the corner could do, she had no choice but to shove it down.

Searching for a distraction, she asked, "How long have you been in this time?"

"Seems like forever," he confessed. "At least two years now."

She stilled. Two years was a helluva coincidence. "Where were you when it happened?"

"My brother Silas and I were climbing—"

Her mouth dropped the instant she registered why he seemed familiar. "I remember you! Wilder and I were going up as you were coming down. We passed you in the middle."

"That was you? Jesus. We were all fucked that day, weren't we?"

What were the odds? But her recall had to be faulty, because there were five people in his group that day. Three men and two women.

"Did the others fall through the portal, too?" she asked quietly.

"Only Julia." By his tone, she was someone important to him. Or had been, anyway. But there wasn't another female hanging with these guys, and it didn't speak well for the woman's chances.

"Who was she?"

He glanced toward the corner, and Abbie followed his gaze.

Morcant had curled into himself and fallen asleep.

Thank the Goddess for small favors.

"She was my sister-in-law."

"Was?"

"The portal kicked us out in different places along the canyon over three days. Julia was first, apparently. We found her body just outside this cave's entrance."

"Oh my god!"

Abbie's stomach rebelled, and the urge to hurl was strong. Her latent power influx had caused the death of Silas's wife! If he ever found out what she was and what she'd caused with her magic… Well, let's say she wouldn't be placing any bets on her survival.

As if guessing her turmoil, Royal pressed his lips to her ear and said, "I feel the tension in your body. But you need to hear me when I say this, Fire Cat. Don't ever let my brother know what you are or what you can do, understand? He blames magic. He'll carve your heart out and leave it to wither beside the husk of his."

"What the fuck do you mean you can't find her?" Wilder had never wanted to destroy shit more. Directly on the heels of Damian's entrance, the trio searching for Abbie arrived to deliver the bad news.

"We searched all through the canyon. If she's there, she's cloaked," Castor replied. The thin edge of anger in his tone suggested he was no happier than Wilder.

"Scrying?" he asked, desperate for a solution.

Their grim expressions said it all.

His legs gave out, and he sank to the floor. "This can't be happening again. It just can't. Christ. Hasn't she suffered enough?"

"We'll find her, son."

"People keep promising, but they've yet to deliver," he retorted before dropping his head in his hands. "God, Abbie."

It only took another minute to register the weighted silence, and he looked up.

"Just spit it out. It can't be worse than losing her a second time."

"We found two bodies on the trail. Bart and Gus," Jonas said.

"How'd they die?"

"Bart's appeared to be an altercation with a rock wall, and the boy was shot in the back," Castor replied, glancing around the room as if looking for a drink. His gaze landed on Damian. "We need your preferred brandy, Dethridge. STAT."

The Aether's brows rose, and he cocked his head as if seeing an unusual species. Perhaps he was. From Evie's stories, Wilder imagined not many people dared such familiarity.

"And you are?" Damian asked dryly.

"Alexander Castor. Your future best friend and pain in the ass."

"I see." His lips twitched, and amusement lurked in his eyes. "You do realize, as a Traveler, you are forbidden from dispensing *future* information. It could see you dead."

"Pfft. It's like you don't know me at all."

Again, the Aether's brows shot up. "I don't."

"Yet."

"There you go with that information again."

Castor shrugged. "What can I say? It's a weakness."

"Hm, yes. I can see why you would be my friend."

"You do? I can't see it. He was a complete pain in the ass the entire trip out and back." Jonas's complaint earned him a glare from Castor.

"I was not. I merely suggested you get your head out of your asses and perform a proper search for my daughter."

"We pulled out all your tops," Draven inserted.

"All *the stops*," Wilder corrected absently as he considered what those might be.

Wordlessly, the Aether held out his hands, palms up. Light flared as a crystal decanter formed, filling itself with an amber liquid. The instant he was done, he held it up to the light and smiled.

"A twelve-year-old bottle of Martell, imported all the way from Cognac. Masters, you might appreciate this." He passed it to Draven. "If you don't mind, please hold this while I conjure glasses for the group. I suspect the Traveler's story will be long, if not interesting."

"Let's take this to Red's sitting room," Jonas suggested. "It'll be more comfortable."

"One moment." Damian held out a hand to Wilder. "You're another Thorne, or so I'm told."

Anger kept Wilder from accepting the help, and he climbed to his feet on sheer determination alone.

"You're upset with me. Why?" Damian asked.

Wilder rounded on him. "You could've helped Abbie at any time, but you didn't. You left her in this hellhole to suffer unimaginable pain and abuse at the hands of outlaws. What kind of person are you?"

Even in his rage, he didn't miss the wary exchange of glances from the others. He simply didn't care.

"I'm working on the assumption you know who and what I am, Thorne, yes?" After receiving a sullen nod, Damian continued. "You should also know I'm constantly under scrutiny from the Witches' Council, the Authority, and the Deities for what my mother became. I cannot afford a misstep for one moment of one day."

"You're not your mother, Damian," Castor said quietly. "You're stronger than she ever will be."

His head whipped around, and his jaw tightened. "Will be?"

"Slip of the tongue. I should've said, than she ever was," Castor corrected with a half smile. "And quit trying to probe my brain for details. You, my dear master mind reader, taught me how to form a wall against intrusion."

"It's quite possible he can't penetrate your thick skull," Wilder muttered. "Can we get back to Abbie now?"

"I appreciate your singular focus."

"You should, she's your daughter, dude." He sighed in disgust. "And look, I'm sorry, but this boys' club shit can wait. We need to find her immediately. And if you aren't willing to help, Aether, then restore my fucking powers so I can search myself."

"You're out of time," Damian replied sharply.

"There's a limited window for requests?" Wilder scoffed.

"I misspoke. What I meant to say was you're out of your natural time. You don't exist yet. Therefore, your abilities don't either."

"As we feared," Castor said. "Can we get a loan?"

Damian barked a laugh. "You want me to loan you my abilities?"

"Sounds reasonable."

"You couldn't contain the power and would be dead in twenty-four hours."

"You forget what I am, Dethridge."

"I don't know you to forget," Damian countered smoothly. "You seem to believe I owe you a debt for being my *future* friend. I do not."

"There's where you're wrong, pal," Castor snapped. It seemed the thread he held on his temper had snapped, and his charming veneer vanished in a heartbeat. "I have never, not once, failed to be there for you when you needed me. I felt I owed *you* for saving me from the streets as a teenager. But I've more than repaid any debt, and I'm asking as a favor. One you'll regret not granting down the road."

The atmosphere around them grew thick with the Aether's ire.

"I will not go against the Authority in this matter," he replied coldly. "It isn't done. And if you know anything about me, you know—"

"That you bloody well do what you feel is right, no matter

what," Castor snapped, his accent coming out with his anger. "In my century, you don't give a flyin' fuck what those manipulative bastards want. You're on the side of justice and the magical community."

"But we aren't in your century, are we?" Damian countered. His silky tone was menacing in a way his shouting could never be. "And you haven't offered proof they are corrupt. You merely strode in here, assuming you can charm me into doing your bidding. I'm no fool."

"That's bleedin' debatable, ya feck!"

In a flash, a knife was in Castor's hand, and he was going for Damian's throat.

Wilder saw their lives flash before his eyes in that one reckless move.

But Damian didn't bat a lash as the Traveler pressed the wicked blade to his jugular.

"And what will killing me prove," he asked with admirable calm.

"Not a goddamned thing, but it will make me feel better for the five minutes before I regret my actions."

"And would you?" he asked curiously. "Regret it?"

With a weary sigh, Castor dropped his arm. "Read my mind, Dethridge. See what you need to so you know I'm right."

"Not necessary." He cocked his head. "You're Irish by birth?"

"Yes. I was born Anton O'Connor—"

"O'Connor," he said flatly. The surname was synonymous with scoundrels and thieves. "Your family isn't well-liked, and yours is not a name I'd be spreading around, Mr. *Castor*."

"I'm aware. It's also why you gave me a chance when I was a starving kid."

"Please stop revealing the future. I don't care to have my mind wiped like your Abbie."

"*What?*" Castor was apoplectic

Wilder could no longer be silent. "Look, I can explain later. Can we focus here? While you two are having a pissing contest, she's out there somewhere fighting for her life—maybe even lost in the desert after wandering the wrong way."

But Castor wouldn't be redirected. "Who the fuck wiped her mind? I thought it was from her injuries?"

"Why haven't you warded this room before telling us that?" Jonas asked with a nervous glance at the windows. "Are you trying to get us all killed here, Damian?"

"Evie did, before I ever entered."

Draven uncapped the decanter and downed a quarter of the bottle.

"Are you mad?" Damian's appalled expression was laughable, had Wilder felt at all humorous. "You don't drink a fine 1850s vintage as though you're swilling rotgut. Are you a bloody animal?"

"Jesus," Wilder muttered. "I can see where Alastair learned it."

"Alastair." Obsidian eyes locked on him. "Why does the man's name continually pop up in conversation?"

"He's our best friend," Castor replied, grabbing the decanter from Draven and taking a swig. "He's obsessed with manners and drinking booze like a gentleman."

"Clearly, we didn't rub off on you," Damian replied dryly.

"Clearly, ya prissy arses," he replied, laying his Irish on thick.

The Aether's laughter was oddly beautiful to a listener's ears, and Wilder would go so far as to say seductive. His voice's soothing cadence, combined with his stunning looks, pretty social niceties, and undeniable power, would be a honeytrap for the unsuspecting. Hell, after hearing it, he was questioning his own sexuality.

Damian shot him an amused glance, reminding him of his ability to read minds.

"I'm devoted to Abbie, so you're out of luck," he said. "Speaking of—"

"You're a dog with a bone, Thorne."

"You know it. And if you entered a warded room, you intended to help us, all along. So let's get to it."

25

Wilder Thorne might have been fifteen years Damian's junior, but he carried himself like a much older man. Perhaps it was the grief he'd suffered from believing Abigail Monroe had passed away during their mountain climbing expedition. Or perhaps he possessed an old soul. But either way, Wilder was joyless, and Damian hoped to change it.

"What do you know of the Arcane Devourer?" he asked.

The Traveler's brows shot to his hairline, and he shared a wary glance with his companion.

"Morcant?" Castor asked sharply. "He's here?"

By his future friend's reaction, the man wasn't wildly popular. "I see you know of him," Damian replied.

"Yeah, so do you. Later."

"What the hell is an Arcane Devourer?" Jonas asked, reading the room correctly.

Damian hated instilling fear in anyone, but cautioning them against the fight to come was imperative.

"He is a powerful bastard who survives by eating the energy

of those around him. The more chaotic and strife-filled, the better," Wilder explained in his stead. Turning his attention to Damian, he asked, "What does he have to do with Abbie? There's a connection, or you wouldn't be here."

"I believe she may be with him."

The long list of expletives Wilder released would burn anyone's ears, but it was Castor's reaction that was the more interesting of the two. He paled and swayed.

If asked, Damian would've said nothing could faze the man, but of a certainty, the idea of Abigail in the clutches of Morcant did.

"We have to find her, right now. That monster, he..." The stark pain in the Traveler's pale-blue eyes affected Damian strangely. A feeling of déjà vu struck him, though they'd never met before. "I know you don't want me to tell you, Dethridge, but—"

"Don't. If you're standing here, things turned out the way they were intended."

"But if I can save you the grief—"

"You have the potential to make things worse, Mr. Castor. Should I do the opposite of what my future self does to avoid an outcome, I've the potential to create an even worse ending." He smiled. "But I thank you for caring enough to try."

"Enough fucking around with chit-chat. How do we find Abbie and off the bastard?" Wilder demanded.

"First, you need to remove your shirt and lie down. I'll finish what Evie began and heal your back fully." So saying, Damian gestured to the bed. "My understanding is Morcant has been searching for the source of the power surges that sent six of you here."

"Six!" Castor shook his head. "No, at most three. Abbie, Wilder, and me. No one else came through with us."

"According to the Authority, they came through in the days

before her, two years ago. Apparently, the portal ejected a total of four people during Abigail's tumble through time."

Wilder paused in undressing. "I don't understand. We came straight through. It was morning on both sides of the portal. Granted, the day might've shifted, but the date should be the same, surely?"

"What was the date you left?" Damian asked.

Wilder and Castor exchanged a glance before he said, "Tuesday, September the second. Why? What is today's date?"

"September the fifth. And if you've been here twenty-four hours, it means you arrived on the fourth, two days after you stepped into the portal."

"It couldn't have taken that long to cross the threshold. That's not how travel works," Castor protested.

"Yet it did. Based on the report, the time disturbance was a total of four days the first time. One for each person, it seems. The first was a female witch. Next, a male, followed by another male the day after, and finally, Abigail."

"But Wilder and I arrived together."

"We were touching. Would it have made a difference?" Wilder asked.

"Possibly. Damian?"

He gave it a moment's consideration and finally nodded. "I agree. It may have been the difference between arriving separately or alone. But Abigail was the only one Stands-in-Shadow found."

"So where did the others go?" Jonas asked. "Why haven't we heard from any of them in two years?"

Damian shrugged. "My source, Isis, has said the first woman, a witch, crossed into the Otherworld. The two mortal men are with Morcant."

"The female, she died immediately?" Masters asked, breaking his silent watchfulness. The probability was high he was trying to stay unnoticed, fearing he'd be called upon to accept his fate.

But Damian wasn't here to push any agenda other than stopping the Arcane Devourer from feeding on Abigail's power to make himself invincible. The Authority realized their cock-up too late in their game. While they'd gambled on her falling into more trouble, they hadn't planned on Morcant. With a Traveler's abilities, he'd be unstoppable, able to pop throughout time to steal what he desired, whenever he wished.

"Yes. She was the wife of a guy by the name of Silas Hastings. He—"

"He's the leader of the Silver City Gang," Jonas finished for him. "Things are dire. Those boys kill first and ask questions later." He met Wilder's worried gaze. "Some don't treat women kindly. Red banned them from The Velvet Ember."

"Why haven't you done anything about them?" Wilder asked. The suppressed fury in his body was something only Damian could feel, and the guy did a marvelous job of hiding it behind a mask of icy calm.

"The posters didn't come through until after they'd left town. They haven't been back," Jonas explained. "The other towns around haven't been so lucky, but their posses usually come back lighter than they went out."

Castor swore. "In other words, you have a lack of recruits willing to bring them to justice."

"*Oui*," Draven said. "But we will this time. *La dame* will not suffer." Meeting Damian's gaze, he asked, "What would you have us do, Aether?"

"First, we heal Mr. Thorne completely, then we set out to find these men. We will divide into three groups and take the surrounding towns."

"Why not scry?" Castor asked him. "Your magic is strong enough to get a result, even if theirs isn't."

"I've tried. The closest I've come is the caves by the portal access."

"What about Stands-in-Shadow?" Wilder asked as he lay facedown on the mattress. "Doesn't he live in that area? Perhaps he saw something? We could teleport to him."

"I'll go," Draven said.

"Wait." Castor downed another healthy sip of brandy, and Damian suppressed a wince. "Abbie's bracelet."

"What about it?"

"Can it be unlocked from here? If she is free to teleport, might she go to where she always ends up, or perhaps back here?"

Damian smiled to himself as he watched these men formulate a plan. Deep inside, he sensed the importance of their coming role in his life, but his ability to see the future was limited to a few months at most. They worked well together, these four, though only two would be needed. Which two remained to be seen, but he strongly suspected they were Draven Masters and Alexander Castor, with their next-level gifts.

"It's a clever idea, Mr. Castor," he said.

"Just Castor or Alex, anything else is annoying, Dethridge."

"Duly noted."

"Al got that from you, too, I see."

Damian couldn't wait to meet the man.

***

"I need privacy," Abbie stated, crossing her arms to show she meant business.

"You're not getting it," Silas replied coldly. "Take Royal or Jennings, your choice."

There was no choice at all. "Royal."

"That a girl. And hurry, we don't have all damned day."

"Dick," she muttered, careful to wait until he was out of range. Royal had been correct; the guy no longer possessed a heart.

Silas paused by his brother to exchange words. Royal glanced in her direction before nodding and striding toward her.

"I hear you need to use the privy. Need me to carry you, Fire Cat?"

"I can walk."

"You can limp," he retorted with a smirk.

"Just show me where it is from here," she ordered, dropping her arms to her sides. "I'll manage."

"Sorry, but Silas doesn't trust you not to run."

"For real?" she scoffed. "He believes I'm able to walk the distance from here to Perdition? I don't even know where the fuck we are."

And it was the god's honest truth, too. Sometime in the wee hours before dawn, they'd blindfolded her and set out for this cabin. They'd only just arrived, but she was hot and sweaty, with her bladder twenty seconds from bursting.

Compassion flashed in Royal's mossy eyes. "He remembered you from the mountain run. Your skills were legendary, Abbie Monroe."

"So you know who I am?"

"It took us a minute, but yeah, we do."

"I'm not so legendary anymore." She hated the mournful note in her voice, but the truth was, the Hastings brothers were out of their minds if they believed she had the strength or stamina to escape with her old skill set.

He tilted up her chin and met her gaze. "If we ever get back to our time, you will be again. I have faith in you. Come on. Let me show you what serves as a bathroom in these parts."

"I suspect I already know," she replied dryly.

"Yeah, I sure do miss the comforts of a hot shower and a quality mattress."

"And cookies from a package."

He chuckled. "Moose Tracks ice cream."

"God, yes! If I were any kind of witch worth her salt, I'd conjure—"

"*Witch!*"

Neither of them had heard Silas approach.

His visage was downright frightening. "You're a witch?"

"N-n-no!" she stammered, seeking Royal's support and not getting it. "I just meant if I *were* one, I'd—"

"Don't you fucking lie to me, lady," Silas growled, reaching for her.

Royal stepped between them. Lowering his voice, he said, "Si, calm down, bro. She's not what you think. If she were, do you really believe she'd have allowed herself to be captured by this crew?" He glanced back toward the yard where the others were working on tack and grooming the horses. "That she wouldn't have already healed herself?"

Though his anger didn't dissipate, Silas eyed her with less suspicion. "Being a witch didn't help Julia. She's still dead."

"I know. But we were talking about the conveniences we miss from our timeline. That's all," Royal said.

"Morcant thinks she's something more. What do you have to say to that?"

"That creepy dickhead can go fuck himself," he growled. "Why are you letting him stick around, Si?"

"He keeps the others on their toes."

"So do you. You don't need him."

Silas ignored him, keeping his narrow-eyed gaze on Abbie. "You'd better be telling the truth, Abbie Monroe, or I swear you'll wish you had." After another long stare, he strode into the nearby brush.

"I know he's your brother and all, but he's—"

"Don't. You can't understand what he's been through."

"Can't I?" she rounded on him. "How about falling off the peak, believing you're going to die, only to find yourself face-to-face with a rattlesnake? How about having strangers take potshots at you while climbing to escape? How about falling a second time within an hour, snapping the bones of your arms and legs, scarring your face, and losing your memory because of it?" Her breath hitched. "How about calling out to the man you love both times, hoping his magic will save you, but it never does?"

"Abbie—"

"How about almost getting raped each time you venture into town, and needing a boy—the one your friend Jennings shot in the back—to be your champion by redirecting his low-life father at every turn?"

"I'm sorry," he said. "Truly."

But she was on a roll. "How about getting shot in the face during a bank robbery by that same man? And how about having your fiancé show up to save you after two years and not remembering him, witnessing his crushed expression?"

"Please stop." His expression was pained, as if hearing of her plight was too hard.

But she couldn't stop.

"Or how about finally feeling the spark return, only to witness the man you love get shot in the back? How about being abducted by a guy intent on raping you and selling you to a band of outlaws to get their kicks? One of which lives off the terror of the victims?"

He remained mute in the face of her rage.

"Tell me again that I don't know suffering, Royal. Please do, so I can kick you right in the fucking balls."

She spun away, searching for the bathroom and fearing she'd soil herself before finding it.

"This way," he said, his tone mild, as if she hadn't just unloaded all her woes on him.

They stopped at an outhouse with an attached outside shower.

"For what it's worth, I'm sorry. Not only for what we've put you through, but for all of it." The sincere apology in his expression was as honest as she'd ever seen, and she could only nod if she wanted to hold it together.

"I'll go in to check for snakes first. Wait right there," he ordered.

Abbie was more than happy to let him take the lead.

"And spiders," she called. "Please remove any tarantulas, or my death will come sooner than either of us expected."

He turned his head, but his grin flashed before he could hide it. The spiteful part of her didn't believe he should get off so easily, but the fair part owed him for repeatedly saving her from the likes of Jennings, Morcant, and Silas.

He returned momentarily with the all clear. "Do you want a shower? I can arrange it."

"Christ. I was trying not to elevate you to hero status, but there you go with the fucking consideration again."

Had there been no Wilder in her life, Royal's crooked smile would've charmed her to no end. But she couldn't forget what he was. A killer wearing a saint's smile. Luckily, he was there to remind her.

"I'm no one's hero, Fire Cat. Besides, there's no hot water. It's my own twisted sort of revenge."

26

bbie had just closed the door to the outhouse and squatted when her bracelet lit up. Slapping her hand over it, she peeked through the crack in the boards, praying they hadn't seen the glow from the outside. That was all she needed! If Silas recognized it as a magically infused item, the jig was up. He'd sign her death warrant, becoming judge, jury, and executioner.

As the one responsible for his wife's demise, she'd deserve it. The weight of accidentally killing a person didn't sit well with her. If she had a way to do it over and save the woman, she absolutely would.

Beneath her fingers, the metal shifted, as if it sprang apart. She dared a peek as the illumination died and the silver returned to its normal appearance.

A rush of relief made every nerve in her body exhale at once.

When she eased her grip, the bottom half sagged on a hidden hinge, and the bracelet plinked as it hit the floorboard.

197

She cringed at the idea of rooting around the shadowy stall's pee-soaked floor to find it.

Inspecting her surroundings, she spotted the pile of toilet paper sheets. Thank the Goddess! Their presence had to be Royal's doing. In the last twenty-four hours, she couldn't help but notice how fastidious he was. Discovering luxuries existed in this hellhole was the only bright light in her otherwise miserable existence.

She picked up her bracelet using another sheet, wiped it down, and stuffed it in her pocket. Fingers crossed, no one would notice it missing from her wrist. As she was about to open the door, she hesitated.

Hope fluttered in her chest. Did the absence of a shackle mean she could now teleport out of here? Possibly back to Wilder?

Abbie racked her brain, trying to recall what he'd once said about the process. How something called a "feeler" was sent out to places one had been or had a very clear image of, so the person jumping from one location to the next didn't embed themselves into an object or, God forbid, someone else.

The imagery gave her a shudder.

Dare she try? What if, by using her untried magic, she caused another death? For certain, she wouldn't be able to live with herself.

A knock on the door caused her to yelp.

"You all right in there, Fire Cat?"

"Yes. Sorry, you scared me." Dare she make up an excuse? "Breakfast didn't sit well. I'll be another minute."

His choked "sure thing" did little to hide his amusement. No matter how old a guy was, he possessed the humor of a twelve-year-old boy. But it bought her a few more minutes to think through her escape. She hadn't outright asked him to return her to Perdition Ridge, but then again, if he were wanted, he wouldn't get within ten feet of an excellent lawman like Jonas.

But what if she could convince him that the others could help them return to their old lives? Would he want to go? Why wouldn't he? It wasn't as if living here in the Wild West was as great as Hollywood made it seem. No, the place was basic and barbaric, with no benefits she could think of.

And why did she care so much about Royal's plight when her own life hung in the balance? Her soft heart would get her dead in this land of guns and grudges, a place that chewed up the tenderhearted and spat out their bones. Look what happened to sweet Gus!

From here on out, she'd only worry about herself. Her next order of business was teleportation and learning what firing up her power required. It lived in the nucleus of the cell, she'd been told. As she dug deep, she absently tapped her thigh, hoping to recall the scraps of science. Not that she'd ever been a great student, but she had a decent grasp of the basics.

A faint warmth spread beneath her palm. She frowned, glancing down, and realized her fingers rested over the bullet wound. The heat pulsed once, twice, then vanished—taking the pain with it.

Royal knocked again, and his tone was harder when he said, "Abbie, wrap it up. Silas is calling a meeting."

"One sec!" Dammit! She'd pushed the excuse as long as plausible, but maybe she could take another "bathroom break" soon and try her abilities then.

She pushed open the door.

Royal's expression held concern mixed with suspicion, and he was right to question her behavior.

As they were heading back to the cabin, she asked, "Will you return me to Perdition Ridge?"

"No."

She stopped. "Why?"

He retraced his steps, and for the longest minute, he said nothing. Finally, he grimaced.

"Silas and I don't split up. Ever. Taking you back means he has to go with us, and he won't."

"Please, Royal. I have to get back to Wilder." She pressed a hand to his heart, hoping to appeal to his softer side. "Please. It's been two years, and we've only just found each other again."

"I'm not immune to your plight, Fire Cat."

"But you won't help," she said flatly.

"If the opportunity presents itself, perhaps. That's the best I could do."

He'd already told her he was nobody's hero. Certainly not when it came down to either Silas or her. He barely knew her, and he wouldn't sacrifice his brotherly relationship for a stranger.

"Let's go." He gripped her elbow, hurrying her along.

She was mounting the steps to the porch when it registered she was moving too freely. Did it mean she'd miraculously healed? Would it raise Silas's suspicions if she didn't limp?

Probably.

Abbie put on a show for anyone watching, hoping the long trek from the outhouse hadn't given her away. She was a fool not to realize the difference in her gait earlier. But then again, neither did Royal, so maybe she'd escaped notice.

"What's up, Si?" Royal asked as they entered.

The group was gathered around a rustic wooden table. Dirty plates leftover from breakfast were scattered about, reminding Abbie how much she missed a quality dishwasher.

A seventh man had joined their gang, it seemed, and he held the place of honor to Silas's right.

She knew him.

Draven.

Somehow, some way, he'd found her.

No recognition flared in his eyes as he looked at her, and she dropped her gaze, hoping she didn't give him away.

"Phil here"—Silas motioned to Draven—"just got word Globe received a silver shipment."

Royal glanced at Draven and frowned. "Phil?"

"You remember Phil. He helped us on the…" Silas glanced at Draven. "Which job was it again?"

The Guardian took a long drag of his cheroot, then blew out six perfect Os, each one encircling the outlaws' heads.

"Prescott," he purred.

Glassy-eyed, they all nodded as one. "Prescott," they repeated obediently.

Group hypnosis. Clever!

"My friend Jonesy will be joining us for this one. Hope you boys don't mind," Draven added with a smirk.

Again, they nodded.

"Excellent." Raising his voice, he called, "Come on in, Jonesy."

Maybe she expected to see Jonas, or even Nate, so when her father, sporting ginger-colored hair and a scruffy beard, stepped through the back door, her jaw dropped.

"You know him?" Royal asked in a low, suspicious voice.

"Uh, no. It's just… he's a beast," she replied. Both true statements. She hadn't met her father in any real sense of the word, certainly not as Abbie, and the guy was freaking huge, standing at least six-five with muscle befitting a gladiator.

"Who's the bleedin' wench?" Castor asked with a scowl, leaning heavily into a cockney accent. He came across as a misplaced pirate, probably perfect for this band of misfits. "I don't hold with no women on board."

"That's a ship," Royal replied dryly. "And it's superstition at best."

"Well, I ain't likin' it now, am I?" Castor grumbled, pulling a pipe out of his pocket and jamming it into his mouth with a harrumph.

It was all she could do not to laugh despite the seriousness of the situation.

"I can wait outside," she choked out.

"Nonsense." Draven waved away Castor's fake objection and rose to his feet.

Whatever game they were playing, she had no intention of spoiling it. She stood her ground as he approached, striving to look slightly nervous but defiant.

"No one could possibly object to so lovely a lady," he said, trailing his fingers along her smooth cheek. Her skin tingled where he'd touched. "But why are you here, with this bunch, when you should be dining in the finest houses, wearing the most beautiful of dresses and jewels?" he asked seductively.

Her breath caught. When he wanted to, Draven could turn up the charm.

Royal put an arm around her, drawing her back. "She's fine where she's at, friend."

"*La dame*, she can speak for herself, *ami*," Draven replied in a steely tone, his annoyance giving away his French roots.

The outlaws shared a wary look, and Silas stood as Draven and Royal's stare-off continued.

"Do we have a problem here, fellas?" he asked.

Royal was the first to relent, dropping his arm. "No. No problem. He's right. Abbie should decide who she wants to befriend and who she doesn't."

"She's our captive. She doesn't get to decide shit," Silas growled. "Damn woman's been nothing but trouble."

"Your man shot *me*," she retorted, taking offense.

Draven and Castor tensed.

"Thankfully, Royal knew what he was doing and was kind enough to dig the ball out," she quickly clarified.

Withdrawing a small bag from his vest, Draven withdrew a

ring. Set in a winding silver vine were a series of tiny blue-violet stones. The ring was delicate and beautiful, exactly the style she preferred.

"May I offer you a gift?" he asked, holding out his hand. "A reward for your bravery, if you will."

With a nervous glance around, she laid her right hand in his, gasping the instant he slid the ring onto her finger. His thoughts, along with Castor's, Damian's, and Wilder's, crowded her mind. The overwhelming barrage caused her to sway, and once again, Royal wrapped an arm around her.

"I hope you will think of me, *ma chère*, whenever you wear this trinket."

"Laying it on there thick, Masters, aren't you?" Castor's unspoken response echoed in her mind, like Wilder's the night they had dinner.

"I must sell it, as Wilder said," Draven replied.

Hoping they could hear her as she heard them, she telegraphed, *"Castor's right. You need to be less charming and more businesslike if you want Silas to take you seriously."*

Aloud, she said, "It's beautiful, sir. Thank you."

"Don't see where no gal like her needs fancy jewelry 'n all," Jennings inserted sullenly. "Ain't good fer nothin', that one."

Royal turned downright feral, jerking him up by the neck. "What the fuck did I tell you about talking down to her?" He shook him like a terrier with a rat before throwing him at her feet. "Apologize, or I'll slit your throat where you lie."

"What? She got a golden puss—" Jennings snarled.

In one smooth but lightning-fast motion, Silas drew and put a bullet between the man's eyes.

Abbie gasped at the ruthlessness and covered her mouth. None of the others seemed to see the issue with casually gunning someone down.

"Anyone else think they're entitled to talk back to my brother or me?" he asked coldly.

The OG crew shook their head, although Morcant's creepy AF eyes gleamed with delight. Doubtlessly, he'd stir strife if he could.

"Good. Wendall, you help Frank remove the trash and clean up this hovel. Royal and I are going to converse with our new friends outside."

As Abbie shifted to join them, Silas froze her with a glare. "Not you. Park it until we get back."

Damn, the man hated her, and she hated not being able to work out why. His brother's attention?

She opened her mouth to object, but Castor's voice rang through her mind, *"Please do as he says. We have a plan."*

"Fine," she said, letting her irritation show. Her sullenness made Jennings's mild by comparison.

Silas pointed to the body. "One dead not enough for you, lady?"

"Was he your bestie? If he wasn't, then I don't see how it's much of a loss," she retorted.

"*Le petit chaton* has very sharp teeth!" Draven crowed with delight.

"Claws," she and Royal corrected in unison.

"Meh. Claws, teeth… what does it matter if they are sharp, *oui?*"

Again, the bizarre desire to laugh struck, but she curbed it.

Silas watched her with eyes that saw to her soul, and she worried he'd tapped into her elation at Draven and Castor finding her.

"No. I suspect he's merely watchful," her father telegraphed, causing her to jump.

"My apologies, Silas," she said in a more subdued tone. "Of course, I'll stay here."

His eyes narrowed as if he didn't trust her, but after a minute, he nodded and led the way outside.

Castor paused in the doorway and shot her an undecipherable glance before making a point to look around the entire room. *"Don't relay fear if you can help it, but if Morcant comes near you, scream as loud as you can,"* Castor warned through their link.

"Yeah, I already know what he is," she replied in kind.

"Good. Have a care, daughter."

Wilder breathed a sigh of relief at hearing Abbie well and back to her sassy self. He ducked into an alley in Globe.

"Abbie?"

"Wild Man? Oh, God! I was worried you were dead."

There was a warmer quality to her speech that wasn't there prior to her abduction, as if she knew or felt close to him.

"Your memories are back?" he asked, afraid to hope.

"Yes. Bart's goons must've jarred something loose when they knocked me out." She paused a second, then added, *"I can't believe you never gave up on me."*

"Part of me had," he confessed. *"Life without you was too hard, and I couldn't imagine continuing down such a bleak path. I didn't want to go on, Abbie. My soul was shredded. I was completely out of options when I stumbled upon your dad at Ebba's."*

"New rule: we both survive, no matter what it takes."

"That's a fucking great rule," he replied with feeling.

She paused for a long moment. *"How's your back? It looked bad."*

"Our friends patched me up. I'll tell you all about it when I see you."

"Your standard line when you don't want to discuss anything deep," she teased.

"Yeah, well, enough about me. Are you safe? Have they hurt you?"

"I'm fine."

"Really? Because I was told they found Gus's and Bart's bodies in the canyon."

"Yes. Bart's demise was an altercation with my foot, and Jennings shot poor Gus in the back when he tried to help me."

Wilder swore.

"I'm fine, Wild Man. Promise."

"I love you, Abbie. With all my fucking heart and soul. I don't know if I ever told you that enough."

"You did. I love you, too." Another long pause. *"Morcant is a creepy motherfucker."*

"A dangerous one, too," he warned. *"Keep your emotions in check around him. He feeds off strife."*

"So I've heard."

There really wasn't anything else he felt comfortable saying with others listening in, but severing the link was too much to bear.

"What's the plan?" she asked, as if she needed to maintain their connection, too.

"I think our friends intend to make it up as they go along."

"Sounds about right for Draven, I think. He prefers to live recklessly."

Draven's chuckle rang inside Wilder's head. *"I'm hurt, chère."*

"I don't know how these guys do this telepathy thing. All the buzzing brain waves are driving me a little insane," Wilder confessed.

"You get used to it," Castor said. *"Now, you two be quiet, so we can pay attention to the heist details."*

Although he hated to disconnect from Abbie, Wilder understood the wisdom of Castor's advice. She was alive and well, with two fierce protectors by her side. Three, if he counted the Royal guy. It seemed wherever she went, she collected saviors as well as enemies. Thank the Goddess for her sense of balance. Because he had little doubt Isis was behind protecting her, despite what the Fates and Authority wanted.

"Damian and I have arrived in Globe," he told their group. *"He's implanting a town-wide suggestion about a silver shipment, so no matter who Hasting's gang asks, they'll get a similar answer."*

"Excellent," Castor replied. *"We'll do our part to get them there."*

Wilder left the alley and made his way to the local watering hole. Damian was in deep conversation with the bartender, and one could only assume it was over the lack of quality booze in the place. The man's fussiness was almost comical, and Wilder could definitely see where Alastair had developed his taste for finer things.

He almost wished Al had come along on this trip, but he was certain the appearance of a man who could be Nate's twin would be disconcerting at best. Threatening at worst.

He caught Damian's eye in the mirror behind the bar, receiving a nod in return. With nothing left to do until Castor and crew arrived, Wilder found an empty table and positioned himself with his back to the wall.

When he was a child, he loved westerns. Books, movies, and television shows; it didn't matter. He ate them up, longing to live in those troubled times. The lawless Wild West had appealed to his reckless nature. Yet, having visited the place and falling victim to the ruthless residents, the constant dirty atmosphere, and the relentlessly oppressive vibe, he could say, with all honesty, his infatuation with the past was gone.

Fantasy and real life were miles apart.

One of an endless parade of sex workers sauntered up to him.

"You look lonely, mister," the girl said, hiking her skirts higher to display a creamy thigh. "I can keep you company for a time."

She couldn't have been more than fourteen or fifteen at most, sporting a world-weary air of someone five times her age. Underneath the grimy clothing, her skin was clean and her ginger-colored corkscrew hair freshly washed. Freckles stood out on pale cheeks, and her large hazel eyes were dulled by a hard life.

The fact that a virtual child was forced to survive by turning tricks in a mining town full of grungy middle-aged and old men soured Wilder's stomach. Hell, *he* was old enough to be the girl's father, and the appeal of someone her age was nil. He battled an overwhelming desire to give her what was left of his gold, but if he showed his stash in this rough crowd, he was as good as dead.

"When did you last eat a decent meal?" he asked.

Caught off guard by his response, her expression became uncertain, and she looked as if she didn't know what to do. She glanced around, then pasted on a come-hither smile before turning back to Wilder. "I could eat if that's what you want, but I'm good for a quick tup, too."

Keeping the grimace off his face was work. "I'm happy to buy you a meal, hon, but I'm not interested in anything else."

"Your tool not workin', mister? I can help. Swear."

He wasn't discussing his "tool" with a child, no matter how worldly, so he gestured to a chair. "Have a seat. I'll order us some food."

"I can sit with ya, sure, but it will cost you a dollar. You sure you don't want to go upstairs?" she asked, apprehension causing her to dart another glance at the person Wilder suspected was her pimp.

"Sit down, child," Damian ordered from behind her.

The command in his voice had her complying, and he slid a bowl of stew in front of her, then offered a second to Wilder.

"Eat, girl, and when you're done, you'll point out your employer."

She paused, spoon halfway to her mouth as she got her first good look at the Aether's jaw-dropping good looks. But she quickly regrouped.

"He'll kill me, sir," she mumbled before shoveling in steaming bites.

"Not on my watch," he assured her.

An understanding passed between them. Damian's calm assurance eased the young woman's fears.

"Tell me about your mother," he said out of the blue.

Wilder wasn't sure where he was going until the girl's face crumpled.

"Ma?" the girl asked. Her lip trembled, giving away her plight, before she bit it.

"What happened to her?"

"She up and died last year. Pox, Doc said." She gave a half-hearted shrug, then tucked into her bowl. "She wouldn't have wanted this for us kids. But Pete, he promised her he'd take care of us. She didn't know he ran girls with Bart."

"Bart? Would that be Bartholomew Mercer from Perdition Ridge?" Wilder asked.

Her nose curled as if smelling something foul. "Yeah."

"I see." And he did. Abbie's fate would've been the same as this child's had people not cared enough to search for her, and had she not gotten lucky in the canyon. "What's your name?"

"Molly Mae." She wiped her mouth with the back of her sleeve and winced. "Ma would be sore at me for doin' that on account it ain't ladylike."

"Molly Mae, you said 'kids' meaning plural. How many siblings do you have?"

"I gots me one sister and a half-brother, Gus. His Pa was a mean'un, though."

Gus. The boy who had been shot trying to save Abbie. Christ, it was a blow. One he wasn't ready to deliver on this poor girl.

Wilder met Damian's considering gaze. "An Evie project?"

"I think that would be best. She'll make it her mission to save the lost lambs in Pete's care."

He grinned, happy to know his great-great-grandmother was a woman of action.

"You want to tell her, or should I?" He nodded toward the first of Evie's 'lost lambs.'

"Please, be my guest," Damian replied with a small smile.

The girl sucked in her breath, causing his frown.

"Must be tough looking as gorgeous as you do," Wilder quipped.

Damian's voice was pained as he said, "You have no idea."

"Nothing wrong with good looks, mister." Molly waved her spoon as if to emphasize the point. "'Specially when you got a handsome heart. Or that's what Ma would say. The two aren't mutually excluded."

"Exclusive," Wilder corrected. "And your mother was right."

A rotund man in a green suit approached. His greasy hair was slicked back, and his graying, bulbous nose spoke of drinking to excess. "Molly's here for work, not sittin' around. You gents want her company, it'll be five dollars apiece."

Wilder was one heartbeat away from ripping the fucker's head off when Damian touched his arm.

"I'll handle this one, Thorne." Rising, he faced the pimp. "Molly no longer chooses to be in your employ, Pete. She has a brighter future ahead of her, as do your other staff."

"If you're thinkin' you can just come in here, an—"

The fucker dropped dead.

One second, he was bristling; the next, his skin turned ashen, and then he was on the floor at their feet.

"Was it something I said?" Damian asked drolly.

More like something he did, and Wilder shared a shocked glance with Molly.

She recovered faster, grinning as she dug into her stew.

Christ, to be so jaded! It reminded him of Abbie's new matter-of-fact attitude.

"Mortals in this century don't have the luxury of softer feelings, Thorne," Damian telegraphed via their link.

He nodded a response, mentally preparing himself for the coming shitstorm.

"Molly, my dear, would you be so kind as to round up your friends to dine with us? I'd like to tell them about their good fortune," Damian said.

She eyed her empty bowl with regret.

"There will be more for you when you return. Promise." After she darted away, he rose and pressed a hand to Wilder's shoulder. Perhaps it spoke to the power the Aether wielded, but he could swear a current swept through him. "I'll leave you here, Thorne. I need to pay a call on Evie and Nate to tell them about their new school for unfortunate souls. Also, the bill for the children's meal will be covered."

"Appreciate it." Wilder waved him off with a grin and dug into his stew.

28

*D*aughter.

How odd was it to discover her father after forty? And to find out he was *the* Traveler, one of the most powerful time hoppers in existence, was mind-boggling. Stands-in-Shadow's moniker for Abbie made sense now.

Traveler's child.

Somehow, he'd known who she was. Perhaps his otherworldly connections gave him an insight few possessed, but she wished he were here now, so she could thank him for his assistance.

As Wendall and Frank wrapped Jennings in a blanket, Morcant watched her, likely hoping to pick up on any squeamishness remaining. He'd be in for disappointment. Abbie's time here had been a lesson in brutality. Other than noting the surprising speed of Silas's draw, she hadn't been upset by his slaying of Jennings.

No, it made a crazy sort of sense to eliminate the disruptive element.

In the short time she'd been with the Silver City Gang, she'd noticed Jennings always questioning orders both behind Silas's and Royal's backs and to their faces. Quite honestly, she was surprised Jennings had lasted as long as he had with a cold-blooded killer like his boss.

Royal was different. Softer, yet not. He had a steely resolve, but didn't possess the cruelty she'd seen in his brother. Maybe Silas's ugliness came from losing his wife. He'd had over two years to grow into the bitter fucker he was.

The second the two grunts hauled Jennings out the back door, Morcant spoke.

"Silas will kill you and your new suitor eventually." His reptilian-like eyes with their hypnotic light were focused on her, as he probed for weaknesses. "What do you think of that, woman?"

She shrugged as if she didn't care, all the while attempting to build a wall around her emotions to keep the Arcane Devourer from consuming her worried energy.

"I'm a novelty. The only woman within miles. There's no real interest on their part," she lied.

His grin was chilling. "You're a terrible liar. You're hoping they save you, but they won't. And eventually, Royal will tire of protecting you, too. Wendall and Frank will enjoy taking turns."

The threat didn't hold water. She'd already gotten a bead on Royal's true nature.

"And I'll enjoy shoving a fork in your eye," she quipped, picking one up from the table and examining it. "You and I can have matching faces. It'll sure make yours prettier."

His gaze narrowed, and he shoved his chair back to stand.

She could remain where she was and let him intimidate her, or she could move like Castor had advised. The smart money was on listening to her father, but she hesitated, not wanting to give in to Morcant's cunning manipulation.

She was so fucking sick of bullies.

He circled the table, never looking away, and she could feel his presence, testing her mental wards.

Morcant was a mere foot away when Royal returned.

"Get away from her," he ordered.

Light flared in the devil Devourer's eyes. His chance to cause trouble had just walked in the door!

"We were about to become friends, Abbie and I. Weren't we, my dear?"

"Not in this or any lifetime, you delusional twat," she retorted.

His hand snaked out and gripped her throat, and as fast as a viper, she stabbed his wrist with her fork.

He hissed his displeasure, drawing back to strike.

The cocking of Royal's pistol froze them in place.

"I *said*, get away from her." Royal may not be the same class of killer as the rest of the gang, but it seemed he wasn't beyond murder if it meant defending those weaker.

Abbie lifted her chin and shot Morcant a triumphant smirk. "Better do as he says, Mor*cunt*."

Rage transformed his visage from creepy to nightmarish, and she experienced an oh-shit-I-went-too-far moment.

Royal read the intent and lined up a shot, but not before electricity flew from the Devourer's fingertips, sending a current straight at her would-be hero's chest. Convulsing, he dropped to his knees, his death all but a guarantee.

Abbie screamed as she dove for him, but Morcant fisted her hair, keeping her in place. Her fear and rage coalesced into a single blast, shooting straight for his center mass, but he absorbed it as if it were ambrosia.

Castor, Draven, and Silas burst through the door.

"She's a witch!" Morcant accused. "Look what she did to your brother!"

"No! No! Silas, it's him!"

"Abbie, calm your mind," Castor ordered, as he bent over a still Royal.

The mournful wail was unearthly as Silas dragged his brother into his arms.

"Let her go, and I will spare your life," Draven warned.

And with his lethal words, Abbie was transported back to the day in the bank. The same sense of doom clouded her mind, and panic consumed her.

"Stay calm, chère, or he wins," the Guardian telegraphed.

She tried. Goddess knows she did! But it felt as if Morcant was drawing her soul from her body. Weakness invaded her limbs, and spots dotted her vision.

"You are a Traveler, daughter," Castor added. *"You have the ability to go back in time to save Royal. Close your eyes and concentrate on the moment he entered the room. Feel his presence, and stop this from happening. If you don't, Morcant wins. He's absorbing your magic."*

With fork still in hand, she borrowed a page from Royal's vicious book and stabbed Morcant in the ballsack.

His high-pitched scream was as gratifying as anything she'd ever experienced.

Replaying her father's instructions, she focused her power, dialing in to mere minutes before.

But the unexpected happened.

Draven and Castor were thrown out the door as the floor opened up, creating a vortex neither she, Morcant, nor the Hastings could escape from.

***

The force with which Alexander landed against the corral fence dislocated his shoulder. Before he could gather his wits, the cabin folded in on itself, sucked into a massive sinkhole.

He scrambled forward, ignoring his pain and intending to do whatever it took to save Abbie. Right as he reached the edge, the earth compacted upon itself, filling the opening.

"Abbie!" he shouted, stupidly, as if calling her name would reverse the situation.

Draven's horrified expression said it all.

Somewhere, under mounds of dirt, Alex's daughter—if alive—was fighting for her life!

His angst traveled through the tanzanite link, and Wilder's frantic voice rang through his mind.

"What's happening, Castor?"

But the shock was too great, and he couldn't respond. He'd foolishly instructed his daughter, an untried witch, to travel in a way it had taken him years to learn, and he had no power to rectify his mistake.

Shell-shocked, he sat frozen.

"Castor! Tell me! Where's Abbie?"

The buzz of conversation came and went, but his mind was numb to anything but grief and failure.

And then, miraculously, Wilder was there, digging through the fresh mound, with all the passion of a starving mongrel searching for a juicy bone.

Alex should tell him not to waste his time, that it would require magic, not manpower, to get her out, if she'd survived the crushing weight of the collapse at all. Yet he couldn't.

Instead, he appealed to Draven.

"You'll eventually accept your role as Guardian, Masters," he said hoarsely. "I don't know the specifics, but I know you will. Please, do it *right now*. Do it for Abbie."

"I can't," Draven whispered his torment. "I can't, not even for her."

"You can at least help part the earth and get her out!"

But he shook his head in defeat.

Wilder's scream was so long and guttural, birds flew from nearby shrubbery. His second cry shook the ground, and the rumble caused the horses to bolt. They tore through the far side of the corral. Lightning struck with his third, and his fourth parted the earth beneath him.

Alex had never seen anything like it.

It was as if Wilder was pulling magic from nature, absorbing the power for his own.

And then the cold reality hit him.

If a regular witch could, Alex, a direct descendant of Zeus, could do the same.

"Gods of this earth related to me,
Lend me your gifts in my time of need,
Give to me now what will one day be mine,
Here, now, this place, this timeline."

Black storm clouds rolled in from all directions, bringing rain, sleet, winds, and snow. The clash produced a funnel cloud, which danced around the three of them for a heart-stopping moment. It cleared as quickly as it arrived, leaving a quartet of Gods surrounding him.

No one spoke as he picked himself off the ground and spun in a slow circle.

"One of ours is down there, buried alive, and I need your grace to save her," he said, well aware that the tears gathering in his eyes might make him weak in theirs.

"You dare a lot, even for one so bold," the most imposing of the four said.

"My request doesn't come without payment, I know. State what you require of me."

A sly-eyed fellow resembling Quentin moved forward, slowly circling him as he took his measure. "A sacrifice, perhaps? Say your son and family?"

"You can shove the sacrifice demand up your ass," he growled. "You want a life? Take mine, but you leave my kid out of it."

Fire flared, encircling the five of them, as anger sparked to life in the God's eyes. "You don't make demands, Anton O'Connor."

"It's Alexander Castor," he snapped. "Anton was a fool of a boy, not worthy of the powers your lot granted him."

"You'll get no argument from us," another said, as if bored by the entire conversation. "Someone tell that poor fool to stop with his earthly endeavors. The woman is not there."

As one, Alex, Draven, and Wilder pivoted to face him. The latter got to his feet and ran for their fire circle.

"Where the fuck is she?" Wilder demanded, oblivious to the danger of commanding an answer from the Gods.

But Alex knew.

"Wilder, wait!"

The younger man froze in his tracks, and his indecision battled his determination.

"Wait," he urged again. To the one who had yet to speak, the one Alex instinctively knew was the King of these Gods, he said, "Zeus, Exhalted One, I'm begging your mercy and indulgence."

"Why should I grant it?"

"Because you wouldn't have answered his call if you believed the Fates were right to send his daughter through time for their own personal gain," Wilder replied.

Zeus's eyes, a paler blue than Alex's own, narrowed as he considered them.

"The woman you seek is no longer on this plane. She has created another portal with her reckless magic."

"The fault was mine, father of our line," Alex said. "I urged an untried witch to perform a service beyond her knowledge."

"Yes."

"She's been innocent in all of this. A victim of others' machinations in both timelines," Wilder added.

He was smart to appeal to Zeus's sense of fair play.

It worked.

"For this reason, you shall not be punished for stepping outside of your roles," Zeus declared. "But you shall not be granted that which you seek."

"You're going to leave us here while she may be lost in some alternate time again?" Wilder shouted in clear disbelief. "Are you fucking insane?"

Zeus crossed through the raging fire ring unscathed, stopping only when he reached him. "Your passion is worthy of heroes, Wilder Thorne, but mistake me not. You *will* show respect for those who grant such gifts to mortals."

Castor's stomach dropped, and he feared for the punishment the Gods would mete out.

Showing wisdom, Wilder dropped to his knee and bowed his head. There was no mistaking that he'd done it for Abbie. If she wasn't a factor, the guy would've told them all to fuck the hell off.

"My pardon for offending you, Exalted One," he choked out. "It will not happen again."

"Rise."

When they were once again face-to-face, Zeus placed a hand on his shoulder. "You are a worthy mate for the daughter of my line, but she must be the one to save herself and earn her place as a Traveler. Do you understand?"

"She's facing an Arcane Devourer. A force not even the Aether could defeat alone in our time."

"The fated trials of who we select are not yours to question, child. It is faith in your mate you must have."

"If anyone can come through your trials, it's Abbie," he replied with a confidence Alex himself didn't feel.

Respect and an emotion similar to approval lit Zeus's eyes.

"You will do." The God then approached Draven. "The Fates have stolen much from you. But you, too, shall prevail."

Before Alex could form the words to ask what the hell he was talking about, the Quentin lookalike was before him, slamming the heel of his hand into Alex's dislocated shoulder.

The sheer agony took him out.

29

PRESENT DAY

"Ｗhat the bloody hell do you mean they went back in time?" Damian demanded. The four-person group winced as a whole, and he dialed back his anger. It wasn't their fault, but he'd damn well give Castor a tongue lashing when the fool returned.

And it wasn't as if he didn't know it had happened. Hell, the memories were merging faster than he could process them. But he didn't have to love it.

He met the individual gaze of everyone present—Laszlo, Ebba, Ronan, and Alastair—before saying, "I apologize."

"Papa?"

He shifted to acknowledge his disobedient daughter.

"Hello, Beastie. I see you've once again ignored my request to stay home in order to poke your nose into adult business." There was no real heat in his words, and likely never would be. Sabrina was willful, and making her behave was next to impossible.

She grinned, and her pixieish visage morphed into pure deviltry. Whenever she got that look, he was reminded of a young Alex. Though polar opposite in appearance, they both loved to push the limits and, along with it, Damian's buttons.

"What was so terribly urgent you needed to follow me?"

"Uncle Alex. He's without his magic."

Damian hung his head, recalling that significant detail as the new memory formed. And wasn't it just his luck? He pinched the bridge of his nose. The struggle to overcome his fear was great. Yes, Alex was as resourceful as a London alley cat, but without the ability to manipulate time or heal himself, he was at great risk.

"Well, here's another nice mess you've gotten me into, Ollie," he muttered.

"Quoting Laurel and Hardy, Dethridge? How droll," Alastair said with a chuckle. "Definitely fitting for our wayward friend, I'd say."

"Did you know he was going back?"

"Not until it was done." With a disapproving glance at Laszlo, he crossed the sidebar and poured himself a scotch. "Anyone else care to join me?"

Sabrina lit up. "I—"

"Not a chance, Beastie," Damian cut in, forestalling her. With ping-ponging warning glares between his best friends, he said, "Put the word out, I'll murder anyone who gives in to her wheedling."

"Sure, and the wee beastie doesn't need our help to get into trouble, Dethridge," replied Ronan O'Connor, Guardian of his children and Sabrina particularly. For a man standing at six-and-a-half feet, he was the biggest pushover known to humankind. One pleading look from her, and Ronan was putty in her tiny hands.

"Okay, so how do we handle this?" Ebba asked. "Laszlo and I have been back to the mountain with Quentin and have found no trace."

"How long has it been?"

"Two months."

Two months? Impossible! In his newly formed memories of the events, they'd only been there a week at most.

"Time is unfolding there and in here"—he tapped his forehead—"simultaneously. I know what has happened, but not what will." And wasn't it frustrating as hell?

Alastair handed off a tumbler. "Which means Alex and Wilder sought you out at some point. What can you tell us?"

Damian sipped his scotch to buy a moment and reorganize his thoughts. This had happened previously when the timeline was changed to save Ebba. The new memories disconcerted him, and he always had to backtrack to make sure what he remembered of the past had happened correctly. If the smallest thing were to change, it could mean vanquished enemies were still a threat.

"Abbie opened a portal to 1875. On the other side of the jump, she encountered a band of half-rate outlaws and a Native American Guide."

"A guide, as in someone hired, or a Guide, as in a spirit walker?" Alastair asked, frowning slightly as if needing to sort it out for the story.

"Wait," Ebba commanded. Turning to Laszlo, she asked, "Isn't that technically what you are?"

"Yes and no. You could say I was until I became a Reaper."

"But Stands-in-Shadow also had Seer abilities," Damian explained. He gave them all a sardonic look. "May I continue?"

"Yes, Papa. Please do. This is so interesting. Don't you find it interesting, Ronan?"

Sabrina was perched on the dining room table with her hands folded in her lap and her legs swinging to a rhythm only she heard.

"Aye," Ronan agreed, but there was laughter in his voice.

It took everything Damian had not to roll his eyes. Thank goodness for centuries of control.

"Abbie and Shadow climbed the canyon to escape," he said. "They were both wounded, however, and she fell. Draven Masters and Jonas Thorne arrived in time to save her."

"Oh!" Hand in the air, Sabrina squirmed.

"What is it, Beastie? What can't wait?"

"Draven. He's like you, Papa. His new memories are forming right now, too."

"Bloody hell, you're right." He glanced at Ronan. "We should call and loop him in."

"Sure, and I'm on it."

"If they saved her, why not send her back?" Ebba asked, sliding a fruit-and-cheese platter onto the table and lifting Sabrina down with a bop to the nose.

They all gathered round for the rest of the tale.

"Abbie's memory was damaged in the fall, and though Nate—"

"Grandpa Nate was there?" his daughter squealed in delight.

"Sabrina Dethridge, if you don't let me get through the telling of this story—"

The air around them grew thick, and a light flared in Ebba's bedroom seconds before Draven and Ronan strolled out. Masters looked like a bear with a sore thumb.

"*Et tu*, Dethridge?"

"Yes," Damian replied with a rueful grin. "I was about to tell them of Nate and Evie's involvement."

And so, together, he and Draven relayed the tale, with him ending his part in the saloon of the Globe.

"I infused Wilder with enough magic to teleport should he get into trouble while I was gone," Damian concluded.

The Guardian appeared sickly suddenly.

"What is it?"

"Abbie, it seems she created another portal," Masters said.

"And that's not a good thing?" Laszlo asked, sharing a nervous glance with the others.

"No. Castor and Wilder were left behind. She made an entire cabin disappear, occupied by herself and two killers."

"Morcant," Sabrina whispered. "He's back, Papa."

There weren't many things able to frighten Damian, but the return of his most evil and hated enemy was one.

"Where?"

She turned her pale face up to his.

"Where, Beastie? Tell me now."

"You can't go to the top, Papa. If you do, he won't be sent back."

There was a *but* coming. There was always a *but* when it came to the Arcane Devourer.

"And if I don't go?"

"Mr. Royal won't live, and he needs to save Abbie."

Draven swore, using every French word in his arsenal and adding some English phrases to boot.

"My sentiments exactly, Masters," Damian said.

The wind on the peak was cutting, whipping the falling snow into a frenzy. Whether caused by predicted conditions or her magical portal, Abbie didn't know, but it was brutal. Worse than the day she'd fallen.

Thirty feet from her, a half-buried body rested. For a brief instant, she thought maybe something had happened to Wilder, and she'd dreamed her entire time travel in a delirium. As if perhaps they had reached the summit during their climb, but were on the verge of death.

The wind kicked up, shifting the snow and revealing blond hair—not brown—and a strong jawline.

Royal.

Fighting the blinding blizzard, she trudged to him.

His skin was pale, leaning toward gray. How long had he been here? Had the portal staggered their arrivals again?

Kneeling, she sought a pulse, and finding none, she hung her head. He hadn't deserved to die like he had. Despite doing what he needed to survive in the past, he was a good man, deep down.

"You can save him."

She spun, falling back against Royal's body.

Silas was huddled by a rock outcrop, tucked away from the worst of the storm. His fingers and nose were a dark purple, and she suspected frostbite had set in.

Did he retain his gun? If so, he was still a threat.

"I don't know how," she confessed. "My magic was latent until the day I fell two years ago. Then a Guardian bound it."

He nodded. "I suspected the disturbance was you. It was the only thing that made sense."

A sob caught her throat as guilt rushed in. "I didn't mean to kill Julia. I swear, Silas, I—"

"You may not have meant to, but you did."

Wishing she could make up for all the death and destruction she'd caused, Abbie nodded and swiped at the ice forming on her lashes. "I know, and I have to live with that forever. I'm so sorry, Silas."

"It's not enough! You were responsible for murdering the woman I love," he hammered.

He wasn't wrong, and if she didn't fear freezing to death, she'd likely have wallowed in the misery of his truth.

Hoping to divert him to survival, she asked, "Where's Morcunt?"

Although his mouth tightened, he didn't respond. Instead, he cupped his hands and blew on them.

"But think about it, Abbie. If you were able to transport us here, you can get us off this damned peak. Maybe send us back before the last jump. Before Morcant killed my brother."

"You know it wasn't me?"

An emotion flickered in his eyes, giving him away.

"You think I did it," she said. "You think I'd hurt the only person in your group who was kind to me?"

A frown appeared before he dropped his head on his folded arms. "I don't know."

Regardless of his belief, she had to save him if she could. He was the only person able to help her if Morcant returned.

"Abbie."

Draven's voice drifted to her as she was halfway to Silas, and she couldn't quite understand how. She spun in a slow circle, searching for the source.

"Abbie."

The ring!

She touched it and opened her mind to the static she now recognized as voices.

"Draven?"

"Hello, chér."

The tight band of tension around her ribs snapped, leaving her shaky with relief.

"Where are you?"

"A base camp, with Ronan and Damian."

"Can you help us? Silas is with me—"

She was almost to him when Draven cut through.

"No, chér. Silas's body is here, with us."

She lifted her head and met Silas's glowing eyes. Terror paralyzed her as Morcant's glamour fell away.

"Abbie?"

His ghastly, evil smile widened as he stalked her backward steps.

"It's Morcant, posing as Silas." Even in her mind, her voice squeaked.

"We know," Damian replied. *"Please do exactly as I say."*

"Okay."

"Visualize the base camp here, where we are. Do you remember it?"

"The cabin just off the parking area?"

"That's the one," he replied approvingly. *"The parking area is empty. No one is about. Picture yourself here, and do it now."*

Morcant was closing in fast, but she couldn't leave Royal to the elements and forgotten like yesterday's garbage.

Turning, she retraced the fading holes she'd made, running as fast as she could. Morcant's evil energy was a pulsing, living thing. A maniacal killer-monkey on her back. She'd always hated it when victims in slasher flicks glanced over their shoulders to see where the killer was. The move was stupid and always resulted in a fall, leading to their death. But damned if she didn't do the same thing!

He was less than twenty feet away, and he'd done the same as her, using her footprints to gain ground.

The hair along her skin lifted as he raised his arms, and a blue light, similar to lightning, cracked between his fingers.

He intended to use the same move he'd done in the cabin!

"Oh, fuck!"

She dropped beside Royal, pulling his body half atop hers with a strength she didn't know she possessed.

The bolt struck him, arching his back and traveling through him to her.

The high-powered jolt was like acid in her veins, and she screamed her agony. Less than three feet away, Morcant threw back his head and laughed as he recharged for another blast.

"Fuck you, motherfucker!" she shouted, hugging Royal to her as she closed her eyes and visualized the parking area below. Her cells already coursed with liquid fire, and the tele-port took all of a second.

When she lifted her lids, it was to find herself surrounded by four magical saviors, two of whom she didn't know.

But she didn't need them this time.

She knew precisely what she had to do.

30

"Can you save him?" Abbie asked the Aether. Odds were, he wouldn't, considering he hadn't wanted to involve himself with her more minor problems. But she had to ask.

"I'm going to do my damnedest," he replied with a warm smile. When she didn't return it, he sobered. "Please accept my humble apology for not assisting you when you needed me most."

"You did what you thought best," she allowed.

He grimaced. "A miserable excuse by anyone's standards. My youthful ignorance kept me from doing what was right, and I'm sorry."

The centuries had been kind to Damian Dethridge, at least in looks. If possible, he was more devastatingly handsome than he had been.

"You saved me from Morcunt," she said simply. "Asking for more seems selfish."

She turned, ready to complete her new mission.

"Don't do it, Abbie," he advised.

She hesitated, then glanced over her shoulder. "Do what?"

"Don't go after him alone. It won't end well for you."

"And who should I take? Or should I let that fucker loose on the unsuspecting world?"

"You'll take Royal, and let him finish what he started."

She looked down at the body of the man who had protected her from his cronies. "I don't understand."

"He has survived Morcant for two years, living under his radar. If anyone can go up on that mountain and not give you away with excessive emotion, it's him. A sneak attack has its advantages."

"But he doesn't possess any magical abilities," she protested. "He's powerless against the electrical blasts. It's why he's lying there."

"And you're not, *chér*?" modern-day Draven asked her.

"Morcunt just hit me with one, and I'm still breathing, so…" She shrugged and grinned up at him. "By the way, I'm glad you're still kicking."

"Me, too, if only to be here for your return."

He hauled her into his embrace, hugging her as if she mattered, and Abbie drank in the love.

"And Jonas?" she asked when he finally released her. "Where is… oh."

The regret in his whiskey-colored eyes shot straight to her heart, wounding her with the knowledge that one of her favorite people was no longer around.

"Evie and Nate?"

"They became Guardians, like Masters," Damian explained. "But they crossed over around the time you tumbled into the past."

"I feel bad I didn't get to thank them," she said quietly.

"They would be the first to say don't stress it," he assured her. "I've known them since I was a small child, and never once did they waver in doing what they believed was right. Unlike me."

In an impulsive move, she hugged him. "Forgive yourself, okay?"

"My offer to heal you is open-ended, Abbie. Whenever you're ready."

With a watery smile and a kiss on his cheek, she nodded. "Thank you. Now, what do we do to save Royal?"

"That's where I come in." A blond man with cool eyes shifted forward. "Well, all of us, really."

"And you are?"

"Trevor Blane. The Aether's resident Death Dealer." He cast a mocking smile Damian's way. "He's our boss."

She looked from one to the other, each man holding himself with an ease associated with knowing his own worth and having confidence in his abilities.

"The three of you work for him?"

"*Oui.* He isn't so bad after you get to know him." Draven winked.

"Your accent has changed." She cocked her head. "But I can't say exactly how."

"I spent a lot of time in New Orleans after you returned home." He tapped his temple. "The memories are still surfacing since the timeline shift."

She froze. "Did I fuck things up? What about Wilder and my father? Were they able to travel back?"

Trevor shot a confused look at Damian. "Her father?"

"Castor."

"Oh, fuck. You didn't tell me that fucking tool would be here, Dethridge," he complained with a hearty sigh.

"He's not. At least not yet." Turning to the third man, who bore a startling resemblance to Abbie's new dad, the Aether said, "And this is Ronan O'Connor. Your long-lost cousin."

The man's grin was reminiscent of Castor's, roguish and

charming, belying the seriousness in his blue eyes. "Sure, and welcome to the family, love. You're a grand addition."

"Thank you, cuz," she replied. "What is your role in all of this?"

"I'm here to help ya send that bastard Morcant back to the past." His expression turned grim. "Sure, and I'd prefer hell, but a man can't always choose these things, yeah?"

"I don't understand."

"You need extra juice to open the portal again," Trevor explained. "Until now, you've been fueling it with fear. You can't risk so strong an emotion. Not with Morcant. He'll snap that shit up."

"Ronan will be your battery pack, and I'm going to shut off your darker emotions until this is all over," Damian added.

"Why can't we just kill him and be done with it?" Her initial plan was going sideways, and didn't it suck? "That's what I intended."

An amused smile curled his mouth. "I'm aware. Thanks to my Oracle daughter, I am also aware of four potential outcomes today. The most promising is the one we are proposing."

"Do I want to know the others?"

"No."

"I'll need to go back to get Wilder and Castor," she reminded him. "What's to stop Morcunt from coming back through after all our work?"

"That's where it's trickier, *chér*." Draven toyed with a coin, weaving it in and out of his fingers in a habitual fashion. Almost like he had a nervous tic, which meant he wasn't as calm and collected as he presented.

"Lay it on me, my friend. I'm a big girl. I can take it."

"You cannot return for them."

His statement was the death knell for her dreams of saving the others.

"Fuck off! I'm not leaving Wilder."

"I didn't say you should," he countered.

"Then what the hell *are* you saying?" she demanded, battle stance ready.

"You leave it to your brother and niece to bring them back."

"No. I'm not involving a child in this mess, and I'm certainly not leaving anything to chance."

"Abbie, you didn't send them through time. The others did," Damian said. "They have to be the ones to return them. Like you have to return Morcant to his past."

It finally dawned on her what they were trying to say. "I was never going to be able to save them?"

"Not alone. Not without your brother."

"Where is he?"

"He'll be here as soon as Morcant is taken care of," Damian assured her. The solemness in his dark eyes registered.

"I'm not surviving this, am I?" she asked as the truth dawned. "Or there's only a one-in-four chance I will. He's the backup to bring my father home in case I fail."

When he didn't answer, she said, "You can't have my brother here right now. Why?"

"In one outcome, Morcant steals both sets of powers."

"Tell me the other three scenarios."

"Abbie—"

"Tell me, Damian. Don't let me go up there unprepared."

"There's only one that matters, love," Ronan said. "And I'm after doin' my feckin' damndest to see you get through it alive."

Buying herself a few minutes to think, she studied her surroundings, noting the slight changes over the years. Ten feet away, a body lay covered by a tarp.

Silas.

"Do we revive him, too?" she asked. "Royal... He'll be crushed by his brother's death."

"Isis is allowing one soul to return to maintain the overall balance," Damian said. "It's up to you which."

"What?" She spun back and stared. "Why me? I can't make a choice like that! What about destiny, or fate, or whatever bullshit thing they like to pull out of their asses?"

The others remained silent, ignoring her dismay.

Kneeling beside Royal, she pressed her palm to his unmoving chest.

"You don't understand, Damian. He'll hate me if I let Silas die. It'll be my fault, like Julia's death was."

The air around her grew thick, and a flash of light appeared as a crack formed in the open space across from her. A veil between worlds folded back like a curtain. Out stepped two women and two men. The guys, she knew. The females, she didn't.

"*Royal?*" she asked in disbelief.

"Hey, Fire Cat."

A sob caught her throat, and she stared mutely as he squatted beside her.

"My death was on me." He wiped the unchecked tears from her cheeks. "I knew better than to walk into the cabin emotionally charged, but my fear for you was too great."

"If I hadn't taunted him…"

"No." His smile was sad. "He lives on chaotic energy, Abbie, but he was losing to your lack of fear. His goal was your power, and murdering me triggered your angst." After helping her to stand, he kissed her temple. "We'll beat him this round."

"But Silas." She looked over in time to see him hug the redheaded woman. It immediately dawned on her, by passing over to the Otherworld, he'd been reunited with his wife. "Julia?"

Silas smiled at her, his first genuine one since they'd met. "You should know her death wasn't your fault either, Abbie."

"I don't understand."

"Morcant got to me first after I arrived," Julia said with a shrug. "He was with rustlers when it happened and recognized me for what I was. He played on my fear, drained my power, and left my body for the others to find."

"All in hopes we were witches, too," Silas added. "He intended to steal from us, too. But we were mortal. Non-magical strife will keep him alive until he can get a stronger infusion elsewhere. And his subtle comments did the trick, keeping me bitter."

Their explanation made a sick sort of sense and went a long way in lifting the guilt from Abbie's shoulders.

"Who are you?" she asked the exotic woman with the black hair. She wore a watchful expression and a flowing teal dress Abbie would kill to own. "How do you play into this mess?"

"She's the Goddess Isis," Damian supplied. Dipping his head in acknowledgment, he said, "Exhalted One."

The others followed suit, and she figured it was best to join in.

The Goddess bestowed a warm smile upon them before focusing on her. "I wish to speak to Abigail. Alone."

After they'd walked some distance from their group, Isis faced her.

"You were thrown into a game not of your choosing, and I believe in fairness above all else. I will grant you a single boon, child, but you must give it plenty of thought before asking. For once gifted, it cannot be undone."

Abbie's mind blanked. What the hell did one ask of a Goddess? Her heart hammered painfully hard at the base of her throat, so heavily, it threatened to suffocate her.

"Do I have to decide right now?" she asked.

"No."

The Goddess produced a delicate necklace. "This is wrought from mithril-gold, a divine alloy only existing on the plane of the ethereal."

The pendant depicted a silver serpent coiled protectively around a five-pointed star cut from a blue sapphire. The serpent's scales shimmered faintly with threads of lapis and gold. In the hands of the Goddess, they illuminated, pulsing in time with Abbie's heartbeat.

"The Serpent represents wisdom and healing, in addition to dominion over life and death. It embodies transformation, such as the shedding of skin. Much like your own will be shed when Damian heals you," Isis said.

"Assuming he will."

The Goddess lifted Abbie's chin with the tip of her finger. "He knows my wishes, and fortunately, they align with his. The Aether will restore you to what you once were."

Uncomfortable under her direct gaze, Abbie gestured to the jewel.

"What does the star signify?"

"Your alignment with cosmic forces, your connection to the Fates, and the divine recognition for what you endured in the trials written for you." Her smile widened. "It represents your ability to rewrite your story through sheer will, thereby defying them."

"I gather they're not happy with me?"Abbie asked.

"You're not to worry about that meddlesome trio, child."

"What aren't you telling me? What does the necklace do?"

"Clever woman," Isis murmured as she fastened the chain around Abbie's neck. "Its Divine Function, when invoked, is to shield you from their direct interference. Their threads will not hold when they try to weave manipulation into your life after this moment."

"I don't understand why you are helping me," Abbie said, staring down at the pendant in awe.

"You bore the brunt of their machinations, and still, you choose compassion."

"No, I—"

"You brought Royal down from the mountain when another would've left him to save themselves." The Goddess cradled Abbie's face like a mother does a child when trying to impart important wisdom with tough love. "That was one of many selfless acts. The *Setarekh* is a star of protection meant for you, and you alone. When you call me, I will come."

And like a parent, she kissed Abbie's marred cheek.

"Be well, child."

"Thank you, Exhalted One."

31

THE CANYON - 1877

"It's about time you came around." Wilder smiled to soften the sting of his sarcasm. "It's only been a week."

"Funny." Castor rolled his shoulder and grunted, flexing it once before lowering his arm, apparently content with the result. "That bastard knocked me out on purpose. I swear, my son gets all his ornery DNA directly from that one."

"Not you?" Draven asked, amusement heavy in his voice.

"I'm not talking to you for another hundred and forty-eight years or more," Castor said sourly. "Your unwillingness to help my daughter is a sore spot."

Wilder snorted. "She wasn't in the sinkhole. Give the guy a break."

In all fairness, he couldn't say it didn't still rankle that Draven didn't do all he could've when they believed she was buried. But he didn't voice it aloud.

"How did you regenerate your powers, Thorne? I can't say I've ever seen anything like it."

"I don't know." He wasn't being coy. One minute, he was at

240

the table; the next, he was bolting for a secluded area, suddenly sure he could teleport. "I think our friendly neighborhood Aether infused me prior to my arrival." He frowned as he recalled the shooting and the infusion he'd felt on the boardwalk. "Maybe not him alone."

"So someone's been amping you up all along," Castor concluded with a nod. "I'm assuming you teleported us here from the Hastings' land?"

"Yeah."

"What happened to the other two losers?"

"Wendall and Frank? Don't know." Wilder shook his head, bemused.

Draven pulled the brim of his hat low over his eyes. "They are probably still in the woods, digging Jennings's grave, *oui?*"

"Or died of a heart attack when they saw tornadoes bearing down on us. Hopefully, they'll believe that's what wiped out the cabin and the others." Wilder conjured a bottle of booze and took a long pull before handing it to Draven. "I don't think I've thanked you properly for all you've done for Abbie. You have my heartfelt gratitude, and I owe you."

Which was why he didn't rub salt into the guy's wound for not accepting what the Fates were pushing.

"She is an easy woman to care about." Draven contemplated the amber liquid a moment before taking a swig. "I shall miss her."

"I have a feeling you'll see her again," Castor said, snatching the bottle from him. "But I'm going to instruct her to punch you in the nuts."

"You are a vicious bastard, *mon ami.*"

Wilder tuned them out as they traded barbs. His mind was too quiet. No buzz of her thoughts, no tether. His panic fought for a foothold. Where the hell was she? Would Zeus help her or leave her to flounder? The questions were a constant barrage, and the urge to scream was strong. Had they truly been in

Perdition less than a week? It seemed like a century or more. And they'd had little sleep, existing on cat naps as they were slammed by one drama after another. He could barely recall the day they'd left to come here.

As Castor handed him the bottle, he froze.

"Didn't we say we would put a C on the rock face if we needed help getting home?"

With his dark-blond brows almost to his hairline, the Traveler gaped at him. "We did! Jaysus! Quentin would be checking back daily to see if we need him."

"How the hell did we forget that little factoid?" Wilder shook his head, disgusted with himself. What might they have prevented if they'd done that first?

Damian's voice rang in his head, *"Nothing. The Fates were involved, Thorne."*

He sat straighter, glancing around.

Jonas and the Aether appeared before them. The sheriff wore a rueful smile.

"It seems you fellas find trouble at every turn," Jonas said. He held his hand out for the whiskey, then returned it after the Aether rejected the proffered bottle. "Is this a meeting of the Woe is Us club?"

"Fuck off," Castor muttered. Gesturing with his thumb over his shoulder, he asked, "Which of you is willing to blast a giant C into the rock?"

"I'll do it," Draven offered. Standing, he dusted his backside and faced the portal. "Anything else with it? Perhaps *Fuck the Fates?*"

Wilder barked a laugh and lifted the bottle in salute.

Damian's tone was highly amused, but his words held a warning. "Ever heard of 'don't tempt fate,' Masters? They aren't the most forgiving lot."

"Speaking of the Fates…" Wilder grimaced. "I've got a story to tell you, Draven."

PRESENT DAY

Royal was allowed a few extra minutes to say goodbye to his brother and sister-in-law before they left for the Otherworld.

Abbie's chest ached for him. For her entire life, her only family had been Beth, and if death ever came for her mother, she'd be devastated.

The job to restore Royal to his body was helped along by Isis. Between the Goddess, the Death Dealer, and the Aether, they reassembled him in true Frankenstein fashion, with electricity sparking through Trevor's body as he pushed healing magic into Royal.

"This is incredible," Abbie said, her voice hushed, goose bumps rising on her arms. "How do they go unnoticed with all the heightened environmental activity?"

"Mortals reject what they don't understand, love," Ronan replied. "Yeah, and if anyone were to witness the electrical storm, they'd dismiss it as an unnatural phenomenon."

Royal sat up, having been reanimated. Although his color was restored, he appeared shaky.

"You'll require a few minutes to get up to speed, Mr. Hastings," Damian told him. With a glance at Isis, he nodded, then said, "We'd like to gift magic unto you, should you wish it."

"I don't understand?"

With a smile able to charm woodland creatures into the open, Isis held out a hand, offering to help him stand.

"You showed true bravery at every turn, Royal Hastings," Isis said. "It didn't go unnoticed how you tried to protect others from your gang's worst instincts."

"Or how you patched up the wounded yourself," Damian added.

"Many times, you thwarted the Arcane Devourer from his

goal to steal the life force of others. The subtlety you applied was noted by him, and it created a target on your back." Isis cupped his jaw. "Despite knowing the powers he held, you showed courage."

"And here I believed myself to be a worthless ass for not stopping it," he replied dryly.

Across the short distance, Abbie's gaze locked with his, and she smiled. "You were a fierce protector, Royal."

"Precisely," Isis agreed. "You shall be known as The Protector from this moment forward. Should Damian be willing, you will join his circle."

"I already have a job…" Royal frowned. "Or, I did. I don't suppose anyone kept my position open, huh?"

"Mine either," Abbie said, realizing for the first time how much would've changed in the time since she'd transported them. What must her mother be going through, losing her only child?

"We need to hurry," Isis said with a ringing clap. "Time no longer runs parallel between the past and present. Too many are not where they should be, and the balance is off."

Abbie's heart beat a hard tattoo. "What do you mean? How is it different?"

"It has sped up here. Three earthly weeks for every day, since the Traveler's grandchild opened the portal. The power of the Three was too great, and misaligned everything."

"The Three? Who—"

Damian cut in to say, "Castor and your other family created a time divergence by using the Heart of Artemus together."

"If it isn't rectified before the third moon cycle begins, the entire population will be in peril," Isis explained. "Each day is faster than the one before."

All for her. Abbie shook her head, certain none of them got the memo that they could set the entire world on its ear. "Okay, so when is the next moon cycle?"

"Tonight."

"Of course it is." She met Damian's concerned gaze. "Okay. Let's get Morcunt back to the past so Quentin can get Wilder and Castor here before moonrise." Glancing around, she searched for anyone with a watch. "How long do we have?"

"Four hours to complete your mission. Although at this speed, that is barely fifty mortal minutes." Isis replied. Her shrug was casual, as if she hadn't just dropped a huge-fucking-problem grenade at their feet.

"That's zero time for planning or contingencies!" Abbie cried. "Like what if that dickweed escapes?"

"He won't," Royal said grimly. "He won't see me coming, Fire Cat."

"No, he won't," Damian agreed. "Stand still, Mr. Hastings. I'm about to create a protective shield over you."

"What about me?" Abbie asked, her voice embarrassingly squeaky. "Don't I get a protective shield?"

The Aether's amused grin was a thing of beauty.

She blinked, forgetting what she'd been on about.

"The protective shield, *chér*," Draven supplied helpfully.

Blood rushed to her face, as heat flooded her body. Dammit! Their link slipped her mind.

"Thanks," she muttered, wishing she were anywhere but there. Her cells warmed, and Draven clamped a hand on her wrist.

"When we're done here today, I will teach you to curb the impulse to teleport."

"It's involuntary. Not something I can control. I wish I still had your—holy shit! The bracelet!" Digging into her pocket, she drew it out. "It stops magic, Draven! Can we use it on the fuckface?"

"That's one alternative from the four," the Aether replied with an infuriating, secretive smile. She was positive it meant, *you're not going to like the other options.*

And she also took it to mean it was the best one because he didn't volunteer any of the others. Turning back to Draven, she asked, "Can you still control it? Maybe alter it a bit so even if he's in his right mind, he can't open it?"

He accepted the offered jewelry and stepped away, likely to consider how to adjust the spell for her needs.

"We are out of time, and Damian must embed the Protector's new power," Isis said.

Dutifully, they stood by as he wove his spells in the air. The sight was wondrous, and sigils lit where only empty space existed before. She didn't recognize any symbols, not that she would've, considering she'd been a mortal before the fall.

Ravens appeared from nowhere and everywhere, surrounding Royal and dipping their shiny black heads in silent homage.

"These creatures shall be your spirit animals. They are wise and able to see what humans do not," Isis informed him. "Are you ready to receive my gift?"

"Yes."

"Excellent. Aether, you may begin."

Abbie frowned. Leaning toward Ronan, she said, "I thought he had."

"Oh, no. Your friend isn't gettin' off so easily, love. I've had magic infused in me DNA, and it's after burnin' like a feckin' bastard."

"But he doesn't know—"

Royal's agonized screams made her blood run cold. She rushed forward, only to be detained by Trevor and Ronan. Abbie struggled against their hold, swearing and sweating, thoroughly pissed off by their sneaky omission of the truth.

Royal's transformation seemed to go on forever, but in reality, it was five minutes of their fifty.

The instant the Aether was finished, Royal dropped to his knees, pale and trembling.

The ravens attacked! They pecked his head, neck—hell, any part of his body they could reach. With the exception of Isis and the Aether, they all froze in shock.

"What the actual fuck—"

But Damian cut Ronan off. "It's ceremonial, and an exchange of blood magic for their ongoing connection. He cannot feel it."

"Blood magic!" Trevor's enraged tone suggested he was ready to exact retribution on Royal's behalf. "Since when do you perform blood magic on Sentinels, Dethridge?"

"Since the Goddess requires it," the Aether replied coolly, one brow raised in challenge. "He must be able to see situations from every angle, or it could cost Abbie and the others their lives."

Arms crossed, mulish expression on his face, the Death Dealer wasn't liking it. "That's fuckin' barbaric," he growled. "Find another way."

"All will be well, Trevor Blane," Isis promised. "Abigail Monroe, step forward."

PRESENT DAY

She was afraid. Like piss her pants terrified.

Speaking of…

Abbie raised her hand schoolroom style.

"Um, can I go to the bathroom first? I'm not going to lie, I'm pretty positive I can't handle anything like that without soiling myself."

Beside her, Trevor choked, and Ronan didn't bother to hide his laughter. Damian compressed his mouth and dropped his head, as if barely able to hold back. Hell, even Isis looked five seconds away from losing it.

"For you, we are only applying a simple spell to remove your deeper emotions," the Aether finally said. "You're already next-level powerful, and there's no need to infuse more."

Her knees went weak with relief.

The birds scattered to the winds, disappearing as if they hadn't nearly pecked Royal to death.

She halted in front of him, sickened by the blood and intending to heal him as Wilder had taught her. But as she reached out, the wounds sealed in bursts of light, like hundreds of paparazzi camera flashes at a red-carpet event.

Royal raised his head and met her horrified stare.

"I'm fine, Fire Cat." He stood and held out his arms, rotating his palms up and down as he shook his head. Awe filled his face. "Hell, better than fine. My body is more alive than… yeah, I don't know when. God, it's incredible, this feeling."

"Indescribable," she replied with a matching smile. She hardly remembered her first infusion during the tumble from the mountain. In her terror, there had been no chance to appreciate the surge.

"Does this new improved me come with an instruction manual?" he asked Damian.

Stepping forward, the Aether traced another sigil on his forehead.

"*Donum scientiae tibi est*, Royal Hastings," he said.

"Yes, the gift of knowledge," Royal murmured trancelike.

"Okay, then." Abbie stepped forward. "I'm ready."

"I need a lock of your hair," Damian said.

Turning her back to him, she allowed him to select what he needed.

"Don't leave a bald spot, or we're going to have an issue," she warned. His chuckle rolled through her, warming her in ways she hadn't felt in a very long while. "That voice is potent."

"Sorry." He didn't sound sorry in the least. "I have what I need."

When she faced him, he was twirling his own hair around his finger. Before her eyes, it lengthened, matching hers. Damian made a snipping gesture with his hand, and the lock fell away, as if cut.

"You're a complete badass."

His lips twitched as he wove their hair together, then fused the braid until it was impossible to tell her white-blond from his black.

*"Through these locks, bind her emotions to me,
So Abbie feels naught, and the Devourer can't feed."*

He ran his palm along the length, encasing the blended hair into a platinum metal band. A second later, he slipped it on his wrist.

"That's cool and all, but what about the others? Royal and my battery-pack cousin?" she asked.

"Royal's new abilities allow detachment during trying times. The ravens will take over when he is in hunter mode." He smiled at Ronan. "And our Guardian friend here is well practiced at keeping emotions in check. He'll not fail you."

"When does this new transference take—oh!" She blinked as it registered she wasn't worried about her new mission at all. "Cool. Do we lure him down or head up?"

"That's your call, my dear. I cannot advise you after this."

"Why not?" Her instant annoyance was swept away, and his shiny new bracelet flared brightly, illuminating the reddening skin beneath it. Abbie froze. "Did my anger just burn you?"

"It's nothing I cannot handle, but if you could keep it in check, I wouldn't be ungrateful."

"Got it. No strong emotions. Now, can you tell me why you're unable to advise me?" she asked.

"Rarely do I reveal the future. It could influence an outcome."

Ronan stepped forward and wrapped an arm around her shoulders. "Sure, and there's the feckin' Fates to consider. They don't love it when our man interferes with their plans."

"But Isis gave me this." She touched her new pendant. "They don't have a say in my life anymore."

"Not in yours," Isis said softly, coming to stand beside her.

"Implying they still do in everyone else's," Abbie concluded. "Got it. All right. Let's fire up our bodies' heat, boys. We're heading up to the peak."

"I've been, so I'll teleport at the same time as you, but at a safe distance. Preferably behind the evil jackass," Royal said. He grinned and tapped his temple. "Thanks to my new owner's manual, I can teleport like a big boy."

Her new cousin grinned as if it were all a gas. "Sure, and you're a grand fit with the Sentinels, ya are. You're as cheeky as Castor and Blane."

"Will the ravens make it as high as the peak?" she asked. "I've seen them while climbing, but I can't recall them at the summit."

"Yes," Isis replied. "These will survive wherever the Protector lives. They are bonded."

"So all that's left is for Draven to alter the spell."

A few yards away, the Guardian was reworking his charm, but the pressing sense she was running out of time was upon her. Abbie thanked the others and drew her two cohorts toward a section of dirt path.

"Royal, in precisely three minutes, I'll have Morcunt's back turned away from the western outcrop of rocks." With a stick, she sketched a layout and pointed upward. "There. You sneak up and clamp the bracelet around his wrist, then I'll signal Draven through our link to have Ronan join us. As soon as I can channel his power, I'll send the dickweed back."

She returned to Damian, who was deep in conversation with the Goddess, but they stopped when she approached.

"Do you have Quentin's number? Can you have him here as soon as I'm done?"

He nodded.

"And if one of the other three outcomes happens, tell him I'm sorry we never got to meet. Tell him…" Her throat tightened, then eased as the band on Damian's arm flared. "Oh, hell! I'm sorry."

"It's fine, Abbie. What else did you want me to tell him?"

"Tell him, thank you for giving me whatever time I had in

Perdition Ridge with Wilder. I'm grateful he allowed us to reconnect, however brief."

"I'll tell him if it comes to that," he assured her.

"Okay. Here goes nothing."

Closing her eyes, she visualized the place in the snow where Royal had been. Using her third eye, she reached for the area, finding it empty. She then scanned the area where Morcant had been hiding from the elements.

Nothing.

"Something's wrong. Either he's not up there, or I'm doing this whole feeler thing wrong."

Damian held up a hand and closed his eyes. His expression was grim when he dropped his arm.

"No, you're right. He's gone."

"Where could he go?" she asked. "He doesn't—oh! I know. Perdition Ridge."

"It no longer exists." His mouth turned down as he frowned. "It's a ghost town."

"But that's better for us. Less innocent bystander fallout." Abbie's excitement bubbled up, and she was happy to feel something for longer than ten seconds. "Can we all interconnect minds like we did with Jonas and Wilder? If each of us can check a different location while linked, we'll narrow it down immediately, right?"

"Brilliant idea," Trev said.

"This is where I leave you to your human coils," Isis told them. "I've been gone too long from my world. Blessings upon you, my Beloved children."

They lowered their heads in respect, looking up only when the flash of light signaled her exit.

Abbie rallied the others. "Let's get this show on the road, fellas. Then later, maybe someone could tell me how the hell the portal kicked me out in an entirely different state."

THE CANYON - 1877

Wilder waited until Draven created the giant C—signaling those back home of their plight—before diving into the treachery of the Fates and what they'd done to them.

He provided the details of Draven and Céleste's story and how the Fates were using Abbie to provoke the Guardian's sense of chivalry, a subconscious manipulation of his long-buried memories. As he laid it out, he hated the taste of the words. Hated how easily they'd all been played.

"I'm sorry, Masters," he said.

"I don't know how to feel," Draven confessed. "*Furieux, oui.* But only at their manipulation. This woman, I cannot remember her."

Wilder wasn't sure if he pitied him or envied him for forgetting. By including Abbie in their games, they'd fucked up his life, too. And the endless memories of their perfect relationship had left him embittered and raw.

"His mother is a Sister of Fate?" Castor asked. His expression was as dumbfounded as Wilder initially felt upon learning of it. "Did I hear that correctly?"

"Yes," the Aether said with a slow nod. "Their games make sense in their convoluted way."

"What are you going to do, Masters?" Wilder asked, silently waiting for the Guardian's explosion.

"I do not know. I will have to give this consideration." His lips twisted humorlessly. "Perhaps I will leave it to the roll of the dice."

Wilder glanced at the others to grasp their thoughts, but

both men were keeping their cards close to their chests. He never wanted to play poker with any of them.

Against his back, the rock shifted. "Shit!"

"The portal is open!" Castor shouted over the sudden whoosh-whooshing wind. Its fierce energy clawed at their clothes. "Stand back!"

"Think it's our ride home?" Wilder called back.

Was Abbie about to step through, or had Quentin created a way for them to return?

Grim determination seized him. "I'm going in."

"No, son. It may not be safe." Castor inserted himself between Wilder and the opening. "You've been granted gifts and can survive here if the need arises. But traveling is what I was created for, so let me test it first."

"How the hell do I get back?"

Castor gestured to Wilder's shirt pocket. "Still have my spell?"

The spell! In all the madness, he'd forgotten. He patted the pocket, sighing his relief when he encountered the vial. How Bart missed it, he'd never know.

"I do."

"If I'm not back for you in a few hours, use it," Castor ordered, and with a questioning look for Damian, he asked, "You see any reason why I shouldn't go in there, Dethridge?"

"No, but don't delay."

"Be kind to the pickpockets," Castor advised with a warm smile and a hearty handshake. "And don't let this one get into any trouble between now and when he returns."

Next, he offered Draven his hand. "My advice? Find the Duval girl. If they are trying to keep you away from her, it's for a nefarious reason. Don't let them."

"Go in peace, Traveler."

To Jonas, Castor said, "Thank you for your kindness to my

daughter. Please extend my gratitude to the others, including Shadow."

"Of course."

Finally, he approached Wilder and hauled him into his embrace. "Thanks for loving my daughter, son. If Abbie returns, my spell will bring you both home. Should I find her on the other side, I promise I'll be back for you."

"Hurry. We both know how unstable that thing can be."

They shook hands, but nothing more needed to be said. Castor pivoted and ran full speed into the swirling blue opening. The portal to Goddess-only-knew-where closed behind him with a snap.

"And then there was one," Wilder murmured. "The non-Traveler lost in time."

"Not lost," Damian said. "You have family here, Thorne."

A crackling zipped through his brain an instant before the buzzing began, sounding remarkably like a Hamm radio.

"Wilder?"

His knees went weak.

"Abbie? Where are you?" Wilder called out, both aloud and through their link.

The others grew still.

"The Hastings' hideout, where the cabin once was."

They arrived in a blink.

Abbie's whole face lit when she spotted Wilder, and the instant her arms encircled his neck, a sense of homecoming enveloped him.

"Abbie," he breathed. His throat clogged, and words failed him.

"Oh my god, Wilder!"

He drew back and cupped her face. Tenderly brushing the hair from her forehead, he asked, "How are you here? Did you pass your test?"

"What test?"

"I'll take that as a no." He spotted Royal hanging back. "Hey, man. Where's Silas and Morcant?"

A pained look crossed his expression. "Silas didn't make the jump."

"Christ, I'm sorry." And Wilder was. He couldn't imagine losing a brother during this insanity.

"Truth is, I feared we'd meet our end with a bullet or noose, so it's much better for him to be reunited with his wife as he was," Royal replied matter-of-factly.

"Still hurts."

"Yeah. It does."

Abbie buried her face in the crook of Wilder's neck, and he rubbed his cheek against her soft hair. Peace, the first since their parting, settled over him. It didn't matter if they never made it home, as long as he was with her, the world could go to hell.

"Morcant?" Damian asked. "You never said."

"We've been unable to find him. He gave us the slip." Royal appeared disgusted by their lack of success.

"Where did you go, and how did you get back here, *ma chère*?" Draven asked.

Wilder didn't have the heart to protest the endearment. Abbie's Guardian was entitled to a slip for all he'd done for them.

She shifted to address the others, not letting go of him. "Heightened emotions trigger my gift, as you know," she began.

"When I was electrocuted in the cabin, she reacted badly, and the entire structure, with the four of us, went through another portal," Royal added.

She glanced up and met Wilder's gaze. "To the present day, up on the summit."

"Jesus!"

"My thoughts exactly." She shuddered, causing him to tighten his arm around her. Giving him one of the loving smiles he'd missed so fucking much, she said, "Silas's body and the cabin landed at the base of the mountain. Royal, Morcunt, and I on the peak. The jackass glamoured into Silas and had me fooled for a minute or two. Once I realized it was him, I got the hell out of there, with Royal's body in tow."

"The Aether and his Sentinels were kind enough to revive me." Royal shot a grateful grin in Damian's direction.

The Aether's expression was pained.

"He's not a fan of spoilers," Wilder said dryly, clearing Royal's confusion.

"Ah, yeah. Makes sense. He refused to tell us anything about this journey either."

"Why did you return without Morcant to this time?" he asked.

"Oh, he's here. Somewhere," Abbie assured them with a frustrated sigh. "We found him in the ghost town of Perdition Ridge, freaked out, which may have given me a bit too much pleasure. We managed to get Draven's magical shackle on him, but the jump through time shorted out the spell. He teleported before we could subdue him."

"But since his return was our main mission, we came to find you and the Fire Cat's father," Royal said.

Wilder's stomach dropped, and he shot a worried glance Damian's way. "Do you think they missed each other in the crossing?"

"Perhaps. The other option is unfortunate."

"So many flipping options," Abbie muttered. She frowned and asked, "What would the other option be?"

"Castor might never have made it back," Wilder replied in his stead. "But why? If the others were on the opposite side, opening the portal, it only makes sense he'd return there."

"They didn't intend to call my brother to open it for the two of you until I was gone," Abbie explained. "We couldn't take the risk Morcunt would steal our combined power."

Damian grew still, as did the air around them.

The hair on Wilder's neck lifted.

We have company, he told the others through their link.

A low hum prickled at the base of his skull, and the air thickened with ill intent.

"Stay calm," Abbie urged in a quiet voice, her knuckles white as she gripped his sleeve. "I've got this."

"Abb—"

She cut him off with a sharp glance. A look he remembered well. One that said, *"Don't you dare argue with me, Wilder Thorne, or I'll murder you where you stand."*

He almost laughed.

It was such an Abbie move!

Wilder released her to do her thing, all the while gearing himself to back her up, whatever it took.

"Keep your fear suppressed, Wild Man," she warned via their link. *"No matter what he does, don't react."*

"Whatever you say, sweetheart."

Abbie shot a glance at Royal, and he nodded, seeming to understand her request. He closed his eyes, lifted his arms from his side, palms upward.

"Find him," he ordered.

Birds rose from their perches, taking flight in every direction at once.

"No need for theatrics," Morcant said, stepping into view.

A series of gun cocks told them he wasn't alone.

"We have a very eclectic group here, don't we?" he purred, as his beady eyes drifted from one face to the next. "Such power!"

"I'm the one you want, Morcunt," Abbie replied. "Come and get me."

The devil cocked his head as if trying to determine what was different about her. She hoped he never figured it out.

He sniffed the air wild-animal style.

"You have no fear. No pain. No anger." Confusion clouded his face. "Where has it gone?"

So much for her hope.

Abbie shrugged and pasted on a taunting smile. "It took a

hot minute, but I realized I'm stronger than you. I don't need to be afraid of a *pathetic* little boy."

"*Be ready, fellas,*" she mentally telegraphed.

Irritation flared on Morcant's gaunt face. "You *dare*—"

His arrogant speech died on his lips as the atmosphere buckled under the Aether's unchecked power. A slow ripple bled through the surrounding trees, and Morcant's mortal men traded nervous glances.

The crawl of energy along Abbie's skin preceded the telltale hum of the Aether's movement. As he stepped up beside her, their gazes locked, and an acknowledgement of their purpose passed between them.

For certain, Morcant wouldn't understand the significance of their shared look, but their team would recognize a plan when they saw one forming.

His voice rang in her head. "*Morcant believes you're the only one with power as significant as his. He hasn't recognized who or what I am. That works in our favor.*"

"*Yep, big mistake on his part. Ready to cage the bastard?*" she asked.

Damian lifted a hand, slicing through the thickening atmosphere. Ancient symbols, likely known only to high-level warlocks, unfolded around Morcant, illuminating and spinning faster than the human eye could follow.

The first gunman fired, but his bullet froze inches from the barrel. Dust particles hung weightless, held in limbo by the Guardian.

When Isis gifted Abbie the charm, it had unlocked an intrinsic understanding of her Traveler abilities. It took her only a heartbeat to thread her magic through Draven's, bolstering the construct and removing some of the strain.

"*Includo,*" Damian commanded, fisting his hands chest level, then slapping his palms together. The echo of his forceful clap was painful to the ear.

Instantaneously, the glimmering light around Morcant solidified, trapping him mid-sneer.

"He's contained."

Abbie exhaled, unweaving the threads and dropping her arms.

Motion resumed around them.

Morcant's hired henchman crumpled where they stood, and their weapons clattered uselessly at their feet.

Suspended inside a column of light, Morcant struggled. His eye movements were jerky, as if he were trying to absorb what he was seeing, and understanding of his plight dawned far too late.

"You can't hold me," he rasped, voice distorted, echoing through the energy field.

Damian regarded him as one might study a specimen under glass. "I humbly disagree."

Abbie's shoulders sagged, her breath catching as the strain of the spell tore through her system. Wilder was there instantly, steadying her.

"You good?"

"Define good." She attempted a smile, but her exhaustion won out. The best she could offer was a tired sigh.

"This thing will hold him?" Royal approached the containment field cautiously.

"For now." Damian brushed his palms together, snuffing out the sigils. "Long enough for The Authority to receive their new guest."

"You think you've won? You think this ends here?" Morcant snarled, his voice cracking with fury.

Abbie gave him a pitying smile. "You're threats aren't original, Morcunt. Monsters always believe they're almighty and eternal. They aren't."

He bellowed his rage, and a hissing steam escaped through the barrier. It was dark, oily, and all kinds of wrong. For a heart-attack-inspiring moment, the prison's glow dimmed, but Damian reinforced it with a flick of his wrist.

"We should move him to the containment center, in case my enchantment is broken," he said, though he expressed no genuine concern.

Jonas and Draven flanked the cylinder prison, ready with their transport enchantments.

"Wait!" she cried. Once she had their attention, she rushed forward to hug each man in turn. "I don't know when the portal will open again, and I wanted to thank you."

Draven squeezed her tight enough to steal her breath. "I am sorry I couldn't be a better protector, *ma chère.*"

"You were the best," she assured him. "You couldn't know I was cursed or the trials you'd face countering it," she teased.

"Be well." His kiss on her forehead felt fatherly, when in truth he was almost half her age. But she supposed his soul was old, making up the difference.

Next, she flipped off the Arcane Devourer—because she could—and faced Damian. "Spoiler: you turn out all right for an uptight rule follower."

"I follow rules for a reason. Perhaps one day, when we meet again, I will explain." He brushed his fingers along her scars, and the tingle traveled through the layers, relaxing the tightly knotted skin. His all-seeing gaze locked with hers. "You've taught us all much, Abigail. I only wish I'd made your stay easier instead of harder."

"I forgive you. But should anyone else like me cross your path, don't be a stubborn ass."

"I make no promise other than to try," he replied with a devastating grin.

"Put that thing away. It's loaded." She tapped his chin. His responding laughter was pure sunshine on her soul, and a little dizzying, too. "Wow! Yeah, okay. I—"

Wilder drew her away with an amused smile. "Come on, you. He's got work to do."

The canyon light shifted, growing darker, and faint threads of gold illuminated the shadows. In a brilliant burst, their prisoner and his guards were gone, leaving only the Aether.

"What will the Authority do with him?" Wilder asked.

"Yeah, please tell us he'll be incarcerated forever," Royal said.

"He'll be held in stasis until judgment is passed," Damian explained. His eyes lost focus, and he stared at some distant spot only he could see. A second later, he inclined his head toward Abbie. "You must go to the canyon. They are ready for you."

"They? Who's th—"

But Damian was already gone.

Wilder looked down at her. "Not ominous at all, right?"

"Not the least little bit," she quipped with an eye roll. "But I guess we should grab Royal and get the hell out of Dodge while we can."

"Perdition Ridge."

"Well, considering how horrid The Devil's Backbone was, I'm glad I skipped history's more notorious places." Wrapping her arm through his, she rested her head against his shoulder. "I'm sorry I didn't get to say goodbye to Shadow."

"Yeah, but something tells me he knows," Wilder said.

The canyon was eerily silent when they arrived. The breeze carried the faintest trace of burnt ozone, hinting deeper magic had recently been performed there.

"God, I'll be glad to see the last of this place." Royal slowly spun in a circle as his raven familiars gathered above them. His eyes traveled upward along the rock walls, stopping on the shelf across the gaping trail—the one where Abbie had first landed.

"Is that your friend?" he asked quietly.

"Yes." She met Stands-in-Shadow's steady-eyed gaze. Kissing her fingers, she placed them over her heart, then sent the energy his way.

"Thank you," she whispered, as he caught the invisible ball and pressed it to his chest.

Though his lips never moved, she could swear she heard him say, "Go in peace, Traveler's child."

Beside her, Wilder withdrew the vial and the written spell.

"Home?" he asked softly.

Abbie leaned into him. "Yeah. Let's go home."

EPILOGUE

SIX MONTHS LATER...

In the hearth, a log snapped and shifted, shooting sparks.

Abbie snuggled closer to Wilder as she considered the change wrought by the last six months. After two years of roughing it, she was finding it difficult to adjust to the comforts of regular life—other than hot showers! Now she took extra-long ones. Fuck the water bill.

"Your mind's buzzing again," he murmured sleepily as he hugged her tighter and buried his face in her hair. "Nightmares?"

"Not really." She ran a hand along his side, up his rib cage, to rest over his heart. The steady beat was calming, reassuring her that this wasn't another phantom dream. Wilder was as real as she was. "It's been half a year, and I still can't get used to a plush mattress. What does that say about me?"

"You like it hard," he deadpanned.

She snorted, trailing her hand downward, finding his arousal, and stroking it lovingly. "That goes without sayin', cowboy." His moan made her grin. "Can I just say how much I appreciate your willingness to make up for lost time?"

"I aim to please, Fire Cat."

Abbie groaned. "Not you, too! I'm never living that nickname down."

Wilder chuckled. "I've seen you in action—in every way—and can say with all truthfulness, Royal nailed it."

"Part of me loves that you're friends now, but I also hate when you gang up on me."

His bark of laughter echoed in the room. "We have to if we want to win an argument. Not that we ever do now that your smartass father is hanging around for every meal."

"He says he's making up for the years we didn't get. Personally, I think he likes a home-cooked meal."

"Yeah, having Royal move in was the smartest decision we could make. The man's an ace in the kitchen."

Abbie gave him a faux sour look. "You're more in love with him than me."

"No, just his baked chicken and homemade applesauce. Oh, and the focaccia. And maybe—"

She pinched him.

"Ouch!" He rubbed his abused nipple. "He's got nothing on your baking, Fire—"

"Don't you say it, Wild Man. Not if you want to live another minute."

Rolling atop her, he pinned her arms over her head. "Hmm, I think you secretly like having two men around to spoil you. Him in the kitchen, and me in the bedroom."

Abbie wiggled, parting her legs to cradle his hips. "And still, you deny my request for a threesome."

"Not funny," he growled. "I don't want to be forced to kill our chef and future climbing partner."

Climbing partner. Something she no longer was.

Suddenly, she didn't feel like teasing anymore, and she focused on the blazing fire.

Sensing her withdrawal, Wilder released her hands, sat back on his heels, and lifted her to straddle him. He hugged her to him so tightly she feared it might limit her ability to breathe. But the closeness was precisely what she needed.

"We'll climb again, Abbie. When you're ready."

"It's our job, Wild Man. How can I train others and teach them to be calm when I can't work through my own trauma?"

Her panic attacks had been crippling to her career, and if it hadn't been for Royal taking up the slack, their business would be bankrupt by now. Somehow, she had to find a way to overcome her fear of falling and failing others. To reestablish confidence instead of hesitating before doing the small, physical things that once came easily—tying knots, balancing, reaching high shelves.

"You fell, not once, but twice, and still, you were willing to go back to the summit to kick Morcunt's ass. That's not nothing, sweetheart."

As she met his understanding gaze, her love for him grew. Wilder Thorne was her greatest cheerleader, and his unwavering support fueled her desire to be whole again. Yes, Damian had removed her scars, repairing the muscle and bone that never healed properly, but he hadn't been able to take away her newly developed fear of heights.

"What if I can never climb again?"

"We'll face that mountain when we come to it," he assured her.

She laughed. "I see what you did there."

"I'm crafty like that."

Feeling oddly vulnerable under his steady stare, Abbie glanced down at the engagement ring on his pinky. "How did Bart miss this?"

"I'm not complaining. This has been on my finger since you

put it there, and it's never coming off unless you take it off." He dropped a light kiss on her nose. "Even then, I'll fight you for it."

"We should make it official, don't you think?" She lifted her gaze to his, grinning at his surprise. "It's been twelve years, counting the two you remained faithful to a dead woman."

"You were never dead, Abbie." He touched his heart. "Not here, where it mattered."

Taking his hand, she placed it on her chest. "Or here, where it mattered. My inner self always remembered you, Wild Man, and it always will."

"True soulmates," he agreed.

"True soulmates." Threading her fingers through his thick, dark hair, she drew his head down to hers. And just before sealing it with a kiss, she added, "Forever and always."

One week later, Wilder pulled to a stop in the parking lot of their climbing center. Through the storefront window, he caught a glimpse of Abbie, grinning at Quentin, who looked to be teasing her again. The two had become as close as siblings raised at birth, and he couldn't be happier for them.

"She's close."

He glanced at Royal, who had their morning coffee order in hand. "Yeah, I think so too, but I've no intention of pushing her until she's one hundred percent ready. That's how mistakes happen."

"Absofuckinglutely." Royal swung open the Jeep's door and, right before exiting, said, "But between you, Quentin, and me, yeah, we're three badass mofos, Wild Man. We're not letting her fall." With promise in his eyes, he said, "You either, bro. I take my job as Protector seriously."

Wilder snorted as he got out and snagged one of the to-go cups. "We're a job to you now?"

"More like a trial," Royal quipped.

A flashy sports car pulled in beside them, and an adorable mess of a woman with a Gucci-backpack-sporting dog climbed out.

"Jesus! Is that an Audi RS E-tron GT?" Royal asked hoarsely. "I don't know who that girl is, but I'm marrying her."

"Too bad so sad, man. According to Cole, she's already got a loser, er, I mean boyfriend."

Royal shot him a sharp glance. "Is he someone we can drop from a cliff?"

Wilder mid-coffee sip choked, earning a pounding on the back.

"Too soon, bro?" Royal asked innocently.

"Why did I hire you?"

"Abbie adores me." They followed the petite woman with the riot of dark purple curls and idiot-looking Frenchie. "So your brother knows her, huh? Think he'll introduce me?"

"No. He'll gut you like a fresh trout." And it was true. Cole was crazy about Luna Lovett. She was the only one who couldn't see it. "But he might look favorably on you if you removed the competition."

"Ah, you damned Thornes and your 'only love once' crap. It's not fair you snag all the good ones."

Wilder laughed. "You don't even know Luna."

"True, but with a fucking ride like that, what more do I need to know?"

Cole joined them on the tail of Royal's comment. "You can know that I'll gut you like a trout," he growled.

"Already told him, brother-mine," Wilder said with a grin for Royal's displeasure. "He's lamenting the fact that we get all the best women."

Cole's eyes drifted across the lobby, landing on his quirky

best friend. "Yeah, well, it will take Isis coming down and bopping Luna over the head to wake her up to the fact that I want to be more than just friends."

"So there's still a chance for me!" Royal grinned and handed over a coffee, which Luna promptly sailed across the room and swiped from Cole's hand, depositing the bug-eyed Baxter in its place.

When her gaze landed on Royal, her smile widened appreciatively. "Oh! Hi! I'm Luna—"

"Goddammit!" Cole unceremoniously hauled her away.

"Was it something I said?" Royal quipped.

Wilder laughed. "I can't say I don't have the same urge when Abbie speaks to you."

"Can I help it if women love a bad boy?"

"Shut up and get the gear ready, Outlaw Joe. You have a client in five."

"Yessir, Mr. Wilder. I'll get right on that, sir!" he said with a tug of an invisible hat brim.

"Jerk."

Laughing, Royal strolled away, pausing to hand off the last two cups of coffee to Abbie and Quentin. With a wicked grin, he swept her into a hug and laid a smacking kiss on her lips.

Wilder made a mental note to cut the rope on their next climb.

***

Thanks for taking the time to read **DISCOVERED MAGIC**. If you loved this story, please leave a review! Also, I have a bit of a surprise for you—an extra epilogue!

If you've already signed up for VIP ACCESS to my world, no worries, just enter your email and get the download. But if you *haven't* subscribed, now's the time because exciting things are coming your way, starting with this **FREE DOWNLOAD.**

https://BookHip.com/BZWPQJK

And if you're fully invested in this series, you'll be happy to know more Thorne Witches stories are coming your way. Although there is no firm release date—*yet*—I have a great idea for the next book, *LATENT MAGIC*, featuring Cole and Luna. I've even crafted the first chapter for your reading pleasure.

READ CHAPTER ONE:

https://www.tmcromer.com/books/the-thorne-witches/latent-magic/excerpt

In the meantime, since I'm sure you've fallen for our resident rogue, Castor, you won't want to miss his story.

PREORDER *THE TRAVELER* TODAY!

https://www.tmcromer.com/books/sentinels-of-magic/the-traveler

Turn the page to learn more about upcoming stories.

NEXT UP is ***WANTON WITCHMAS,*** book 2 in These Boots Are Made For Witching. With laugh-out-loud antics and a plethora of inappropriate characters, it's sure to entertain!

Expected Release: mid-December 2025

https://www.tmcromer.com/books/these-boots/wanton-witchmas

FOLLOWING THAT is ***THE TRAVELER,*** book 4 in the Sentinels of Magic series. It's the Alexander Castor story everyone's been waiting for.

Expected Release: May 2026

https://www.tmcromer.com/books/sentinels-of-magic/the-traveler

BOOKS BY T.M. CROMER

Get your printable list here!

PARANORMAL ROMANCE

The Thorne Witches®:
SUMMER MAGIC
AUTUMN MAGIC
WINTER MAGIC
SPRING MAGIC
REKINDLED MAGIC
LONG LOST MAGIC
FOREVER MAGIC
ESSENTIAL MAGIC
MOONLIT MAGIC
ENCHANTED MAGIC
CELESTIAL MAGIC
EVERLASTING MAGIC
CAPTIVATING MAGIC
DISCOVERED MAGIC
LATENT MAGIC

The Thorne Witches: Happily Ever Afters:
ENDURING MAGIC
BOUNDLESS MAGIC
FRACTALED MAGIC

The Unlucky Charms:
<u>PINTS & POTIONS</u>

<u>WHISKEY & WITCHES</u>

<u>BEER & BROOMSTICKS</u>

<u>COCKTAILS & CAULDRONS</u>

<u>WINE & WARLOCKS</u>

<u>HIGHBALLS & HEXES</u>

Sentinels of Magic:
THE AETHER

<u>THE DEATH DEALER</u>

<u>THE SEER</u>

<u>THE TRAVELER</u>

THE SIREN

These Boots Are Made For Witching:
WICKED WITCHMAS

WANTON WITCHMAS

The Angels of Legend:
<u>LUCIFER</u>

CONTEMPORARY & ROMANTIC SUSPENSE

Stonebrooke:
<u>BURNING RESOLUTION</u>

<u>HIDDEN RESOLUTION</u>

The Holt Family:
<u>GOODBYE TO YOU</u>

<u>THIS TIME YOU</u>

<u>*INCLUDING YOU*</u>
<u>*A LIFE WITH YOU*</u>

Fiore Vineyard:
<u>*PICTURE THIS*</u>
<u>*RETURN HOME*</u>
<u>*ONE WISH*</u>

T.M. Cromer is a multi-award-winning sorceress of the written word and fearless architect of high-stakes paranormal romance. With a flair for twisty plots, slow burns, and swaggering heroes hot enough to scorch the page, she conjures stories that hook readers and refuse to let go. From her cozy PNW lair, flanked by two Hellhounds and an unholy amount of caffeine ambition, she weaves love, danger, and humor into every page. Whether it's witches, sirens, or magical assassins, her characters never behave, and neither do her stories.

When she's not dreaming up new ways to ruin her characters' lives before crafting their HEA, she's daydreaming about swimming with orcas or cackling over a particularly clever line of dialogue. Come for the magic, stay for the heartbreak, and maybe fall a little too hard for a man who only exists on the page.

Want to stay current on what's happening in T.M. Cromer's world? Subscribe to her newsletter to receive release news and promo alerts.

SIGN UP: https://www.tmcromer.com/newsletter

You can also join her VIP reader group on Facebook to chat with her, take part in polls, and stay up to date on what's happening. Become a member today!

http://www.facebook.com/groups/cromerscarousers

FOLLOW T.M. CROMER:

facebook.com/tmcromer
instagram.com/tmcromer
tiktok.com/@tmcromer
pinterest.com/tmcromer
amazon.com/stores/T.M.-Cromer/author/B011QK3WXY